Viola, A Woeful Tale of Marriage

Horatio sat stunned. Mistress Wilds was proposing adultery, a punishable offence. He cried out mightily, "I'll not be poxed, nay I shall not."

The woman's eyes widened. "I ain't poxed, Mister Sharpe. I am an honorable woman."

He could not get his brains around what was happening. "Why are you doing this?"

She took a deep breath. "I am a woman, Mister Sharpe. Women must have children. 'Tis what we do." Her breasts heaved. "Me husband reckons I'm barren. But I ain't!"

Wings

Viola, A Woeful Tale of Marriage

by

Katherine Pym

A Wings ePress, Inc.

Historical Novel

Wings ePress, Inc.

Edited by: Joan Afman
Copy Edited by: Joan C. Powell
Senior Editor: Pat Evans
Executive Editor: Marilyn Kapp
Cover Artist: Pat Evans

All rights reserved

Names, characters and incidents depicted in this book are products of the author's imagination or are used fictitiously. Any resemblance to actual events, locales, organizations, or persons, living or dead, is entirely coincidental and beyond the intent of the author or the publisher.

No part of this book may be reproduced or transmitted in any form or by any means, electronic or mechanical, including photocopying, recording, or by any information storage and retrieval system, without permission in writing from the publisher.

Wings ePress Books
http://www.wings-press.com

Copyright © 2009 by Katherine Berryman
ISBN: 978-1-59705-541-3

Published In the United States Of America

July 2010

Wings ePress Inc.
403 Wallace Court
Richmond, KY 40475

Dedication

For Richard

One

London, November, 1659

Viola Sharpe stood astonished as her husband stomped to the opened door. His arms were full of clothing. Breeches, hose, and shirt sleeves dangled to his knees. A shoe fell and he kicked it over the threshold, which caused his sleeping gown to drop. Growling, he kicked this, too, out the door.

She cried, "Are you coming back?"

"Nay, I shall not," he hollered, and picked up what he had dropped before storming down the lane.

He never looked back.

Viola sank to the settle to have a think. The little coin she had hidden away in a chink of daub and wattle wouldn't last long. The rent was due, the coal bucket empty, and she might be with child, for she had missed her terms.

Amongst all things that soundly rattled her though, one did not. Viola would never turn to whoring, not never or evermore in her whole life. She'd find another way of surviving in a world where one walked the narrow path between being a poor, drudged slut, and an honorable woman.

Suddenly, she was stark mad. Damn the filthy rascal. How could he have done this to her?

They'd been married less than a year. In a clandestine way, of course, and not to the liking of the Puritan Commonwealth, but Viola was almost completely certain it had been honestly and legally done.

Her sister, Paulina, had asked, "Art thou a true parson?"

The man winked. "But of course, little lady, as honest as this gold coin in me hand," and he bit into it with a grin.

Since the onset of the Republic and Protector Cromwell, the Church of England and anything Popish had been suppressed, sending proper clergymen out of work. Half-starved, many found themselves in Fleet Prison for debt. To their unhappy peril, parsons performing a marriage the Anglican way could be prosecuted, nevermore to minister for three long years.

It put middling couples into a tight pickle, for contracted marriages could be costly. Clandestine was far cheaper, and safer, as long as the fellow who married them *promised* to be a true church official, *and* read from the Book of Common Prayer. It was even more binding if the rite were performed in a church, although hers hadn't been. She and Roger had been married at her papa's house on London Bridge.

Not that she had wanted to but she was definitely with child at the time. Her papa had become vexed when he heard of it, and shouted at Roger, "God damn your soul, I shall shoot you with me pistol if you do not marry the girl."

True affection had never been part of it, but his pole and cods rested mighty fine with her privy parts, until he showed his true colors. After they had flung the stocking from their marriage bed, he became a most vicious fellow as he flipped her over to ride from behind. She'd been fearful he'd wanted to do her ill, which was truly wicked and a criminal offense.

She had cried, "Nay, you'll not do it in me backside as if I were a stallion to satisfy your needs. Leave off."

He only laughed and entered her lusty parts to ride her like a cur. He was base horrid, plundering her with his cock in such a manner, and then casting her aside when done. At first, she rolled away and wept from the lack of a true cuddle, but after months of it she lost interest. He may as well have plunged his prick into a tub of lampreys so little good it did her.

Viola sat up straight. She was better off without the scurvy beast, and must make the best of it. She lost the first babe, but this one might live, and she would stand on her own legs to raise it right and proper.

She rose from the settle, and chucked her apron. Swinging a cloak over her shoulders, Viola resolved to visit with her papa to discuss Roger's knavery and seek his advice.

If he were able.

Her papa had been in an accident last summer which turned him very strange, indeed. Riding along in a coach through the City, a wheel broke off, tossing him to the ground where he hit his head on a rock. The dent on his forehead had been very deep and turned into a large, soft bump.

The physician only shook his head. "I can't tell you why your papa lies like one dead, but ain't."

Paulina cried, "He's been like this for days. What should we do different?"

The Leach pulled his hat down round his ears. "Just tend to him until he awakens, or dies. Keep him comfortable, and out of the sun. Give him castor oil twice daily."

Viola gasped. "He ain't with child needing to give birth, nor do we want him shitting all over the bedclothes."

With a stern frown, the physician tsk-tsked her. "Apply it to his wound, Mistress. To the bump." He swept to the door. "I'll be back in a week or so. Send me word if he dies."

Paulina tended their papa for weeks, not even his finger stirring, until of a sudden he awoke to gaze at her with unblinking eyes. It gave Paulina a sharp fright, and still, after all this time, he looked upon them mighty odd. Even his speech was different, of a singular pitch and singsong.

He was no longer the boisterous, angry papa Viola had known, but a simple, whimsical fellow who sat at a workbench intending to create things. He would stare at the bits and bobs on the table all blurry-eyed as if filled with drink. He rarely started a task, and never completed anything.

She skipped up the cobbled lane and onto London Bridge.

Leaving behind the empty expanse where a fire had burned houses several years earlier, Viola entered into the shadow of houses cluttered along its edges. The road not more than twelve feet wide along its full length, it seemed more a tunnel.

It was always a maze of people, carts, and horses amongst the houses, shops, and chapels, and a troublesome coil, but the only way to her papa's house. As she strode along, the tide rushed out to sea. Its furious current caused the roadway to tremble beneath her feet.

She dashed up the stairs to her papa's door, turned the latch and burst into the house that was of proper size for a modest family. Viola gazed around the room, a goodly chamber that was sitting room and kitchen with a hearth large enough for two boiling caldrons on wash day.

Once a month, Paulina and she, along with the maid, toiled all day and far into the night over the hot caldrons. If her papa was not working with Alderman Bird in the City, the heat of it drove him up the narrow stairs to his bedchamber and away from the drudgery of women's work. Late in the afternoon, Paulina hollered up the stairway, "Papa, you must go to the cook shop hard by for victuals afore we all die of starvation and thirst. 'Tis the only way you'll eat this day."

And growling, he thundered down the stairs and out the door, but not anymore. Now, he just sat on the bench to tinker, or stared at them as hot steam filled the room to rest damp on all surfaces.

Viola shrugged. No use thinking on how it had been, but how to carry on this very moment.

She smiled at her sister who sat hunched against the table. Paulina stared through paper optic tubes affixed to convex spectacles, trying to put delicate touches to her needlework, whilst their papa sat at his workbench.

No one said anything to her. After the day she'd had, it was vexing, but not unusual. Viola strode to the table where she fingered Paulina's embroidery, a very fine bit of artistry, and waited for her family to notice her.

Paulina finally dropped the needlework, and gazed at her above her heavy spectacles. Viola announced, "Roger has left me, and I'm with child. What shall I do?"

Paulina jumped to her feet and ripped off the optic tubes. She took hold of Viola and hugged her hard. "You're well rid of him. He's a beast and a corrupt rogue. I don't see how you stood him this long. Did you know he tried to debauch me?"

"Nay, I did not."

"Aye. I came to visit one day, but you were at market. I had to slap his hands away and threaten to cry up the bailiffs. Mark me words; you're better off without him."

Viola turned to her papa who continued to regard his table. "What do you say, Papa? Am I better off as Pall says?"

He stood up from the bench, and wiped his hands with a rag. He took a deep breath, raised a finger, and declared, "I am scientific, me girl, and I shall make the world a better place for it. Soon, all will know James Wilmot, Esquire, as a noble fellow, and the Lord Mayor will give due recognition for me valor."

Greatly stumbled and not knowing how to answer him, she nodded as Paulina's mouth fell agape. They looked at each other for a moment then back at their papa.

Viola said, "Uhm, we look forward to it, Papa. Just how will you do this?"

Grabbing his cloak from a hook, he said, "I'd thought to scrub the river water as it's so horrid filthy, but that can wait."

Paulina leaned forward. "What then?"

"You know the heads on pikes atop Bridge Tower?"

Viola stared at him. Everyone knew of the heads on pikes at the south end of the Bridge. Villains, highwaymen and government fellows who fell awry of those in power ended up there until the flesh rotted afore being plucked off and thrown in the river. Wherrimen did not take passengers to that side of Southwark when workmen were up top, making room for the next batch. To be clapped on the skull by a rotted head was not a happy way to cross the veil.

James secured the cloak over his shoulders. "I'm resolved to fetch heads from the river to see if they are pink and fresh as Sir Thomas Moore back in King Harry's day." He straightened his cloak ribbons and opened the door. "If I find a head such as this, I shall bring it back to life."

And out he strode, leaving the door open behind him.

Two

They watched their papa leave, Viola shaking her head. "He's base strange, he is. That fall from the coach put him right over the edge, it did." She closed the door and turned to her sister, "What shall I do, Pall, now Roger has left?"

Pall shrugged. "You must come back here, of course. It'll be as afore when we shared the work and made mirth after dinner with singing and playing of cards. I'm also dead tired of sleeping with the servant. Jane snores something terrible." She picked up the optic tubes and peered through them, lifting her work to study the needled stitches. "I've missed you, Vi, especially since papa went peculiar. I'm glad Roger's gone. Do you know where he went?"

"Nay, I do not. He said he ain't coming back, leaving me in a pitiful taking." She stamped her foot. "I tell you, Pall, no matter what happens, I'll not be a whore. Never shall I be one."

Pall returned to her needlework. "Are you of a mind to become someone's mistress, then? That wouldn't be so bad, I think."

Viola shivered. "I don't want anyone to touch me, ever again in me life. Being with Roger was rank terrible. I'd rather be thrown in gaol to rot than ever be with a man, again."

Pall raised her needlework closer to the light of the window. "That doesn't leave you much choice, then. When do you begin a life of thieving?"

"Aye? What're you about? I ain't of a mind to be a thief."

Pall sighed. "You must see to reason, Viola. There ain't much you can do without a husband or papa or brother. We have no brother. Our papa's gone base creaking odd, so..." She shrugged. "You must marry again. Find a husband who has a shop here on the Bridge or in the City, and when he dies you can keep it and be independent." She raised her head, smiling, the optic tubes looking very strange a' popping out of her face.

Viola cocked her head, and narrowed her eyes. "You may have forgotten, but I'm already married."

"Oh fie," her sister said with a wave of the needle. "If he's really, truly gone, and I hope he is, then what does it matter?"

Viola stared at her sister amazed, and said very slowly as if she'd gone the way of their papa, "It would be bigamy, Pall."

"Pish fie, it happens all the time. I know an old woman who's been married several times, and even ran into one of her husbands not long ago. She just ignored him as he walked by." She gave Viola a significant look, and added, "He was with another lady, most likely a wife."

Viola sat down on the bench across from her sister, and rested her arms on the table. "How can you blather so? Caught in bigamy, you can be sent into slavery or your hand will be burned. Ain't you a wee bit tetchy someone would cry your sin to the church courts?"

Pall gazed at her. "If you remember, there ain't no Church of England since the Roundheads came to power." Returning to her needle, she sighed. "It's been so very dull and foggy with no music, no frippery during the service. I shall never understand the way of the world."

Viola couldn't understand her sister. "But it's the law, ain't it?"

"Bah!" Pall cried out. "It's Puritan swill."

"But we're bound to service twice on Sunday, ain't we?"

Paulina frowned. "Forced to those sermons puts me in a right melancholy. I never hear a word they say."

Viola laughed. "'Tis a good thing you ain't apprenticed, for masters ask after the sermons. You'd most likely be clapped soundly about the ears for not answering proper."

Pall stood, pulling off the optic tubes and made her way to the end of the table. She assumed a stance that was tall and stern. She screwed her face most grim.

She snorted a couple of times, cleared her throat, and pointed to the ceiling. "Led by the burnt hairs of God's Providence, we throw ourselves upon the mercy of the Lord's most glorious feet for a blessing of our privy parts…"

Viola burst out laughing. "Nay, stop, you're too loud. We'll be tossed in the clink for blasphemy."

Of a sudden, Pall shook her fists and slammed them on the table. "Fine and dandy, then. I shall tell you in the highest manner I'm glad the Protector is dead and his son, Tumbledown Dick, is dragged out of office to the country."

Viola waved her hands in warning. "Shhh, Pall, not so loud. There are spies everywhere."

"Nay, I shall not be quiet. With Lambert, the military fellow, dissolving the Rump Parliament last month, I vow this beastly Commonwealth will soon be over."

She danced a small jig, twirling around. "Ha! Can you imagine the old Long Parliament who killed the king trying to stay in power? There's good reason the townsfolk call it the Rump. They're all right asses, they are."

Again, she twirled around, this time wiggling her backside. "I'm of a mind to stick some garlic in a rump of beef and roast it ever so gently over the fire. Cook it until the Rumps are all dead and gone. It'd be jolly good eating, ain't that right?"

Viola never knew her sister to be in such high temper over the state of the government. She thought it best to change the subject before someone pulled the door off its hinges and arrested them on the spot.

The tide rushed below the floor, rattling the crockery hanging on the wall. The window shook in its casing and a tool slid off their papa's workbench, dropping to the floor.

She stood to open the window to see the water higher and fiercer than she'd seen it in a long while. Spotting something in the water that cried out very loud, she looked closer to realize someone had fallen in. The poor sod would be dead soon as he was swept screaming toward the Bridge, his arms flailing above him. She stood on tiptoe to see him disappear beneath her.

His screams suddenly stopped.

It gave her the jitters. "Pall, someone just drowned below us."

Shrugging, Pall picked up her needlework, threads, and shears from the table. "Have you forgotten the unholy din of those poor folks' screams? That, with the clatter outside our door, it's a wonder we can think."

Soundly rattled, Viola cried, "How can you be so base cold?" And she suddenly had a fretful thought. "Where's papa?"

"I don't know, but I'm hungry. We should go and bring him back, stopping at the cook shop for some dishes. What are you of a mind? A venison pasty would be nice, as would a pot of ale."

"I think a collar of brawn would be brave eating," Viola remarked as her mouth watered. "Let's get along afore all the good food is purchased and gone."

Pall swept on her cloak and retrieved a basket. "Let's to the cook shop afore we search for Papa."

Viola was suddenly mightily peckish, having had only a piece of bread with cheese the whole day. "Aye, but let's to the Dog and Bitch where we may sit and eat, and order take away for papa."

Pall grinned. "With papa's idea of retrieving a head from the river, I'll be wanting a full stomach afore dealing with that troublesome brew."

Viola turned thoughtful. "What if we send papa to Leather Lane Spa? Mayhap, the sweat tubs and drinking of turpentine would help his addled brains."

Pall swung around to gape at her. "But those baths are for the cure of the clap. Papa doesn't have the clap." She tied the ribbons at her neck, and then asked, "Does he? Would that make a man base strange?"

Viola shrugged. "I ain't one to know, would I, if he does or not? The place couldn't hurt, I should think."

Pall shook her head. "'Tis something to mull over, but another time."

Agreeing, Viola said, "Aye. After Roger leaving today, I cannot ponder it."

Pall shut the door forcefully then bolted it tight.

They held hands as they swerved in and around pedestrians, carts, and sedan chairs, and headed south to the inn that was very near the great stone gate and the bear statue. Viola noted a pile of offal in their path and pushed Pall out of the way before she slogged through it.

The zigzag took them off course where they came straight to an old Scottish covenanter, harking doom to the passersby. Waving his arms, he bellowed most harsh, "Hear me, brave folk, hear me words, for the Lord wilt cast the whole lot of this London and her suburbs into the seething pit of hell.

"We must rise to demand Lambert bring back the sainted Rump. Skies darken as the Lord's glory weeps with the loss. Mark me words, if the Rump don't come back, fire and brimstone shall fill the air with its noxious fumes. 'Tis God's way. Bring them back."

Snorting, Pall shook her fist at the old man. "Get thee gone, thou filthy rogue. Can't you see people ain't interested in your sodden ways, or of a mind to be sprayed with this twaddle? You ain't wanted, here on Bridge Road or evermore, anywhere."

Viola glanced around, alarmed. Her sister was hollering blasphemy, again, and this time in the open, a dangerous thing. Even with Cromwell dead, the Commonwealth was still alive, and all manner of men loyal to it could take offense and drag her to the clink where all sorts of dirty folk dwelled.

"Pall, halt thy tongue. Say no more." People stopped in the road and stared at them. She snapped, "'Tis dangerous, it is. Stop spouting such high words for the world to hear."

Pall shook her head, her face pinched into full annoyance, and declared, "I shall not. This old man must go straight to the devil afore someone throws him off this here Bridge."

Viola began to feel fearful. There were apprentices about, who stared and licked their chops for a riot. If she couldn't stop Pall, they'd be in a hopeless coil.

She grabbed Pall's arm and tugged her away from the man shouting prayer words. "Stop causing such a naked frisk. Don't you see everyone staring and lollygagging for a brawl? We daren't be picked up by the magistrates. We must find papa."

Pall shrugged away from her. "I'll not stop ranting as you demand, Viola. I'm sick to the teeth of the dull Puritans and their ways." Turning, she spat, "Aren't you?"

Truth to tell, Viola had never thought on it, and it was worrisome her sister was so off her hooks by the ways of the government. After all, neither of them had known anything but the Puritan ways for as long as she could remember.

If she weren't so anxious about their papa, she would wonder why her sister was so remarkably intense on the matter. She said, "Nay, I am not. There's nothing we can do about it, anyway. Let's find papa for I'm afeard he's come to harm."

"What about our dinner?"

Viola was suddenly cruelly vexed. She snapped, "Well, you've made a right mess of it, haven't you? Caused everyone to stop and stare like we're a pair of curs causing riot. If you don't come with me, then do as you please. I'm going in search of papa."

She stomped off in the direction of the great gate, no longer caring if Pall came or went. She'd had a ragged thorn of a day, and was completely discontented.

Pall could rot.

Viola tramped off at a furious pace and sped through the gate and onto the streets of Bankside. She touched the bear statue for good luck as their papa would do for safe journey whenever passing on an errand, for this side of the river was no longer the best place to roam. The spot where the Globe had once stood now boasted a froth of brothels, and pox ridden places they were, too.

But she wasn't going in that direction. Instead, once she cleared the Bridge, Viola turned to Southwark bank and to the river stairs.

As the sun sank low, this side of the Bridge fell in deep shadow. It took a moment for her eyes to adjust to the boats and stairs. Ladies waved for wherries to take them across to London town while men hazarding life and limb, hollered boisterously as their boats shot through the Bridge arches to fall like toys onto the water below.

The closer Viola got to the stairs where the river ran so furiously, it was hard to hear anything but the roar of rushing water. As she stared into the dim dark, someone cried out in mortal terror, and everyone turned to gape as a man holding a dead head above the water was swept away with the current.

Three

Viola screamed, "Papa! Papa, come back!" She turned on her heel to the stairs.

Paulina dashed off the Bridge and skidded to a stop as Viola raced past her. "Oiy, what's the fuss about?"

Viola made strangled sounds in her throat as she panted and puffed. She ran up the stairs to follow along the bank as their papa sped away in the current.

"A pox on it," a man hollered, running after her. "You'll never meet him with all the tangle of brush along the river's edge. Get thee to a wherry afore he's altogether gone."

Viola wheeled around, running down the stairs to a wherry that bounced and bobbed in the water, Pall at her heels. "Don't leave. We're coming. Quickly, now."

Raising her skirts, Viola leaped onto the boat, scrambling to a seat. Pall fell behind her, breathing hard. "Forsooth, what's the hullabaloo? Why are we in a roaring brawl to be drowned in this here high river?"

Viola fought the urge to clap her sister soundly round the ears as the wherriman plied into the current with mighty strokes. Her hands snapped into tight fists. It made her stark mad how base frivolous her sister was.

"If you ain't such a damn turkey-cock, gadding about all fired up with Lambert and the knavery Parliament, you'd see papa has gone missing in this here river. We're off to fetch him if we can afore he drowns this very moment."

"What? What's papa doing in the water?"

"Gone to find a dead head I reckon. Must have slipped or something, fallen in, what do you think?"

Pall sat still for a moment, then over the roar of water, hollered, "Which way did he go, then?"

"Down this way in the current, you blathering fool. I just hope he snags against something so he's not swept to sea. That'd be most horrid."

Pall studied the swirling eddies. "Aye."

They rushed down stream far enough so the deep shadow of the Bridge was behind them, the sun marking their way. Clustered ships with tall masts bobbed and pushed together. Water swooshed between the hulls as rigging creaked, decks moaned, and bells clanged. Rubbish sped by, some banging against the wherry and the sides of the ships to veer off and rush away, again.

Viola narrowed her eyes in an attempt to find her papa amongst the swirling water and debris.

As the sun dipped lower and the Bridge shadow moved down river, water and flotsam turned dark. It was hard to distinguish what was what. Everything looked the same, forcing Viola to close her eyes and listen to the sounds above the crashing water and creaking ships.

And then she heard it, her papa's cry.

Opening her eyes, she turned in its direction, searching for him. Viola leaned against the edge of the boat, concentrating on the sound.

Pall asked, "What do you see?"

Viola waved her sister away. "Shhh. I think I hear him."

Pall went quiet, and then with a shout, she pointed. "Oiy, over there. I see something against the rear of that ship."

Viola squinted and tried to see what Pall saw. It was getting dark. Rubbish bobbed in an eddy near the aft of a ship, making it near impossible to pick out her papa.

"Over here," he cried. "I'm drowning."

Pall leapt to her feet and hollered, "Do you still have the dead head?"

Standing up, Viola swatted her sister. "Blast it, not now."

The wherriman slapped the water with an oar, sending a cascade into the boat. "You're vexing me straight to the gut, you are. Sit down the both of you. Do you want to be tossed overboard?"

In unison, they pointed and cried, "He's over there. Quick, now."

"Hang me, not afore the both of you sit the bloody hell down. I ain't about to toss us overboard while you're a raving and pitching us about like lunatics. I've got a reputation to keep. I ain't drowned no one yet, and I ain't about to, you ken?"

Viola grabbed her sister's wrist, and forced her down as she sank to the seat, praying the man would hurry to their papa before he disappeared in the dark waters. The sun was sinking fast on the other side of the Bridge. Once down, it would cast all into pitch night, and her papa's voice sounded dim.

The boatman pulled hard right, his strength turning the wherry around, and he rowed up stream toward the ship. A piece of rigging had snapped from one of the ships, snagging under the ship next to it, and trapping anything that coursed too close.

Their papa held tight to the rope with one hand, the dead head in the other. He gasped and spat water as debris bobbed around him. Both Viola and her sister leaned over the edge of the wherry as they drew near, their arms outstretched to grasp him before he went under.

The wherriman sucked in his breath. "By God I shall forsake you both if you don't get back in this here boat. As I do all right imaginable in saving the damned blockhead, I shall not have the two of you pitch us into the drink."

Viola clamped her mouth shut, and squeezed Pall's wrist to keep her quiet.

The wherriman grunted and rowed against the tide to the aft of the ship. Viola and her sister stretched their arms over the side, Pall grabbing hold of the snagged cable while Viola swept aside the rubbish with her hands.

The water was very cold.

The wherry edged toward the ship, the boatman heaving from the effort. "Pox on it, grab him afore I lose hold and we spin away."

Together, they stretched over the rim for their papa. Viola snatched for him but she pulled away with a cry as a dead cat bobbed across her arms.

The man growled in his attempt to keep the boat steady. Viola cast her hands back into the debris, reaching for her papa's coat while Pall pulled his stiff fingers one by one away from the cable. As he came loose, they dragged him to them.

There was no getting him in the wherry.

The wherriman lost his grip on the fast water, and the boat spun away from the ship. It dashed into the current, their papa's weight dragging it lopsided. Viola and Pall clutched him as the wherry sped downstream, the boatman cursing boisterously while it took on water. Grappling with the drag and the current, he finally got hold of it again and rowed them across to London side.

They landed at Tower Stairs.

"Get thee gone," he yelled. "I never want to see thee evermore. You're a doom to me business, trying to sink me dead when I saved the rank fool from drowning. Lot of thanks I get."

Viola still held tight to her papa. Everyone was wet, and cold, their breaths vaporizing in the near dead dark. She said, "I give thee many thanks, and will take you to dinner, if you help us get papa out of the water."

The man harrumphed and spat, then he nodded. "Well, that suits me fine. I'm a bit peckish after that little spin," and he bent forward to grab their papa's arm.

The dead head popped up, their papa holding it by the hairs, and the boatman cried in surprise. He sprang away, and the head plunked back into the water.

"Nay, you shall not, Papa," hollered Pall. "Drop it this instant. You'll not be taking it into the house."

Shivering with cold, he raised the head, his fingers clamped tight in the hair. Viola knew if they didn't get him out of the water, he'd die right soon of the blains.

"We must get him to the wharf. We'll pluck away the head once he's up the stairs."

The three of them pulled and dragged him from the side of the wherry and up the slick stairs, almost dropping him as Pall slipped and fell.

"You alright?" Viola gasped.

"Aye," Pall said as she scrambled to her feet. "Scurvy greasy, though."

With the wherriman's help, they hauled the heavy weight of their papa until everyone stood shivering and shaking at the top.

Their papa's teeth clacked as he raised the head before them. "You plucked me out of the grave, you did, and I thank thee."

"You shall drop that head this very moment, Papa," Pall commanded. "It ain't to enter our house, do you hear?"

"Aye," the boatman groused. "Everyone can hear you, I reckon."

Pall glared at their papa. "Well, then? Why are you still holding onto it?"

"A cause me fingers are locked, ain't they? They're frozen into the hairs of this here dead person."

Viola grimaced. Someone would have to wrench the head from her papa's hand. She wouldn't do it, and she looked to her sister who shook her head and stepped away.

A link boy, holding a lit lanthorn, sauntered up to them. "Couldn't help but hear. I'll do it for ten pence."

"Oiy," the boatman yelled. "Best not forget you owe me a shilling and a supper for the saving of this creaking sod."

"That's robbery," Pall cried. "It shouldn't be more than a few pennies."

"Nay, 'tis a shilling and a dinner, or I'll cry off to the bailiffs."

Viola and Pall reached under their cloaks for their purses as hands stretched toward them, Viola hoping they had enough between them to handle the affair. They doled out coin and seeing there was enough for dinner, Viola nodded.

The link boy raised the lanthorn and grabbed hold of the head. He wrenched it out of their papa's hand, who cried out in pain.

"Oiy, don't hurt him," Viola said as the dead head went whirling into the water with a loud plunk. She nodded. "Well, that's done. Pall, you see to papa, and I'll take this gentleman to a cook shop for a dish."

Pall twirled toward the river. "Oh no, I've lost the hamper. Must have dropped it on the stairs at the other side. How'll you carry the dishes back?"

Tired, hungry, and wet, Viola did not care.

Four

Horatio Sharpe stood near the Tower stairs watching two women argue with a wherriman, always unpleasant business. Their guild was strong, and when in a mood, they could be as unbridled as the apprentices rioting in the streets. He was about to enter into the fray when it seemed everyone came to terms and money was exchanged.

Not knowing what the bit of turmoil was about, it amazed him when a link boy furiously wrenched something from the hand of the old man. He gazed closer, then he saw it. The lanthorn flashed clear light on the thing, and he coughed in surprise as it was flung in the river.

Now, that wasn't a sight seen every day, nay it was not, and it made him curious as to who these people were. He did not move when the lot of them approached, and he watched with a grin as they entered the road, squabbling like hens. They did not give him a glance.

One of them looked to be a right fine woman, and he reflected it had been some time since his wife had died. It had been even longer before that, for he would not touch her privy parts after the betrayal. His sacks were heavy, and he could do with a frolic, but there were strict Commonwealth laws against fornication. If found with his breeches down, he could be thrown in the clink for three months, if not more, depending on the humor of the judge.

Watching the women walk away from him, he sighed. The government had always been tiresome, but it was even more so since hope ran swift the tide would soon turn.

The desires of change were so high in his heart it was difficult to focus on one thing for more than a moment. His sleep at night was prone to fits of distemper, awakening him with excitement almost like gusts of lust.

He was afraid of going rackety mad, but he couldn't help himself. The past year and a half had been a delirium of precedents: Cromwell and his Puritan Commonwealth were in chaos, and it looked more and more like King Charles II would be brought back from exile.

Horatio was a Royalist, and had been since the killing of Charles I. Since the end of Tumbledown Dick Cromwell, he'd been swept into the undercurrent of Royalist agents who were in communication with the young king, even taking packets of letters and documents to him on the Continent.

As an intermediary, he had made several trips to the exiled court since the summer. During his travels, he learned England was looked upon by other nations as a country of regicides, knaves and rogues. It was a black mark on his land, one he hoped would soon be blotted out.

It had been two months since he'd gone overseas, and his restlessness caused distraction in all things, including his bookshop.

Just that afternoon, James Finch who owned the printing press in his shop, blocked the door and cried, "Where art thou going?"

Horatio tried to move past. "Out."

"Nay, you may not. Me wife ain't your servant when patrons come and purchase printed sheets."

Vexed, Horatio snarled, "Once sold, it ain't so bad when Charlotte asks you to print more, now is it?"

The man had softened. "Nay, but that ain't the point. You're a' gallivanting all over the place, throwing your shop open to the apprentices and all sorts of mischief. I ain't to be held responsible for anything that goes amiss."

Horatio pushed past him. "And so you won't."

That had been several hours ago. Now, his restless soul kept him in the streets that were loud and wretched with the stench of rubbish and swill. He stood for a moment and thought where to go, next. If it were earlier in the day, he'd find his way to a coffeehouse to hear excellent discourse on the latest news. After a dish or two of coffee, the stuff being so strong and bitter, it was a wonder anyone could see past the jitters and speak with clarity. Several spoons of sugar worked for him, but if he drank it in the evening, he could not sleep at night.

Horatio frowned. It was a filthy circle, it was.

A man brushed by him. The basket on his arm punched him in the back. Horatio snapped, "Oiy, there, mind where you're going."

"Then get out of the way," the man retorted without a backward glance. "Can't you see you're in the busiest part of the lane?"

Horatio decided to go to an ordinary in Covent Garden. The food there was good, the rum full-bodied. It was a meeting place for news not far from the New Exchange and Whitehall. Loud, too. Men could whisper subversion without being overheard.

Picking up his step, he entered the City at Tower Street. It was full dark now, and glad he was to have a long sword at his side, plus a dagger. The way could be fraught with danger, cutpurses and the like, but he was too on edge to take a wherry. He would walk the couple of miles.

Striding at a fast pace through the City, he neared St. Paul's Cathedral and slowed his step, thinking for a moment to go into the church. The middle aisle of the nave was a mix of businesses and promenade, but then he resolved not to. It was also a place of thievery, and more so in the night with the underworld roaming up and down amongst the pillars.

He patted his sword, and continued to Ludgate where the press of merchant carts, sedan chairs, coaches and folk harking to leave the City was thick. Moving into a place between a sedan chair and a family pushing a grocer's cart, he waited with the rest to pass through the gate.

Horatio felt a sudden pull beneath his cloak and swung around, slapping a nearby woman with his sword. As the woman hollered her backside had been stabbed, he grabbed hold of a lad clutching his purse, the strings still anchored to the points beneath his petticoat breeches.

Behind him, the woman continued to cry foul, but he took no measure. He seized the lad by his neckerchief and shook the very devil from him. "Oiy there, you damned impertinent knave. You want to swing at Tyburn for your troubles? I shall cry up the bailiffs and have you thrown in gaol for the whole world never to see you again except in the gibbet."

Horatio tightened his grip on the neckerchief until the lad looked half strangled. "Do you want that?"

The lad's eyes were wide in the torchlights of the gate. He made choking noises, but was able to stutter, "Nay, nay."

Horatio snatched his purse from the lad, gave him one last hard shake, then let him go. He collapsed into the muck of the street.

Horatio growled. "If I ever see you with your hand under another's cloak again, be resolved to die."

The lad coughed harshly, shot to his feet, and bolted into the crowd.

Turning around, he faced a man who was roaring and spitting at him as the woman beside him bawled high she had been murdered.

It vexed Horatio to be so nettled. "What's this, then?"

The man cried, "You've stabbed me wife with your sword, nearly killing her, you have. What'll you do about it?"

"Pox on it man, I ain't hurt the prating woman. 'Twas the flat of me sword that touched her as I swung around. Had to grab hold of the young thief, didn't I?" and he shouted at the woman, "Shut thy screaming banshees. Me hairs are burning right off me head with your caterwauling."

The woman gulped to a stop.

Horatio pressed himself into calm. "I am most aggrieved to have clapped you with me sword, Mistress. You ain't hurt, now are you?" He bowed to her, showing a lusty leg.

The woman's scowl melted into a smile. "Ain't you a fine one? Thank thee, sirrah, for your gracious kindness. We'll be going, now." She took hold of the still grumbling man and dragged him through the gate.

Horatio pulled his gloves tighter, then strode out of the City and into the suburbs. It would not be long to Covent Garden. Only a few more blocks.

Reaching the ordinary, he pushed through the door. It was steamy hot and crowded with noisome folk. It always brought a smile to his face as he regarded the full benches and tables. A shout rose over the din, and he looked in its direction to see an old schoolmate, Harry Sattler, waving from the side of the room.

He returned Harry's gestures with a smile, and suddenly hungry, worked his way to the counter to order a pasty of boiled hare with gravy sauce and mushrooms. Horatio bent over the counter to regard the stock of ale, since the Puritans frowned on the drink.

Of occasion, the barrels would go missing while the magistrates prowled establishments, giving long sermons on the evils of the spirit. Once the prating fellows walked out the door, barrels would reappear, and all would drink to their fill.

He fancied a pot of ale with his supper, and seeing a barrel with its bung loose, Horatio was cheered to his very heart. He paid for a pitcher, and took it to the table where he sat down and gazed at his friend who grinned at him like a madcap.

"What's afoot, Sattler, so jolly on such a cold night?"

Sattler raised his cup of ale. "'Tis a right troublesome coil our government's in, that's what I say, what with people standing up for the Royalist cause and the Puritan armies all a' frenzy. Forsooth, there'll be a battle afore long, but in the end we'll be better for it. What do you think?"

Horatio looked around the table filled with people slurping their food. Even with the changes coming, one had to be careful.

Sattler waved a hand. "Have no fear. No one's listening, and if they was, what could they do to us? Everyone's tired to the gut of the bloody carcass government."

Shrugging, Horatio said, "One can't be too cautious, but what you're saying is old news, me good fellow. Learnt of the frenzy yesterday."

Sattler squirmed on the bench with so much eagerness, he was near to Morris dancing, another thing most frowned upon. "Don't you see?" he cried. "The events are moving ever so quickly. I expect Monck to leave Scotland soon and come to London. It should be a battle right at the City gates, I think, and am resolved to prime me pistols for the event."

Horatio raised a brow. "You think it'll come to that, then? Nay, I shall not join you. The Puritans can haggle themselves dead for all I care."

Sattler leaned forward. "What'll you do, then? How will you lean?"

"The royal way of it, and it'll be all right imaginable. The King shall return to rule his kingdom, and high time, too."

"Aye, I understand." Sattler nodded and winked knowingly.

"What do you understand?"

"You were part of the Sealed Knot and the effort to bring back the King a few years back, ain't that so? I'm resolved you're about to do it, again."

His friend knew him well, and he nodded.

Rumors were rife. Commonwealth spies were everywhere, gaping through keyholes or infiltrating societies. They had worked their way into the Sealed Knot which eventually became a hindrance to the monarchy effort. Horatio had long since disavowed them.

If Parliament ever sat again, and made the decision to bring the monarchy back, he fully intended to be part of the excursion to fetch the King. Aye, indeed, it would be a wonderful thing.

Horatio answered, "Aye, but not with the Knot."

A grimacing old man with short cropped hair, a Roundhead by the looks of him, dropped Horatio's pasty to the table, mumbling of the Saints' ordinances. He pulled out a wad of tobacco and stuck it into his mouth as he wobbled away. Sattler chuckled at his retreating back.

"Well, must be off, then," Sattler said. He pushed away his trencher and emptied pot. "Have to see to the wife. It's our fifth, you know. Every time I touch her, she gets with child. Puts me into a right merry pickle," and he grinned.

Horatio laughed. "You runneth over with a froth of goodness, 'tis seems." But still wanting good company, he said, "Nay, stay. I've a full pitcher a' waiting to be drained."

Sattler stood. "Nay, must be off afore she finds something to fault me with and goes all gloomy. Mayhap, after the babe is born…."

Raising his cup to Sattler, Horatio said, "Aye, we'll do it then."

With his friend gone, he dug into the pasty, savoring the rich gravy. Ah, it was sprinkled with crushed peppercorns, very brave. He drank from the ale pot, and noticed a familiar woman standing amidst the slathering patrons, staring at him most strange.

Now, who was she? Aye, he remembered. She was his neighbor, an honorable lady married to Robert Wilds, and he thought as he thought every time he saw her, *poor woman.* Wilds was a rigid, religious fanatic who was at least twenty years her senior.

As he gazed at her she appeared all tetchy, clutching her cloak to her chest. Of a sudden, she nodded sharply then walked with quick strides to his table.

Her cloak still bunched against her, she asked, "May I sit down?"

Horatio lowered his cup and smiled. Seemingly a virtuous, modest woman, she was very handsome with pink cheeks and bright, red hair. He always thought Irish when he saw her, and his privy parts stirred. "Aye, Mistress Wilds, what can I do for you? Would you like a cup of hardy ale? 'Tis most brave, and will give you mirth."

She sat down and released the cloak. Her hands shook. She clasped them together and slid them under the table. "Aye, Mister Sharpe, I would very much like that."

Taking Sattler's emptied cup, he poured her ale, and wondered what was afoot. "What can I do for you?"

Mistress Wilds held the cup firmly and drank from it. She ran her tongue over her upper lip, and Horatio's heart thumped. He wondered what it was like to touch her breasts, to fondle her privities.

She said, "Uhm, I knew your wife, Mister Sharpe. Very sorry about her passing. Was it childbirth?" She looked at him with high appeal.

Bringing up his wife put him right off his hooks. "Nay, it was not, Mistress Wilds. She was stricken with smallpox. The physician said the disease putrefied her heart. There was nothing he could do."

Looking distressed, Mistress Wilds' head sank almost to the table top. "I'm very sorry to hear that."

"Nay, don't be. Now, I'm resolved you did not seek me out to discuss me wife. What's amiss? May I attend you in some way?"

Her back straightened, and she looked him in the eye. "I followed you, Mister Sharpe, all the way from Tower Hill."

"Why would you do that? 'Tis dead dark out there, dangerous for a woman."

The woman did not heed him. "When Mistress Sharpe was alive, she told me she once had a child, but he died. Were you the father, Mister Sharpe?"

She was an impertinent jade to ask something so personal. "What's it to you?"

Mistress Wilds finished off the pot of ale. "Was the babe yours, Mister Sharpe?"

Knowing it was before his wife turned sour and went rollicking off with his younger brother, he was assured the babe was his. He answered, "Aye."

Mistress Wilds glowed. "That is joyous to hear, Mister Sharpe."

Horatio was astonished. "Aye? And why would you say this, Mistress Wilds? 'Tis most unseemly."

She smacked her lips. "Well," she paused, and then took a deep breath.

"Aye, Mistress Wilds?"

"Me husband does not seem to, uhm, have the strength to sire a babe, Mister Sharpe. We've done the honorable give and pull, but..." She shrugged.

Horatio sat taller on the bench, his pasty forgotten. "Aye, Mistress Wilds?"

She stared him straight in the eye. "I've a proposition for you, Mister Sharpe. I must have a child, and am resolved you are the man to do it."

Five

Viola stepped onto the Bridge when the boatman hollered in high discontent. "Nay, for me troubles, we'll to the Old Swan for a trencher of meats and a pot of rum. Nothing else will do." He grabbed her arm, and pulled her across Fish Street towards the tavern.

"Why?" Viola cried, struggling against his strong hand. "There's a perfectly good ordinary on the Bridge."

"I like the Old Swan," the boatman said most stubborn like. "The tail there is fine, too."

"What?" cried Viola, and she wrenched from his grasp. "I'll not be paying for you to be treated kindly in a brothel."

"It ain't a brothel, lass, but a tavern with lassies to serve us, and mayhap, one to soothe me battered brains after the ride on the river just now."

"Well, I ain't paying for anyone to soothe your brains, sirrah, that I vow this very moment. Only a chine of beef and a pot of rum, that's all you're getting."

"Pox on it, lassie, don't get yourself into a tangle over the matter. I ain't asking you to do any such thing."

As they drew near, it stank of fish for the Old Swan was on the edge of the river near Fishmongers' Hall, and Viola's heart perked up. Mayhap, she'd get a fresh dish of fish for their dinner. That would be lovely, indeed.

The boatman said, "Ah, here 'tis. Come along, now," and he pushed through the door.

It was full as an egg with all sorts of folk popping about that included a troublesome group of apprentices, crying for food and drink.

"Well, then," the boatman said as he meandered amongst the tables then suddenly halted. "Here's a bench for us. Sit thee down and I'll fetch a maid."

The benches were bursting with lads, leaving only a space or two for the boatman and herself. The table was soiled with grease and spilled ale. Discarded trenchers were piled with bones, larded fat, and gristle.

Viola grimaced. It was an unappetizing view, and put her right off her hooks for food as she squeezed into a narrow place.

A young apprentice looked up at her, his eyes drooping very odd like. It gave Viola a sudden start, afeard he may have the plague, or the flux, or something else horrid. She asked, "Oiy then, art thou well?"

The apprentice blinked. "Aye, just full in the belly. Am thinking of seeking me sleeping pallet, for me master's a hard one to please, and afore times come quick."

Viola nodded. She, too, generally rose afore dawn to commence in the drudgery of the day. "What sort of business are you apprenticed to?"

The lad frowned. "I prentice on the Bridge and must make needles, you see, from dawn to dark. It hurts me eyes until I've a banging head, and I ain't so good at it, neither. Look."

He placed his hands before her face, spreading his fingers. Indeed, there were bloody scrapes and slashes all along the length of them.

The lad tucked his hands under the table. "'Tis base horrid what I go through every day, stabbing me self with the damned things. Me master claps me about the head saying I ain't going fast enough or they ain't buffed enough. I'm thinking of running away to prentice with a chandler, I am. Then won't stab myself every day, or be forced to two sermons on Sundays and listen to all that blather nonsense, doom and damnation."

He worked himself into quite a state, and Viola watched with fascination as his eyes screwed up and tears spurted down his cheeks. She took his melancholy as overtired, and quietly asked, "How is it you wouldn't to church with the chandler? Is he a rank atheist?"

The lad sniffled. "Nay. He's me sister's husband, ain't he? Not mean like me master. I'd not be forced to sermon, nay I would not."

"Nay," Viola said with a shake of her head. "We must all to church, mustn't we? It's strictly done, ain't it?"

The lad shrugged. "Don't know, do I?" He rose from the table with a wide yawn. "I'm off to me pallet afore I'm found gone." Away he went, walking with purpose toward the door.

Viola sat quiet a moment then realized the boatman was taking his sweet time returning with the maid. She stretched to gaze round the tavern, but could not see him, and she shrugged. She'd wait one more moment and settled to regard the rest of the lads at table.

One fellow gave her a grin. "You were talking hard serious with Sam. He's always so gloomy. Gets right up me nose, he does."

Viola smiled. "What do you do?"

"I'm apprenticed, ain't I?'

Viola rolled her eyes. "I reckoned that. What sort of prenticing do you do?"

"To do a fine hand and be a clerk, don't I? One day, I'll be a scrivener in Westminster Hall."

Forgetting about the boatman, she wondered about the lad. He was short and stocky, seemingly not fit for anything but to be a fisherman or an ironmonger, and her gaze sank to his hands. They were delicate as a woman's which was very strange. His shirt sleeves and fingers were stained with ink, and her gaze ambled up again to his face as she contemplated the mystery of it.

She asked, "And what sort of fine hand do you have, then?"

The lad puffed out his chest. "I've copied Scriptures and our Protectorate's speeches, I have. Me master has taken the papers to a high shop at Paul's where he'll have it put to special bindings. I've the best hand he's seen since afore the old King was beheaded." His grin went wide.

She gazed at him, his face and body, and realized he was not a lad but a man. "How long afore your contract is up?"

"Two years, if I ain't found frolicking with Lucy."

"Who's Lucy?"

He wiggled his eyebrows. "Me master's daughter."

Viola's eyes widened. "Ain't you the rake shamed rogue?"

Grinning, he nodded. "Aye, that I am."

With elbows on the table, Viola rested her head in her hands. "So, what'll you do, then, if you ain't caught?"

"I'm resolved to get established with a lord or MP."

Viola sat taller. She was getting an idea. "How do you expect to go about getting a position with a lord or Member of Parliament? Ain't it dangerous, what with all that's happening by the likes of the Commonwealth and such?" She waved a hand. "You could find yourself discontented in the street."

He declared, "Nay, I shall not, for I shall continue punctual in all dealings with those in power and be seen forthwith as a brave clerk in anyone's employ."

Her idea was clarifying, and her heart began to beat with untold joy, thinking she may have a way out of the pitiful taking of a run off husband. "How did you get the position with your master? What did you have to do?"

"Me pa did it. He knew me master from afore. Paid him good coin to take me on."

She frowned for she may have broken into calamity. Her father could not plead for her, and there was no money to give a potential master.

Shaking her head, she resolved to overcome it, and asked "Who is this fellow, your master? Is he hard like the lad's who just left?"

"Me master is a dull Puritan, righteous in all his dealings."

"Who's your master, then? What's his name?"

He quirked a brow. "Why'd you want to know?"

She leaned forward. "Because I might have someone who could prentice with you."

"There mayn't be any space, for he's got three as it is. We're all on pallets in the loft. With such a crowd, 'tis troublesome to go a' frolicking with Lucy, I can tell you." He smiled and wiggled his brows.

Suddenly vexed, she snapped, "Don't be impertinent. Just tell me your master's name, and be quick about it."

"Oh, all right, then. Don't get yourself all caterwauled over it. His name is Providence Smythe, up at Royal Exchange, and a right scholar, he is, too. He's very good at Scripture, a near conventicler, if you get me drift."

Viola nodded, then clapped hard eyes on him. "What do you mean? Is he a filthy, cruel varlet? Does he go to secret meetings with the same?"

"Nay, just a melancholy, fanatic Puritan." He stood up and made a small bow. "Must be off, now. Dawn comes quick."

Viola watched him leave, then noticed the tavern had emptied of folk. She stood up, and turned a full circle, sweeping her gaze around the common room. Now, where did the filthy boatman go to? Viola trod around the tables to the tap rail to fetch what was left of the evening fare.

When she reached the counter, the publican was in a froth of heartburn, and hollered high for a maid who'd gone missing. Viola's mouth sank into a frown for she knew right well the maid had gone off with the wherriman.

She leaned over the counter, and waved a hand for the publican's attention. "Oiy, there, any food left in the kitchen?"

The publican turned to her with a snarl. "Not much. 'Tis been a busy night."

"I've a purse of coin, and will take what you have."

A bit later, the door of the Old Swan closed behind her. Forsaking the boatman, she had purchased what was left, a dry chine of beef wrapped in a bucket of warm coals, a barley loaf and a pot of ale. It would have to do.

It was dead dark, and not liking this part of the wharfs, she quickly walked to the Bridge. Once amongst the houses, it was lighter with the windows lit against the night and bright lanthorns a' swinging in the breezes.

She slowed her steps with the revelation that had come to her. She would become an apprentice. It would keep her from being someone's mistress or to whore along the lanes, and she burst into the house all joyful.

After laying the food on the table, she informed Pall of her decision.

Her sister stopped sorting wooden trenchers. "Are you mad? Has the leaving of that dirty cur addled your brains?"

Viola fell into a droop. "Why not? I'm small enough to act the part, frail looking almost. Too often Roger said I was more a starving lad than a woman, afraid he'd break me during a tumble. Me womanly parts are apparently very little for a man to hold onto. Or see."

Pall stepped closer. "What about the babe, Viola? Once you begin showing, you'll be dragged in front of the courts for falsifying the prentice contract. The child would be born in gaol. Do you want that?"

Sinking onto the settle, Viola began to sniffle. She'd had a cursed, devil of a day, and now Pall had stricken her marvelous idea to dirt. "I'd rather risk apprenticeship—and the gaol—, than go into slavery or have my hand burned for bigamy. I shall never set to whoring, Pall, never."

Paulina sat on the settle and hugged her. "Only the upper types get dragged to the courts for bigamy. More coin, you see. 'Tis perfectly safe for us middling persons to forget a marriage and marry again."

But Viola did not think so, and she wept piteously against her sister's neck.

Six

Horatio sat stunned. Mistress Wilds was proposing adultery, a punishable offence. He cried out mightily, "I'll not be poxed, nay I shall not."

The woman's eyes widened. "I ain't poxed, Mister Sharpe. I am an honorable woman."

He could not get his brains around what was happening. "Why are you doing this?"

She took a deep breath. "I am a woman, Mister Sharpe. Women must have children. 'Tis what we do." Her breasts heaved. "Me husband reckons I'm barren. But I ain't!"

Not convinced, Horatio poured more ale into their cups and watched as she drank full of it. The emptied cup landed with a thud on the table. She had a desperate gleam to her eye as if she would use every bit of power to sway him to her side.

Looking at her, he admitted she was most handsome fair, and he felt the heaviness of his sacks press against him. Considering the opportunity she laid before him, he knew at that very moment he'd risk the clink to unload them.

Mistress Wilds took a deep breath. "Me husband's gone Presbyterian. He's always been a dull and foggy type. Now his head is forever buried in Scriptures." Shaking her head with the greatest of passion, she declared, "I must be with child, sirrah, or die in the making of it. Nothing else will do."

"How do you intend for this to happen?"

Her mouth dropped, and she stared at him for a long moment. "Why the only way, wouldn't it be?"

Horatio shook his head. "Not what I meant. You'd not have a fellow come to your house, would you?"

Her face was a mask of determination. "I've thought it over quite thoroughly, and I've a plan. Me husband will be ignorant, Mister Sharpe. He won't never, evermore know he ain't the father of the child."

Horatio frowned. "We don't look anything alike, Wilds and me. How'll you explain that?" He cleared his throat. "If I agree to do this, of course."

Mistress Wilds' eyes brightened. "Beyond the Scriptures Mister Wilds is all blurry eyed. He'll not see the child ain't his."

He did not see how that could be since Wilds was a thin, shallow-chested fellow. Horatio was a head taller and quite shapely for a man, if he did say so himself. He was especially proud of his pleasantly shaped calves, not requiring padding in the stockings.

Wicked thoughts, most wondrous, rollicked across his brain. Pouring the last of the ale in their cups, he asked, "How will we go about it, then?"

He listened intently as she told him what they would do.

~ * ~

Horatio awakened rock hard, knowing all would be right with the world by the end of the day. It had been near a month since the offer to get Mistress Wilds with child, and a difficult time it had been, too.

He'd agreed to bed the lady, and since then suffered for it. Knowing his lustful needs would soon be appeased, the anticipation for the feel of a woman caused him troublesome anguish, and he wrestled with his pole so as not to mortify himself upon their meeting.

Very quickly he lay abed relieved, allowing him a clear think.

They were to meet at the Mitre, a public house and inn on Fenchurch Lane which suited him well as it was a known royalist establishment. After the killing of Charles I, the publican had draped black cloth over the swinging sign outside the building, and left it there. It put the publican in great peril during the stiff Cromwell years.

Mistress Wilds informed him her sister was married to the cunning fellow which set mighty well in his books. Being sired in such a place as the Mitre, the babe could only follow the righteous path as a man, and be a Cavalier.

Horatio had been often to the inn, and it stirred his heart to joy for the old days. The place sat large and proud on the street. The lower floor boasted a brave kitchen and tavern. Above the tavern was a music room, in disuse during the Cromwell years, and several sleeping chambers, some of which were alcoves. He hoped Mistress Wilds did not select one of the sleeping alcoves for their meeting, which was not the least bit private. The last thing he wanted was to be discovered by anyone who knew Mister Wilds.

Horatio had his face barbered, shifted into newly brushed clothes, and arrived at the Mitre before the scheduled time. He intended to scan the place for any Parliament men searching for ragged trouble. Times were hard for the Commonwealth, and spies were vicious.

All he saw was a comfortable inn. The coal fire was warm, and the place was crowded with low murmurs from the patrons.

Ordering a pot of mum-beer, his favorite of late, for the taste of the brewed wheat settled nicely on his tongue, he took a seat at a table near the fire. The days had gone frosty with a furious wind that whistled around corners, marking winter was upon them. He had taken to wearing a baize cloth shirt under his suit to keep from getting the colic, and sitting there in a near hot place awaiting Mistress Sharpe, he hoped he wouldn't go too hot and sweaty.

He scoffed. Damn and a pox on it, why should he be bothered if all she wanted was his pole and cods for a babe, and he took another sip of his beer.

Time ticked away and the lady's presence should have been made known to him. Horatio's good temper began a slide into discontent. After all this time, wherein notes had come and gone betwixt them blathering high hopes for the future, and all would soon be well, if she came down with the frets and did not meet him, he would be vexed to the very gut.

Attuned to all activity in the common room, he suddenly heard a scrape upon a stair, and saw a door open.

A woman looking very much like a plump version of Mistress Wilds beckoned to him from the doorway, and straightening his back, he gazed around the tavern. She cleared her throat, and beckoned to him again, bringing him to his feet.

The long awaited moment had come. His cock reacted to the knowledge, and he blessed the activity earlier in the day.

He followed the woman through the door and up the stairs to the upper rooms. When they reached the top, he gazed around the alcoves for people in residence. There were no shoes or packs on the floor by the curtains, and he let out a breath of relief.

The woman took him into a chamber that was small with shelves along a wall, stuffed with folded linen. Buckets and brooms sat in a corner. She plucked a stack of linen off a shelf, and thrust it into his arms. Reaching through the vacant shelf, she snapped open a latch, pulled the shelving toward them then pointed to a door.

Taking the linens from his arms, she said, "I'll give you two hours, then come up here to retrieve you from the priest hole. It's just above the brewery, so some noise will not be heard, but much noise will." She looked at him in the dim light of the room and added, "Good luck to you."

With a sharp nod of her head, she ordered him into the chamber then closed the door. He heard the rasp of the shelving and the click of the latch. He was totally enclosed.

If there were windows, they were blocked off, for it was like pitch except for a small burning candle. Horatio gazed around the room, his eyes adjusting to the dark. Not just a priest hole, it was more an old storage loft.

A disembodied voice said, "Afore the time of Bloody Mary, this was storage for the brewery grains and other sundries. Since then, this here place has seen papists, Protestants, and Royalty."

Horatio gazed toward the origin of the voice and saw a bedstead naked of curtains. Being on top a' rump-scuttling would be cold to his backside. "Mistress Wilds, art thou ready?"

"Aye, Mister Sharpe. The feather coverlet will warm us for the task at hand. Come join me."

With a grin, he did.

~ * ~

Afterwards Horatio walked with a quick step back to Tower Hill and his residence, feeling mighty fine. The frolic had been far better than anticipated, for her privy parts had a hunger that sent him to the heights of debauchery.

He feasted upon her with such desire he thought his very heart would burst from pride. How could her husband be so staid and gloomy, and not enjoy her? The man's melancholy was to his boon, however, for he had emptied his sacks in her until there was nothing left.

In between times, they shared ale and a plate of anchovies, then he dived between her legs until she gasped and cried, and he was spent. He left her there on the bed with her tail propped on a pillow. She said it was to make certain all his seed met the mark. He grinned.

Pulling on his boots, Mistress Wilds had said, "If me terms come, I shall be sending you a note for another meeting. Will that do well with you?"

He turned to her with a smile and a nod. "Aye, indeed, Mistress. I shall very much enjoy another meeting with you."

Seven

"Are you to church with me?" Viola asked as Pall swept through the sitting room.

Paulina pulled her cloak off a hook, and replied, "Nay, I'm to an Anglican church in the City."

Viola frowned. It was against the Commonwealth to attend popish services. "I'm to Magnus the Martyr to hear Doctor Stern give a sermon. Heard he's a fine speaker."

"Bah!" Pall snapped, suddenly all festered. "He's like the rest, harking doom from the pulpit. 'Tis a wonder good folk don't jump off the Bridge at the end of his sermons. Everyone's going to hell, anyway." She secured her hat on her head with tie ribbons, and glared at Viola. "Why do you bother?"

Each day Viola grew more astonished to see her sister's vexation so high against the Commonwealth. She shrugged. "Because it's expected?"

Pall snorted, and was about to walk out the door when she paused. "Why don't you come with me? It'll be a lark. On our return, we'll pick up that collar of brawn you've been so desiring." She smiled.

Viola stared at Pall, not understanding the constant flares of high distemper, then flat calm. It took her breath away.

Pall stamped her foot. "Well?"

Viola blinked. It might be just dandy to attend a service where the minister didn't constantly hark everyone was heading straight to the fires of hell, but she had to ask: "Art thou a Malignant, a popish person? It ain't allowed, you know. How'd you find one of these here churches?"

"You'll not speak that word, again," Pall barked. "'Tis ignorant to call us Malignants. It's from the Cromwell days, anyway." Pall pulled her cloak ribbons more securely around her neck. "I'm to St. Dionis Backchurch, near Gracious Street. As for Anglicans, I dare say there are many all over England, including London City. Even though the Roundheads want it, Royalty ain't dead." She gazed hard at her and asked, "Where have you been that you don't know this?"

Thinking on Church dogma and its rules caused Viola's brain to go all soggy. Then, she had never been concerned with the workings of the government, who ruled it or the Church. Royalty or Parliament men, Aldermen and the Lord Mayors were all corrupt rascals, and she wanted nothing to do with them.

She shrugged. "Ain't interested, and me hands have been full with Roger."

Pall took hold of the door latch. "Well, you can come or not, suit yourself," and she walked down the steps to Bridge Road.

"Oiy, wait for me," Viola called as she plucked her cloak from the hook.

~ * ~

They walked into the City and strode up the hill to Gracious Street, Viola panting with the effort. Her sister walked too fast. She was at a near run. "Oiy, Pall, hold on. What's the rush?"

"We must get there afore the ceremony begins."

"Ceremony? What you talking about?" She grabbed Pall's cloak to slow her down.

Pall crooned, "It's all the liturgy and trappings of the service, you ken? Like a ceremony, and ever so nice." She leaned close to whisper, "Sometimes, there's even a bit of music, most extraordinary."

Viola had never heard of such a thing. *Music during a service!* "What do you mean, music?"

"It's so very lovely." Pall sighed. "Music so airy is very pretty in a church."

Appalled, Viola sputtered. "I should think it's horrid wicked to have music during service. If spies are amongst us, we'll get thrown in dungeon and never be allowed out." She lowered her voice. "Does the music give you a very fine feeling in your heart?"

Pall's eyes were shining. "Aye, it does. Let's to it afore we miss anything."

The church loomed large and seemingly on top of the street, but before they entered, Pall took hold of her arm and pointed. "That there, across from the church is the royalist inn and tavern, the Mitre. After the service we'll just go there for a drink and look-see. What do you think?"

"But we ain't with a man, are we? Can't just go Morris dancing into a tavern alone and unattended, now can we?"

Pall snorted. "Pish fie, with the Commonwealth almost done and no strength left, we should be fine going in there. It'll be most brave to hear royalist talk, and the Mitre's been that way since day one. No one's pulled down its walls or plucked the doors off its hinges. I reckon men *and women* go inside all the time." Squinting an eye, she conceded, "But if we must, we'll find someone to take us in there."

They walked up the stairs and were last into the church. An attendant closed and bolted the door behind them. Everyone was quiet, and the heels of their shoes clacked loudly against the stone floor as they found places in a pew.

Viola glanced around. There were no cushions on the seats to mark ownership of parishioners, and she thought it probably wise in such dangerous times.

Bells tinkled and everyone stood. The service was beginning, the church crowded. She and her sister were in a pew behind some very tall fellows, forcing Viola to crane her neck to see the ceremony.

Pall whispered, "Every time I come here, 'tis more full. As you can see, Royalty and like thinking ain't dead." Her smile reached her eyes that sparkled and were happy, forcing Viola to smile in return. She patted Pall's arm.

The minister wore frippery of color as he stood at the altar with his back to the people. He chanted and raised a gold cup above his head, all the while singing his prayers. The people responded in quiet song, amazing Viola with the heady danger of it all. Oft times they knelt on a bench, very popish. The sermon was not of doom and calamity but about having the duty to give good example in all ways throughout the day. It was uplifting, and Viola's heart was gladdened.

Then the minister turned to the congregation, asking all to come forth to the railing where he began to dispense food and drink to the people.

Pall made a movement to follow, Viola grabbing her arm. "Where art thou going? What's afoot? Is it the popish way to feed us?"

Pall gazed at her with a shrug. "Nay, 'tis something to do with eating and drinking of the Lord."

Viola went stiff with horror. A shiver racked her to the very heart. She cried, "'Tis positively savage. How can you eat of God? He'll strike you to the pit of hell, He will."

"Nay, 'tis not savage, but jolly interesting. The wine ain't watered down, neither. Come along and try it."

Viola would nevermore, ever touch the flesh of God, for she was certain it would kill her dead. "Nay, I shall not."

Paulina shrugged. "Suit yourself," and she sauntered off down the aisle.

As Viola thought very stern on the riddle of eating God, she heard a chuckle behind her and turned to see a man with a wide grin on his face. She whispered harshly, "I beg your pardon, what's so mirthful?"

"You are, Mistress. You will not be stricken down when you take communion."

"Communion?"

"Aye, the taking of the host and wine is a symbol of the Last Supper."

"And why aren't you eating of this food?" she asked. If he weren't afeard, he should be down at the rail with everyone else.

"I've already partaken once today," he answered as Pall tripped back, all happy as you please to kneel on the bench.

Viola regarded her sister most closely, waiting for the flesh to shrivel off her bones and crumble in a heap right there before her. Time ticked away, but she did not die nor shrivel. Pall sat on the pew all calm and happy like.

Extraordinary.

The ceremony was done with the parson walking from the altar into an inner sanctum. It gave everyone leave to mill about in the pews or converse in the aisle as the door was unbolted and thrown open. Pall turned to the man behind them and smiled, showing her dimple and batting her eyelashes.

Viola sniffed, disgusted.

Her sister was an impertinent jade as she flirted, then was so bold to ask: "Oiy, there, and who are you, sirrah? We are Mistresses Paulina and Viola."

The man bowed. "I am Mister Horatio Sharpe, at your service, Mistresses Paulina and Viola. How may I serve thee?"

Pall talked to the man, but taken aback by his name, Viola did not hear what was said. She gazed hard at him, wondering if he were related to Roger. They were both tall, both with dark hair, and both had dimples in their chins. She knew Roger had some brothers, but she had never met them, or any of his family for that matter, and she suddenly wondered what else he had been hiding.

Pall nudged her. "Art thou coming?"

Surprised, she hollered, "What? Where?"

"Why to the Mitre with this gentleman. He'll be our escort." She gazed at the man and batted her eyelashes again.

Viola was hungry. "Is it open for business on the Sabbath?"

Mister Sharpe chuckled. "But of course, now that the service is complete."

She shrugged. "Alright then."

As they walked out of the church and down the stairs to the street, she pulled her sister to the side and muttered, "Pall, I've been with you all me life, but these past weeks have made me afeard you've gone rackety mad. How is it you've changed so? Has papa's accident made you base strange?"

"What do you mean? I ain't strange as papa, and you do me injury to say such."

Viola was insistent. "I don't remember you being so high against the government, taking risks to attend popish ceremonies. 'Tis most odd."

Pall glowered at her, suddenly angry as a hen. "It near breaks me brains thinking you so false afore the whole world. Don't forget, you attended the ceremony, too." She sighed, and with a glance toward Mister Sharpe, added, "Well, let's to the inn, then. It'll do no harm to have a dish or two. Afterwards, we'll go home."

They followed Mister Sharpe into the inn where Viola watched with interest as he greeted folk all pleasant and jovial like. He shook hands with the publican and bussed his lady-wife's pink cheeks, who was in high mirth.

Viola looked about and saw an effigy of Charles I perched on a corner cupboard, draped in black cloth. There were candles and a prayer book on the same shelf. It was a shrine.

A fellow leaned close to her and muttered, "Our brave publican, here, will have that corner in mourning until the rightful heir returns to run our country."

Viola turned to the man who was fitted all fancy in a coat of color, the woman at his side in a gown of equal color, and her face painted very bright. Mayhap, she was a saucy slut, and Viola's gaze went strong fixed on the couple.

The man was not bothered by her stares. He said, "The publican is Mister Clarkson, a fellow of stout beliefs in what is aright in this here world." He gazed around the large common room and added, "None of the government authorities ever bothered him these many years when one would have thought their staunch republican ways would rule over all. I've determined it showed weakness in their resolve." He gazed at the painted woman. "Ain't that so, me lovely Charlotte?"

Charlotte sent him a thoughtful gaze, as if she loved him extraordinary. "Aye."

Viola watched this with interest, for the painted lady no longer seemed a saucy slut but a woman of gentle breeding. When Charlotte turned to her with a smile, her blue eyes were very kind. Viola's heart warmed, and she smiled, too. She instantly liked the lady, Charlotte, and wanted to know her more.

Another lady walked up to Mister Sharpe, her smile happy. She greeted him with a loud kiss, which he returned with gusto. It made Viola think they were a couple, but thought no more on it when the publican's wife announced to all around: "Oiy, welcome to the Mitre. We've a side of lamb and a lovely collar of brawn gently roasted. The ale is hearty and the wine robust. Come, make yourselves comfortable."

Viola was delighted to hear of the brawn. Her mouth had watered over it for quite a long while, now, and for it to be roasted made her very merry, indeed. She followed everyone to a long table near the hearth, expecting to have one of the bravest of meals in the whole of her life.

Mister Sharpe stood at the end of the table. "Let me introduce everyone afore this worthy banquet begins." He gazed fondly at the woman who had kissed him on the mouth and said, "This here is Mistress Elizabeth Wilds, me neighbor on Tower Hill."

Mistress Wilds nodded her head. The red swirling curls at her cheeks bobbed prettily.

Mister Sharpe moved down the table. "This here are Mister and Mistress Finch, who own the press in me bookseller's shop."

The Finches smiled and nodded.

"And here are me new friends, Mistresses Paulina and Viola. We just met at the Anglican Church service next door. They are resolved to shake off the grim, Puritan Scriptures."

Paulina laughed while Viola frowned. She had no intention of throwing off the government's accepted dogma to eat of God in a popish service. Saying nothing, though, her thoughts quickly spent themselves on the surfeit from the collar of brawn and mum beer. After the brave meal, she hoped to eat a syllabub, a dessert of curdled cream and wine. Very nice, and she smacked her lips.

It was a merry feast, and afterwards, the publican stood afore their table with a pitcher of new beer. "Aye, would you like to join the lads and ladies going to sing in the music room?"

Music room? Another reason to be thrown in the clink, but Viola also knew it was hard to drive singing and rollicking out of folk. She wondered at that, but suddenly yawned. Stuffed with much food, she could do with a nap.

Paulina shook her. "Come on, then, for a jolly round of music."

"Nay, it ain't allowed."

"Aye, 'tis," Mister Sharpe responded. "Unless you're of a mind to seek the magistrates," and he gazed at her with an uplifted brow.

"Nay, that I'd never do."

Mister Sharpe pulled his hat more firmly round his ears. "Good, then come and join in. There are instruments in the music room, and a pair of virginals." He wagged his eyebrows.

Viola's eyes widened. "Can you play such instruments? What a wondrous gift."

"I can tinker," Mister Sharpe said. "But Mistress Elizabeth can play. She's very good."

When Viola entered the music room, there were people scattered about on benches and straight chairs. There was a table with a barrel of small beer and filled pots next to it. Viola took a pot of ale and sat next to Pall whose temper was very mirthful. She clapped her hands and giggled, and gazing at her, Viola wondered if she didn't see a tear or two.

The violins and violas were tuned, with the virginals tinkling to their tuning. It went all quiet, and then a fellow cried, "A' one, a' two, and a' three…"

The musicians struck their first note in unison, after which all went in different directions, creating the most beautiful of sounds. Viola gasped with pleasure, and tears sprang to her eyes. It was the most wondrous thing she'd ever heard in her whole life. She could die this very moment and go straight to heaven.

She allowed the music to engulf her whole being, then Mistress Wilds stood up and began to sing. Her voice was a meadowlark on a summer's day, and wonderful. Viola sat on the bench and wept.

Eight

"What a lovely day," Paulina exclaimed as they walked back to the Bridge after the afternoon of music and song. After a few pots of beer, the whole room of people stirred to sing, thumping their feet with the rhythm. Mistress Wilds and Mister Sharpe even took up dancing a jig in the center of the chamber.

Viola had to admit it had been fain wonderful. "I did pleasantly sing a song with Mistress Elizabeth, didn't I?"

"Aye, indeed," Pall said with a sigh. "You sing most handsomely."

"As do you," Viola said. "Together, we should learn a piece and sing it in the music room afore all the others."

"Nay," Pall answered as they skipped down the hill. "I'd like to learn to play an instrument, though. Maybe, the virginal."

Viola laughed as they neared the Bridge and their house. "That would be lovely."

Chattering loudly, they burst through the door, coming to a sudden halt at a sick, horrid smell. Viola coughed as Pall cried, "What is it?"

Their papa tinkered at his bench, and looking up at their entrance, hollered as if they were deaf, "I told you I'm scientific, but you wouldn't believe me. Nay, you would not, throwing the dead head away from me. Well, this day I went back to the water whilst the tide was out and all calm, and found this one in the mud." He grinned and showed them the head. "'Tis newly dead, and still pink. Come and have a look-see."

Pall fell to screaming while Viola, filled with horror, sank onto a stool, suddenly sick. All the food and beer she'd taken in soured horrid within her. Why couldn't she have an ordinary, dull road life? Why must there be such a furious clamor all the time?

Still screaming, Pall ran around the tinkering table to the dead head, trying to grab it away from their papa, but in his madness, he was agile and determined. He raised it high, the muck of it drizzling on top his hair. "Nay, you shall not have it. 'Tis mine to keep and to bring back aright to life. Leave off or I'll clap you soundly about the ears. Don't think I won't."

Someone pounded on their door. "What the devil's going on there? I'll cry the bailiffs if you ain't more quiet."

Almost like his old self, their papa yelled at the closed door. "Nay, you shall not. I have me rights, and me rights say I can be scientific and clap me daughters until they're once again proper, so leave off!"

"Nay, I shall not," the man shouted from the other side of the panel. "You'll go quiet or suffer for it—that I promise."

"Nay, you shall not," their papa cried as he lowered the head and stomped to the door. He yanked it open. "Get thee gone from me house or I'll cry the bailiffs that you're trespassing."

Viola knew the man to be their neighbor, never a friendly fellow. His gaze sank to the dead head in their papa's hand, and his eyes widened. "What the devil is that?"

"'Tis a dead head I'll bring to life as Godly Thomas Moore during King Harry's day."

"That never happened. Once someone's dead, they're dead. You must be mad. You should be thrown in a dungeon."

The two men bent toward each other and hollered into each other's faces as Pall stepped on the table bench and opened the window. Watching her sister, Viola swallowed again and again as the sickness got worse, the bile rising into her throat. Pall sneaked around to the back of their papa, and in a sudden movement, grabbed the dead head, clambered onto the bench, and threw it out the window.

The hideous whiff of death did Viola in, and bile rushed up her throat. She scrambled onto the table to retch out the window.

Later that night whilst tucked in bed, and as Pall snored heavily beside her, Viola mourned the loss of such a fine day, and her papa acting so strange. Once he realized the head was gone, he wailed and bellowed to the ceiling like a stark animal.

It had been base dreadful with the neighbor running off all afeard, and Pall forced to take control. She slammed the window shut, then ran to the door, and out of the house in search of an apothecary for a drug to settle him. They left their papa on the floor beside the warm hearth, droning in a melancholy manner with his eyes closed, and sought their bed. She could still hear his moans through the planks of the floor.

Viola rolled over, but could not get comfortable. Pall snored loud enough to shake the mice out of the daub and waddle. Viola turned to find a better spot, and Pall's snores stopped, but almost immediately resumed their racket. Even though she could not eat a morsel after being sick, Viola felt overstuffed and hot, and suddenly cramps crawled through her belly.

She turned to her side, hoping not to be sick, when hard pains gripped her. Viola realized with a sob she was losing the babe. She moved the curtains aside, and scrambled off the bed to the corner privy-chair where she sat and groaned against the sharp agony that tore at her lower parts.

As she expelled Roger's babe into the privy pot, fear gripped her for it was far worse than the first loss. Blood gushed out of her. It filled the pot, then overflowed onto the plank floor. She keened and grunted. Her body was clutched in a vise of searing pain, and her agonies awakened Pall who jumped out of bed and ran to her side.

Pall held her tight, gently rocked her, and wept. Against her ear, Viola heard Paulina beg God not to let her die.

Nine

Horatio walked through the dank lanes to Tower Hill. His sword slapped comfortably against his leg, and a brace of pistols nestled neatly beneath his coat. A bell tolled in the distance, and the watchman cried: "Eight of clock in the night, and all is well."

It had been a lovely day, from the Anglican Church services to the singing and dancing at the Mitre. His belly was full, and his cods were empty.

Earlier, and after dinner when all had dispersed to their homes and whatnot, he'd settled alone all comfy in the music room. He sat on a settle with his foot on a stool. Drowsy, his eyelids growing heavy, he heard a foot on the floorboards, and Elizabeth Wilds stood before him. His head was all a buzz with mum beer and heady wine, and with a smile, he patted the bench.

She said, "Me husband's gone with the Presbyterians, beating the Bible and shouting of doom and damnation."

"Ah, then, we are alone."

"I am spending the night under the protection of me sister and her husband."

Horatio winked. "Come along, then, Mistress, and I shall rub your back."

"Thanks to you, sirrah. This I will do."

When she perched on the edge of the settle, he massaged her neck and back between the shoulders. He asked, "How art thou? You look fine and dandy."

She relaxed at his ministrations, and that made him feel ever so good in the heart. Her joyous reaction to him—to his hands, his pole—puffed him up like a turkey cock. The fire was still warm from the afternoon, and he kissed her neck, running his hand down the front of her bodice.

Melting into him, she murmured, "Me terms have not yet come."

He took her in his arms, running kisses down the front of her neck toward her breasts. As his pole got hard, he breathed in her scent. She was a handsome piece of tail, and a kind, noble lady, too.

She leaned her head back and gave him more room to explore her wonders. She turned around and said, "I ain't wearing any drawers." She kissed him hard.

Horatio's heart hammered in his chest, knowing such fierce desire, he was afraid his hairs would burst to flame. He couldn't think, couldn't breathe.

"I'll lock the door, shall I?" Elizabeth said breathlessly.

While she was up, he shifted his clothes to release his cock, thick and hard, and his cods, heavy with need. Coming back to him on the settle, she lifted her skirts to straddle him, and he gasped with pleasure.

~ * ~

Afterwards, she rested her head on his lap with her ankles hanging over the arms of the settle. She wanted his seed to hit its mark, and he hoped his seed *never* hit the mark. He basked in the joy of the toss, his breathing still heavy.

She said, "I shall miss this when I'm with child."

He leaned his head against the back of the settle. "Must we stop?"

"Aye," she said with a note of sadness. "It would be best."

His thoughts were becoming clearer. "I must be away on business within the week, to see the King."

She sighed. "Me husband has been having strange fits of late. He either roars of the Scriptures and how all will come to the ends of the world and to the devil, or goes all quiet like, and writes secret code along the margins of his Bible."

Horatio sat up. "What? Is there mischief afoot?"

Elizabeth shrugged. "I know not, but as each day passes, he blathers much of the way of the world and how it must come to a halt."

"Does he send out messages, letters? Do any come back to him, all secret like?"

Sighing as if sleepy, Elizabeth nodded her head against his leg.

Cruelly troubled, Horatio went into a hard think. Wilds was always a rank fool. With the chance of the King returning from exile, all Royal folk must cast their eyes against any roguery, and protect their sovereign.

~ * ~

As Horatio climbed Tower Hill toward his house, he realized Wilds might very well be part of a treachery. He had worked too hard for the return of his monarch to allow anything to stand in his way, and decided to walk by the Wilds' front door to have a look, it being so close.

Wilds' shutters were still open, and there was no fabric covering the glass, very strange. The servants should have closed everything against the dangers of the night. It put him on guard.

At first, it was quiet with very little light from inside, then he saw a moving shadow. Elizabeth had said Wilds would be out, and he reasoned whoever moved about could be one of the servants. Horatio crept closer to the house.

Like his own, the first room was the entry. It was dark. Empty.

The door leaving the entry was open, showing a room beyond lit with candlelight. He stretched taller, and wondered if it were the servants or Wilds in there. Suddenly, a man filled the open doorway, dragging a trunk into the entry.

Horatio quickly ducked out of sight. He listened as the man dropped the chest with a grunt and slapped his hands. It was not Wilds, a thin, sallow fellow, but one who was big and burly, like an ironmonger.

Was this the work of thieves? The door was not ajar or off its hinges, and removing his wide brimmed hat, he slowly straightened to see in, again.

Wilds came into the entry. He thumped a book and wagged a finger at the big man, then stopped as if something caught his eye. Turning toward the window, he jerked, and hollered, "Someone's outside. Quick, go get him!"

Ten

February, 1660

Viola walked through the wet lanes of London City, holding in her hand a forged letter. She was taking it to Alderman Bird, the man her papa had worked with afore his accident. He was well known along Lombard Street, and she thought he'd be able to provide a place for her as an apprentice.

Staying under the overhang of houses to keep dry, Viola breathed in the dank air of the City, glad to be healthy again. The loss of the babe almost killed her dead. The midwife, in fear and desperation for her life, sent for the surgeon who admitted the only way to keep her from crossing the veil was to leech her everyday for a sennight.

That was in December.

Still too weak in January, her illness made her miss the Twelfth Night party, but Pall told her she had found the pea in the cake, making her queen for the day. Viola did not know who the king was as her sister had gone completely Royalist, and trotted with different folk. She was away much of the time, but when she was at home, Pall smiled greatly. Viola wondered if Mister Horatio

Sharpe were not one of her new friends, and she resolved to ask Pall the question next time they were together.

She frowned. If they were serious, if they had frolicked, and he was Roger's brother, it would be incest and a troublesome coil.

Viola came to Alderman Bird's house, and dashed across the street amidst much traffic. Along the way, she noticed people harking up and down the lanes, very happy, bits and bobs of them crying out, "Kiss my rump", which had something to do with the old Parliament.

Pall was very high on the matter, but this was the first Viola had seen of the City residents all festered over it. What had happened, she did not know. After giving the letter to the Alderman, she would go along the lanes and find out the reason for so much mirth in the streets. She pulled the bell rope and waited, hoping this business would soon be put behind her.

While abed for so many weeks, Viola racked her brains how she would carry on without Roger, and the only thing she came up with was to become an apprentice. If she could make it work, she'd not be forced into another marriage or onto the lanes as a whore.

Knowing Pall would not support her until forced, Viola concocted what she thought an extraordinary plan, but she wanted full into it afore she told her sister. Once the time came, Pall would help her look like a lad.

The door opened and a tall man squinted down at her. "Aye, what do you want?"

Her gut clenched. She forced a smile, and curtsied. "I've a letter for the Alderman from me papa, Mister James Wilmot, if you'd be so kind to give it him."

The man harrumphed. "He's in. Come this way."

The invitation was unexpected, and Viola swallowed heavily as she entered the house. Looking around, it was very large and well appointed, and she remembered how her papa had once said the man had more money than he could count, and lived that way, too.

She saw portraits on walls, carpets on furniture, and even turkey cushions on chairs. She could not imagine how very comfortable that must be for a person's backside.

The man turned to her. "Stay here, and don't touch nothing." He entered a chamber and closed the door.

It was very quiet as a clock chimed the hour somewhere in the house. Viola gazed with horror at the letter in her hand. She had crumpled it in her fretfulness, and was attempting to straighten it out when the door opened. Chagrined, she looked up to see the tall man bid her enter.

Alderman Bird was at his desk, smoking a pipe. He gazed at her for a long moment, then said, "So, you are Wilmot's daughter. How's he doing?"

His face was warm and welcoming, and Viola relaxed a bit. "He's base strange, Your Honor. That clap on the head near pushed his skull into his brains."

Bird shook his head. "Very unfortunate. My man said you had a letter from him?"

Viola handed him the sealed letter. "Aye, Your Honor. He's requesting you find a place for a lad we know." She smiled, and hoped he wouldn't ask for money to do the deed.

Taking the letter, he broke the seal and read the short message. "Ah, Wilmot wants the lad to follow in his own footsteps, to be in the employ in a house such as mine." He turned his gaze to her. "If he's so base strange, how'd he write this?"

Egad, she shouldn't have blathered so about her papa. "Uhm, Your Honor, he can still read and write when he's clear thinking. He tells everyone he's scientific, now, and tinkers at a bench. He writes of his work in a journal."

"This does not look like your father's hand, me girl."

Filled with so many lies, what was one more? "Everything's changed, Your Honor. His voice, *and* his hand."

Bird grunted and reread the letter. "Hmmm, well, it's been hopeless around here without your da, so I'll grant his wish. As it turns out I know of a man who has space for a prentice, but the lad must read and write. Can your lad read and write?"

Viola chirped, "Aye."

"It's to learn the clerking business. Would he be up to that?"

"Aye, Your Honor. He's a bit frail looking. Ain't of a type to do heavy work, like being a fishmonger, or a steelyard worker, or such. He'd do just fine learning to be a clerk," and she grinned.

Bird gazed at her, his eyebrow hitching high, and she cursed herself for blathering, again.

Taking a quill and dipping it in ink, he scratched hastily. "Send the lad to Providence Smythe at the Exchange. He has a shop there." He looked up at her.

"Mind you, the man's a strict Puritan, a near conventicler. If the lad does not hold to his dictates, he'll be cast out."

Viola was not bothered. She was resolved to make certain all was right and imaginable with the world, and with her master.

He asked, "What's the lad's name?"

She gulped, discarding the earlier name she'd picked, for it would no longer do. She thought fast, and having been around Puritans all her life, she put two names together. "Dothgood Scroope, Your Honor."

Bird grinned. "Well then, the two of them should do right well together," and he finished the note with a flourish.

Eleven

It stopped drizzling as Horatio walked down Lombard Street. All he hoped for seemed very close. The Commonwealth was near dead with everyone siding for a free Parliament, and against the old Rump Parliament. The only option was to bring back the heir and King from Holland and set him happily on the throne of England.

Horatio's excitement built as he marched quickly down the busy lane, his sword thumping in rhythm at his side. He heard a door shut and looked over to see a woman on Alderman Bird's stoop, all happy like. She looked familiar, but he was of no mind to reckon why. The times were too exciting to bother with such trifles.

General Monck finally arrived from Scotland late January, and still no one knew which way he would go, to support the King or no. It made everyone afeard of a ruckus, especially when Monck's men filled the town and abused poor folk, amongst others, the Catholics and Quakers.

This month of February began in a most extraordinary way with the foot soldier revolt at Somerset House. The whole force demanded a free parliament and their back wages, which Horatio heard was a vast amount. Then the apprentices rose to support the soldiers, and that caused a tempest in the streets. For days, there was a great show of short rifles, pistols and swords, the citizenry of London all afeard it would end in a great trounce.

Horatio ignored his bookseller shop at the Exchange in his keen joy to keep abreast of these wondrous times. Besides what was happening in London, he had been several times to and from the King with letters.

He'd met behind closed doors with Royalist agents who declared for the return of the King, but still wondered mightily at General Monck's intent. Everyone was very high on the matter, for it did not help when the General sent his men into the City to have important citizens slapped in chains. In the end though, Horatio believed the man would declare for the King and all would be right in the world.

Horatio paused at a street corner, watching a roar of people. As the afternoon gave over to darkness, the rejoicing in the streets turned clamorous.

Middling and high folk hollered against the Rump Parliament, and church bells rang in constant staccato. To his merriment, he walked along and saw bonfires spring up and down the lanes. Rumps of meat roasted on spits, giving him a most contented feeling.

Doors were thrown open, and the owners of houses and shops welcomed him in for a drink in celebration. He climbed to a third-story garret, and was astonished to see small fires everywhere, in all lanes, streets and tight alleys. The smell of roasting meat overpowered the stink of the City, and made his mouth water.

Back to the street, again, there was laughing and cheering along the way. A woman thrust a pot of ale into his hand as he zigzagged around bonfires only a few feet apart from each other. People reveled and danced around them. He came to a man at a spit over the fire who gave him a portion of cooked meat on a stick. "There you go, laddie. Have a taste of this here gently roasted rump."

Horatio took it with a grin. "Aye, so I shall, and I thank thee." He took a bite. It was one of the finest he'd ever tasted in his life.

The man laughed. "Kiss my rump with the fine eating of it." He returned to the meat at the fire, and guffawed at his own joke. "Aye, kiss my fired up, roasted rump."

Horatio smiled and walked away with his meat.

It was near nine o'clock. As he made his way toward home, and his bed, Horatio strode down Fenchurch Street. The Mitre was all lit up with torches on either side of the door. Rowdy hollering and singing reached the street, and he decided to seek his bed later. His heart filled with joy, he stepped into the tavern.

It was a full house with unbound gaiety. People sat and drank, ate from more roasted rumps, and sang with great mirth. He greeted the publican's wife with a sound bussing. She looked all tired from the day of revelry, but indeed happy.

"Oiy, there, how you be?" he asked.

"Very fine what with the swift change these days." She spread her arm to indicate the patrons. "Everyone's of great mirth the King will soon return."

Horatio grinned. "Aye, that'd be an extraordinary thing."

"Some of these here folk are seeking their homes, so you'll be able to find a place easily enough. I'll bring you a quart of wine gotten from the Venice House just today. 'Tis robust and ain't watered down." She gave him a different look, studying him like, then said, "I've a letter for you, by the by. Need to know your thoughts on it by the end of this evening."

She turned on her heel, back to the tap rail, leaving Horatio to wonder greatly what that was all about. Shrugging, he strode through the tables, looking for a place to sit, and nodded to people he knew. He came to an open space next to Mister and Mistress Wilds.

Every time he saw Wilds—who had never caught him, or recognized him as the one staring into his window—Horatio wondered what the man was about. He'd tried to follow him on occasion, but Wilds was a cunning fellow who easily disappeared in the crowds. It was cruelly vexing.

Mistress Wilds gazed at him with sparkling eyes as her husband sat next to her, all dark and dreary. Horatio greeted him with a nod, but the man remained stiff and frowny, barely civil. With a glance at Elizabeth, Horatio raised a brow, shrugged, and sat on the bench next to her. He was resolved Wilds should go straight to the very devil.

He pressed his hat more firmly on his head. "Mister and Mistress Wilds, how art thou this night?"

Mister Wilds stood. "Not so well, sirrah. Must needs to seek me bed for I'm off to Oxford on the morrow." He gave his wife a stern glower. "I ain't at all happy you'll be staying here whilst I'm gone, Wife, this being a den of unsaintly clamor, but as I've no choice in the matter, me having no one else to watch over you, what must be, must be."

He buttoned his coat to his chin, then more softly said, "Take care of the babe within, for I shall want me heir healthy to follow aright in the Presbyterian ways."

Elizabeth Wilds smiled happily as she gazed at her husband, and Horatio's heart burst in a froth of pride. He looked away afraid the man would notice, and waited for him to leave the tavern.

As soon as Wilds was gone, he turned to Elizabeth and exclaimed, "What's this I hear? Art thou with child?"

"Aye," she responded with a broad grin that showed the dimples in her cheeks.

He sighed. What a lovely lady she was, and now all was finished between them. Even though it started out selfish enough, he'd come to care for her in a way more than providing seed for a babe. They did well together, were satisfied in each other's company, and her response to him as they frolicked had been most delightful.

"Well then," Horatio said as the publican's wife sat a quart of wine and a glass before him. "What'll you do, now?"

Elizabeth's regard moved to her sister. "Margery and I have a proposal for you."

"Aye," remarked the publican's wife as she sank to the bench beside Elizabeth.

Horatio went cautious. "What's this about?"

Margery motioned for him to move closer, and the three of them went into a huddle. She whispered, "Had it in the letter, but burned it. Thought it best not to write what we've a mind to on paper." She gave him a significant look.

Horatio frowned. This sounded like a wicked deception was afoot. "Aye?"

As Margery was about to speak, Elizabeth stayed her and said, "Before we give you our proposal, I would like to thank thee for all you've done. I'm a most happy woman, and as this will be the last we'll speak so bold to one another, I'd like to give you proper thanks by a full night of frolic."

His pole reacted with the greatest of desire, growing hard immediately, and he shivered. His heart pounded in his chest, and he thought with alarm he might be on the verge of loving the woman. That would not do, and he steeled his thoughts against it.

Margery said, "Aye, you'll have the priest closet, but Elizabeth for the last time."

Now, what did that mean? Horatio had never understood women, talking so cryptically all the time. They would give him a look, as the publican's wife was at this moment, expecting him to get the full drift of what was said.

Well, damnit to hell, he did not get the drift. "Speak plainly, woman," he snarled.

Elizabeth chirped, "We've of a mind to go into business, Mister Sharpe."

"And?" he prodded.

"We want you as part of this here business."

"Me?"

Margery nodded. "Aye."

This wasn't getting him anywhere, and he snapped, "Well, get on with it, then. What's this about? Don't be all foggy about it."

Elizabeth said, "The business will be nothing of baseness or dishonor, sirrah, but very needful. As you know, me husband could not provide well and get me with child. There are others just like me."

Margery leaned closer. "Aye, 'tis a shameful calamity out there. Husbands are confused, accusing their wives of being barren when in fact, 'tis they who are empty inkpots."

"'Tis their manly pride that will not let them be truthful in the matter," Elizabeth added with a certain confidence.

Horatio was stunned. "You want a stud service business—with me as the stud? Am I hearing you aright?"

Both women grinned. "Aye, and you'll be paid a fine percentage."

"As I am doing all the work, I should think so," Horatio grumped, realizing he'd probably do this. After all, it would be a discreet way of appeasing his lusty parts, and since Elizabeth, he knew how sorely he had been with need since his wife's betrayal.

His head snapped up. "I'll not have the clap! You shall provide me with clean women."

The ladies beamed. Margery asked, "You'll take part in the stud business?"

"Nor do I want the women harking at me door, later, saying I'm the father. I'll not be part of this adventure unless this is firmly resolved."

The women nodded, and said in disjointed unison, "Aye. You can be assured. No harm will be done."

~ * ~

A month later, Horatio had no idea the women of the local environs were so pitiful in need, and he wondered what the cause of it could be. The stud business was without the publican's knowledge so he was forced up the backstairs, and he was always in the priest's chamber prior to the woman entering, the fee already paid. A taper burned in a corner, keeping him shrouded in dark.

He could only marvel how easy it was, once their clothes were off and he set to work. With faces obscured by shadow, he became joyously aware their privy parts were *not* all alike. He experienced short and narrow, long and narrow, short and tight, long and not so tight.

One was large enough to sail a boat in and around, most difficult, and another by her feel, came to him several times. He knew not if she just liked it or if she were indeed not having any luck getting with child.

Not that it mattered. It gave him comfort as he fondled and frolicked with them, and finally not able to hold back another moment, did his part of the bargain by spurting his seed into them.

Twelve

March, 1660

It was washing day, always terrible hard, and Viola was glad this type work was finished for her. Her apprenticeship was to begin day after tomorrow, but she had yet to tell Paulina of it. She would have to speak of it tonight, after their dinner, a daunting thought given her sister's temper this day.

The servant-maid dumped too much soap in one of the washing caldrons. The suds overflowed and tried to douse the fire. Pall was stark mad at the wench, bawling her out with each round of suds that slopped onto the hot coals.

It took her sister a good long while to settle calm after a heartburning, too. She was a passionate woman, but worse than a fishwife when hog high and bothered.

Today, she was extraordinary tetchy and annoyed, and Viola wondered what was afoot. Her sister awakened in this black temper, and Viola gasped when the maid was boxed terrible on the ears. "What are you about, Pall, beating the girl? She ain't done nothing but obey your words."

The wench screamed and sobbed loud for the whole world to hear. She ran out of the room, her hands covering her ears.

Pall's dirty gaze followed the girl. "She must have dumped a full pound of soap in this here caldron. We'll never get it out of the clothes, and I ain't of a mind to fetch more water from the water carriers, nor do we have enough coals to do another rinsing."

She stirred the clothes with a stout, wooden rod, then lifted it up to show the room a pair of breeches dripping with suds. "See? We'll never get this out, and the wash will be dirtier than ever come next month."

Viola could not respond as she watched her apprentice breeches drip suds from the wooden shaft. She gulped heavily when Pall turned to regard them.

"What's this?" and she jerked the rod with the breeches away from the hearth. "These ain't papa's. Too small."

Turning to face Viola, Pall marched to her and placed the breeches against her, never mind steam rising as soap and water dripped on the floor and her shoes. Pall cried, "Ah-ha! You wicked jade. You've gone and done it, anyway."

Viola grabbed the rod and threw the sopping fabric back into the caldron. She faced her sister, arms akimbo, for she'd brook no intolerance on the matter. She'd be a prentice, and that was the end of it.

"If you ain't of a mind to help me, Pall, then I'll do it myself. The articles are already signed with Master Smythe, and I'm going there with or without your approval."

Pall sank to the table bench. "What are you about, then? Why can't you just find another man to marry? It won't hurt nothing."

Viola found it very strange her sister could not understand her, and very carefully stated, "I-shall-not-be-with-another-man, Pall, nevermore, *ever* in this world. They are too rank and horrid."

When Pall didn't say anything, she crossed her arms in front of her. "Do you understand? Will you help me?"

Shaking her head, Pall answered, "Aye, I'll help you. What do we have to do?"

Viola sighed loudly. "Thanks so much," and suddenly topped with excitement, she plopped onto the bench across from her sister. "Once we get the washing done, and Papa's put to bed, you must cut me hair as a lad. You already know about the breeches, and I've been to the market and second shops. I've the breeches, shoes, shirt, coat and cap. They were all afoul with nits and crawly things, so I threw them in the caldrons when you weren't looking." She smiled.

Pall grunted. "That's terrible horrid. The dirty vermin will be floating dead on the water."

Laughing, Viola dashed up from the bench and kissed her sister on the cheek. "Good thing for all the soap, then."

Pall joined in the giggle, but it soon turned into snuffles, and tears perched on her lashes. Viola was stricken to the heart. "What's wrong? Why has your temper been so high this day?"

"Because I'm in love, and he ain't returning it," her sister wailed to the ceiling.

"What? Who?" Viola sat on the bench next to Pall and embraced her. "Is it Mister Horatio Sharpe, then? Was he the twelfth night king? Did he find the bean in the cake with you as queen and your pea?"

Sobbing against her neck for a bit, Pall suddenly stopped and choked. "What pea? What bean?"

Viola patted her sister. "Never mind, then. Mister Sharpe's a beast not loving you back."

Pall pushed away from her, swiping tears from her cheeks. "What the devil are you talking about? The man I love ain't Horatio Sharpe, but another Royalist who I found out yesterday is married with several children. Their house is just along the lane hard by Cornhill Market."

Pressing Pall back to her bosom, Viola patted her head. "So, he won't have you as his mistress, then? What a filthy blighter."

Pall laughed against Viola's bodice. "He's not wealthy enough to have a mistress, but in any case I don't want all those children running about me feet. The very idea makes me ill." She sat up, again, grinning.

Viola smiled and shrugged. "There's nothing for it, then, you'll have to find a courtier and move into Whitehall when the King returns."

Paulina gave her a strange look. "So, you believe the King will be restored to the throne?"

"Aye. Did you see all the merriment in the lanes and the bonfires?"

Pall patted her belly. "And had some fine roasted rumps, too."

"Do you think the King will come back?"

"I've been having a full month's mind onto it, Vi, and believe it will come to pass. Very strange when only awhile ago, we could be thrown in clink to say his name. Now all are cheering for him and his return."

Pall stood, and paced back and forth. "In troth, my brains are full of desire for him coming back. I cannot abide Puritan restrictions any longer. Gives me a terrible gripping of the guts, they do. Before this swift turn of events, I even thought to France, a horrid Papist country. But now, me dreams have completely shifted, and I rejoice to think of it."

Viola sighed. "Well, best get back to the washing, then. Why don't you fetch the maid and give her your regrets? It'll be a happier house with all working nicely together."

Pall nodded, turned on her heel and strode to the stairs. Viola returned to the caldrons, agreeing it'd be troublesome to get the soap out of the clothes. Already the rinsing caldron was too sudsy to do any good.

Later that evening, as the laundry was hanging to dry about the house, she and Pall sat at the table, sharing a pot of thin ale. They'd sent the maid off to the cook shop for a take away dinner, and as they waited, Viola could feel weariness creep over her. Her arms ached, and her hands were red and stiff from wringing the heavy fabric.

Women's work was base terrible. It made her glad Roger was no longer in her life.

As she sipped from the pot she suddenly realized papa had gone out somewhere, not even remembering when he had left. "Where's papa?"

Looking around Pall's brows creased. "Don't know, now do I? Didn't see him leave, did you? Mayhap, he's upstairs in his bed."

"Nay, that's not like Papa, even though his brains have been boldly stirred. I hope he's not gone and done something stupid."

Pall started to rise when they heard a boot scrape against the front stoop, and she settled down again on the bench.

Viola knew that sound. It was their papa returning.

As the latch moved, Pall asked, "Wonder what he's been up to?"

He walked in with an arm behind his back and Viola groaned, hoping it wasn't another dead head. He stopped before them, his cloak smelling of acrid smoke and piss. It was terrible awful, and she knew he'd been in the tannery section of the city.

"What've you got behind your back, Papa?" Pall asked.

"I ain't of a mind to tell you."

Pall's face curled tight. "And why not?"

"I'm afeard you won't let me keep it."

Afraid there'd be a brawl, Viola said, "We already know you've got something, Papa. May as well show us."

Their papa sighed. He screwed up his eyes, squinting at her and Pall. It made Viola tetchy he was holding something very nasty.

He shrugged. "I remember great trouble by you lassies when I'm of a mind to be scientific. Since everyone's so vexed at me dead heads, found this here hare newly killed." He brought it out to show them. "I'll be bringing the poor creature back to life, and none of you are to stop me."

Pall laid her head on her arms, and lamented, "I must have a courtier take me away from the filthy hovel of papa's madness," while Viola felt glad she was to vacate the house nearly the very next day. She was resolved never to return.

Viola said, "You must hang it out the window when you ain't bringing it to life." A lovely thought struck her. With it outside, mayhap the birds would take it away. "Will you do this?"

Their papa released a great breath, and he nodded. "Aye, this I shall do."

Thirteen

The day was near upon her. Pall had cut Viola's hair short, just above the collar, and made a thick fringe of hairs that tickled her forehead. The breeches and stockings she wore were stiff with soap, and without long skirts, she felt curiously wicked.

Viola tied the strings on the last shoe and stood straight. "How do I look?"

Pall stopped pulling at the bed linens and turned to her. Her eyes went wide. "Well I must say you look the lad alright. Have you bound your breasts?"

"Aye, I have. Wasn't easy, but I've put buttons and loops onto starched linen. It's tight enough to flatten everything." She plucked at her coat. "I hope the stitches are sturdy for it's mighty snug. I can hardly breathe. What do you think?" and she opened her coat to reveal a loose shirt.

Walking to her, Pall said, "Turn around."

As Viola did her bidding, and she faced her again, Pall asked, "What'll you do when your terms come? How will you hide the rags?"

She lowered her eyes. It had been months since the loss of the babe, and still her terms had not returned, thinking in the dark of night she might have been damaged by the babe business.

She gazed at her sister. "I shall look upon the trouble when it happens." She shrugged. "If it happens."

Paulina patted her arm. "Well, you've done a fine job of turning into a lad. When do you leave for Master Smythe?"

Suddenly afeard of getting caught due to never being around lads, not knowing how they worked or thought, she gulped. "I must be at the 'Change tomorrow at dawn."

The next day, Viola was up afore times, the window showing the outside dark as pitch. It had been a hard night as she tossed and turned, and listened to Pall's snores. She was vexed by the lack of sleep, knowing it would be a long, strange day. She lit a candle in a small lanthorn to see by as she shifted herself into the lad's clothes, her satchel of goods sitting on a chair.

No one was up and about when she descended to the main chamber. The coals were dim embers in the hearth which she was not fain to stir. She pulled some cheese and bread from the ambry while pouring a pot of small beer for her morning draught. She was not hungry but knew to eat something, not knowing when the master would allow her a meal.

It was time. Viola shut the door behind her, took a deep breath, and walked towards her new life.

~ * ~

The Royal Exchange was not far, just up Fish Street hill. It was a large building full of shops with an open courtyard. Rich merchants and traders from outside London and many foreign countries plied their trades there. The East India Company stored spices, peppercorns, and the like in the vast cellar. Viola always liked it, and she thought the tower clock and grasshopper weathervane swinging in the wind especially cunning artistries.

She strode to the building, and saw the early morning sun lightening the balconied galleries. Viola expected to meet all sorts of interesting people while learning the clerking business, and she was all afire for it.

As she walked to Smythe's shop, a great bustle and clamor met her. Lads and men labored in and out of the next shop, hauling goods to carts waiting along the lane. Master Smythe struggled with a large pile of leather bound books, taking them to a cart, all the while barking orders to his prentices to get a move on.

Not sure what to do, it put Viola in a pitiful pickle.

As he dumped the books onto the planks of a cart, Smythe looked up to see her. His face crumpled into notable lines of annoyance, and Viola choked in misery. Not a good start to her apprenticeship.

He hollered, "Dothgood Scroope, you're late."

Viola frowned. She was not late. His orders were clear when the arrangements were made: be here at dawn. The sun had not passed to the roof of the building. Was he to be an unfair taskmaster?

Not wanting him to see any defiance, she lowered her eyes. "Very sorry, sir, won't happen again."

"Nay it shall not," he decried loudly. "Get thee to assist. We're moving this here shop, and ours, to Paternoster Row. There is more room with lodgings atop."

Someone tapped on her shoulder, and she turned to see a young lady. "Howdy-do, I'm Lucy, the master's daughter. I'll take your satchel and store it in a safe place. We'll be abed at the new place tonight."

"When did this happen?" Viola asked. "I thought to work at the 'Change for me prenticing."

The girl shrugged. "Ain't for me to know, is it? Me pa nevermore tells me what he's about. I just do as he says."

Viola's eyebrow hitched, doubting the girl's words. Lucy didn't appear cowed and guessed the girl had a quiet will of her own. For a woman to survive in this here world amongst men doing as they pleased, abusing women and lording over them, a girl had to be arch clever.

She'd know soon enough and gave over her satchel with a smile. "Thanks to thee. I'll be about the business of prenticing, now."

Later that afternoon, hungry and thirsty, she wondered if she'd ever apprentice as a clerk. So far, all she'd done was lug chairs, tables and books, paper, heavy bits of a printing press to the street for all to be cast into a cart. There had been several rounds to and from Paternoster Row that day, and she was sore fatigued.

It hadn't taken her long to learn two shops were being cleared, one a booksellers' with a mighty heavy press, and Smythe's clerking shop. She had yet to see any of the bookseller people, and wondered if Smythe owned it all, but as the day wore on, she did not care. The labor was no better than a full-up washing day.

With the sun setting behind an ominous bank of clouds, Viola sat on a stool at the back of a cart as it lumbered through the tight streets. Her new home was almost to the other side of the City, very near the wall, and Ludgate that would take one into the suburbs, foreign places. She didn't know about this new place and was all gloomy having been forced to leave the 'Change.

How was she to meet new and interesting people?

A fellow leaned forward and thumped her on the knee. "You're a strange one. Don't talk much, do you?"

Viola regarded the lad who shared the cart with her. He was tall and gangly, a right troublemaker, if she judged right. "What do you mean? I talk fine."

"Nay, you do not. Where do you come from? You a City lad?"

"Nay, I'm from the Bridge."

The lad grunted. "That's better than the pit of Southbank, but you're a foreigner alright. Can see it right clear, I can. It'll bring you ill to let others know of it. Best keep all quiet like. I'll keep your secret if you pay me two shillings from your pocket right this very minute."

Viola squawked. "What?"

"Aye, mean it, I do. Will cry to the whole world you ain't from around here. It'll be troublesome, I can promise you that. I've seen foreigners hanged on lampposts, I have. You want that?" He smiled.

His face was gaunt with red spots on his cheeks and chin, his teeth scummy green. His smile gave her the jitters, for she saw him as a true wicked fellow.

Master Smythe came alongside, striding in pace with the cart and clapped the lad's ears. "Thou shall not torment the new lad, you hear? I'll send thee to the stocks, don't think I won't. Thou art a devil, and a bane to me business. Another jumble with prentices, and thou shalt be thrown in the street, don't think you won't." He clapped the fellow, again, and walked brisk to their new shop.

It was at the end of Paternoster Row with St. Paul's hard by. Before that day, Viola had never in her life traveled so far away from the Bridge. Of course, she'd lived in the City with Roger, and even though her papa had taken a coach that fateful day, she was still close enough to the Bridge.

Now, being such a distance, she didn't know how she could travel to visit Paulina and her papa. With a weary sniffle, she thought she may nevermore see them, ever again.

The wicked lad thumped her on the knee. "What you doing, crying like a babe? Ha!"

Suddenly vexed, Viola leaned forward and with a curled finger, her nail being jagged sharp, stuck it in his nose and wrenched it out, again.

He barked in pain. "Oiy, what you do that for? You've brought me to blood."

"Nevermore treat me so basely ever again, you filthy cur, or you'll feel more than that while you're asleep sound in the night and not expecting a right nasty thumping. Don't think I won't."

Cupping his nose in his hand, he gave her a wary regard, then turned away. Heavy rain started to fall, and the cart picked up speed as they neared the new shop.

As soon as her feet hit the dirt of the lane, she was set to work. All the goods were to be pulled with haste onto the lower floor and away from the downpour. As she helped shove heavy pieces out of the way and into the shop, the rain and wind blew foul. The furniture and baskets, the heavy press sat in a jumble just beyond the front door.

It was past time for dinner, and with no servant-maid in the house, Master Smythe sent two of the lads to a cook shop with a large hamper for hot dishes. In between dragging pallets and the like up the stairs to the upper levels, she noted Smythe, his temper, and how he went about business.

She must tread carefully as he seemed a melancholy, no nonsense man. During the day, she realized he was used to four apprentices, but one had gone, leaving him all ruffled. Her master bemoaned again and again throughout the day there was too much to manage in this here cruel world.

Later, while sitting on the floor with a wooden trencher balancing on her knee, Viola watched the others pick their teeth with the tips of their knives, and trying to be a good lad, followed suit. She had finally eaten, and her full belly settled fine.

The wicked boy, whose name she learnt was Isaac Knollys, stood up and stretched. He asked the room, "When's Simon returning? I ain't seen him in awhile. Has he gone off to sea or something?"

"Mind thy manners," Smythe snarled. "It ain't none of your business where the lad goes, only mine."

Isaac shrugged. "Just hoping he ain't dead or nothing, 'tis all."

She watched Lucy turn all bleary eyed while Smythe hollered, "I said, it ain't none of thy business. Now, all of thee off to thy pallets afore my hairs burst aflame."

Viola ran after the others up the narrow sets of stairs to the loft, and gathering a pallet stuffed with pea shucks and straw, she threw it down near a curtain left by the previous lodgers.

She paused. By the smell coming from behind it there had to be a privy pot. The curtain would suit her very well, knowing lads and girls did things differently. She started toward it but was knocked aside by Knollys. "Out of me way you sodded calf. I've a need to piss."

Viola hit the wall with a puff. Rubbing her arm, she knew she'd have trouble with the dirty rascal, and listening to him piss loudly against the pot and the floor, she knew not to walk in there without shoes fixed tight to her feet, neither.

~ * ~

During the night, she groped her way behind the curtain to use the piss pot, then back at her pallet, again, she undid the buttons of her make-do breast band. With exhaustion set in from the day, and able to breathe, she slept soundly.

It did not seem long. She awoke to rats scampering in the walls and on the floor where she slept. Several bolted over her, and she gasped. Near panic, she tossed her feet and the blanket to cast the scurvy lot away from her.

She laid her head down, again, and blinked in the darkness while rain hit the roof. As she listened to the boisterous scurry of rats, and the loud snoring of the lads, a rat ran over her legs. Viola sat up and pulled her knees close.

This would not do, nay it would not. She was resolved to ask Master Smythe to bring in ratter cats this very day, for it weren't safe with the rats around. With a cry of horror, Viola jumped to her feet as several of the horrid things jostled across her pallet.

Not able to stand another minute of it, she worked her way down the stairways to the lower level where she stirred the embers to fire, and dumped new coal on top. With the rain blowing hard against the windows, it seemed it would be a sore, damp day, and a warm fire would help.

She lit a candle lanthorn as the night gave way to a grey dawn, and used it to sweep light through the cluttered room. It would take all day to sort out.

A coach rumbled to a stop on the lane outside the door. Viola heard loud voices, with a lady laughing and a man chuckling. Keys jangled in the lock and the door swung open. Viola raised the lanthorn to see Mister and Mistress Finch, the Royalist couple she had met at the Mitre that day she'd attended the popish service with Paulina.

Now, what were they doing here so early of the morn, and in a Puritan's shop, to boot?

Fourteen

Mister and Mistress Finch stopped dead at the doorway and stared at her, the door still open and rain pouring in. Viola raised the lanthorn and gazed at them.

Mistress Finch smiled. "Ain't you the green one? Who are you?"

Viola blinked. "I might ask the same of you, for this is Master Smythe's clerking shop, and we ain't opened yet."

Mister Finch shook off his wet cloak. "We know what it is, lad."

Smythe, who appeared from nowhere, shoved her away and yanked the lanthorn from her hand. Still in his sleeping gown and cap, he gave the new arrivals a dark look. "Let them in, Dothgood, let them in. The rain's soaking the floor as 'tis." He raised the lanthorn. "Where the devil hast thou been? Yesterday, thou were to direct the joiners in the breaking down of the press."

Mistress Finch closed the door whilst Mister Finch stepped to Smythe. "We're here now, ain't we? When the joiners arrive this morn, we'll direct them to the rebuilding of the press. I've already chosen the site where it'll be braced to the ceiling."

"Not in here, thou ain't," Smythe growled. "'Tis too loud for me clerking lads."

"Nay," Finch replied. "Our press will go into the other room where the bookseller shop's to be. 'Tis large enough for a printing alcove, that's why we chose it. I've hired carpenters, and a wood turner to build me a new screw and bolt for the press. We'll be busy the whole day." He looked around at the room that was becoming lighter but still dismal grey. "Where's the maid-servant? Could do with a morning draught."

"I sacked her whilst thee was gone. Haven't had time to raise another." Smythe jostled Viola. "Go to Lucy and raise the sloth from her bed. 'Tis high time we begun the toil of the day."

He raised his hand as if to strike her, and she ducked out of the way. She moved quickly to the stairs. He hollered, "While you're about it, get the lads up, too. I can't abide the laziness I see afore me."

As she climbed to the next floor, Viola found it very strange a father would send a lad to his daughter's bedchamber. She shrugged. 'Twas a strange household.

But for the rats, the first floor with the sitting room was empty, as was the kitchen, and she marveled at the grand sight. In all the houses she'd ever lived in or visited, she'd never seen one with a kitchen. Looking around, none of the hearths were alight, and she wondered what was amiss that Lucy was still abed. She climbed the stairs to the next level.

It was dark as a dungeon, and cold. Viola felt the damp settle on the back of her neck and around her ankles. All the doors were latched, and at first, she only heard the rats in the walls, all else being quiet.

It gave her the creeping jitters. Something was wrong, she knew it, and not wanting to stumble into Smythe's bedchamber, she went all still like, and listened.

She heard muffled crying, and something else that sounded horrid. Stepping to the door, she knocked on it, but there was no reply. Viola opened the panel to see Lucy bathed in tears and retching in a pot. Viola cleared her throat.

Lucy continued to retch in the pot.

Viola asked, "Is there anything I can do? Fetch your papa or something like that?"

Her head still in the pot, she wagged it.

Viola could not stand there letting the girl drown in her own slop. She took a bracing breath and stepped into the chamber. She knelt beside Lucy and held her until she finished.

Lucy wiped her face with a rag and then wrapped her arms around Viola and sobbed. It was heart-wrenching, and forgetting to be a lad, she rocked the girl to and fro as they sat on the floor. The tears slowed, and Lucy's breaths came in small grunts. Viola's shirt was wet, and suddenly Lucy gurgled with laughter.

Viola was troubled, thinking Lucy had gone split mad. "What? Are you aright?"

Lucy snuffled against her shoulder. "Your shirt smells of soap."

It took Viola a minute to comprehend, then she laughed.

"What's this all about?" Master Smythe shot as his meaty hand clapped Viola hard about the ears. "I've sent thee to get the sloth out of bed, not lay with her."

Viola gasped and sprang to her feet while Lucy groaned, and crawled to her mattress still on the floor, for the joiners had yet to rebuild all the beds. "I'm terribly sick, Pa. The lad was only helping me."

Smythe's face crumpled into lines of dismay. "By the Lord Almighty, thou shalt not die as thy mother. I'll not have it."

Lucy only groaned as she sank into the feather ticking. "I'll be up and about soon. You must do something about the filthy rats. Please, let me rest a moment."

Smythe grumbled deep in his throat, clearly not sure what to do. He turned to Viola. "Dothgood Scroope, get thee out of me daughter's bedchamber. Can't you see she's all flimsy like? It ain't proper."

Viola scuttled by him as quickly as she could. "I'll up to the loft to get the others, shall I?"

Smythe's thoughts seemed to be on his daughter. He mumbled, "Aye," then closed the door.

Viola ran up the stairs. So far, she'd done nothing but lug and slave, staggering under the weight of heavy goods. She wondered when she'd get to the clerking part of the business, and gazed up the ladder to the loft. She took hold of the ladder rungs.

The snores could be heard afore she reached the top. As she stuck her head through the opening, she saw the loud din of sleeping lads did nothing to deter the rats. They cavorted and carried on as if persons on the floor were the most natural thing in the whole world. It almost broke her brains to think on it.

She scrambled into the attic and shook a young fellow by name of George Herbert, but she left Knollys alone. "Up you must get, young George. Master Smythe's calling for you."

The lad snorted awake, sat up, and rubbed his eyes.

Viola started back toward the ladder. "Smythe is wanting us all down to put the shops aright. Wake Knollys afore you come."

George yawned. "Aye."

To the bottom, again, she found the Finch's had left the shop to break their fast, not waiting for Lucy. Gazing around, she had no idea what to do, or where Smythe wanted the wares and furniture placed, so she perched on a stool and waited.

The lads drifted down, then Smythe, all of them dressed to face the day, her master wearing his wide brimmed hat snug on his head. He gathered them together. "Bow your heads. We must pray no evil come to this new house. Already, the demons of the dark clamor against us. Our Lucy is ill."

Viola regarded the rain slashing against the mullioned windows and shivered. Sliding off the stool, she bowed her head to gaze at her feet as Smythe droned against the fires of hell, then praised Scripture and the Lord on His throne. He rattled on and on with the prayer, crying against fire and brimstone. As he gained momentum, he threw off his hat, pulled at his hairs, and blathered to the angels in heaven.

Her feet started to ache as weariness traveled up her legs to the small of her back. Viola reckoned he'd gone on near an hour when the door pushed open, the wind and rain slashing a cruelly doused man.

"Oiy there," he said his eyes full of laughter. "Have I stumbled into a church or a bookseller's?"

His arrival put the dull prayer to halt. Viola held back a grin. She thought him a mad, merry fellow, and glad she was to have him disturb the dismal service. She turned to regard Smythe who glowered most peevishly at the rain-soaked floor.

"Who art thou and what does thee want? Thou hast left the door open with the rain drowning the whole chamber. Close it this very minute."

The man obeyed, then turned to them with a flourish of his sodden cloak. "I am Daniel Hammer at your service, Mister Finch, come as you requested."

Smythe frowned. "I ain't Finch but Smythe. Why art thou here?"

Daniel Hammer looked a bit ruffled. "Well, I'm the hammer man, who until yesterday, was a coin maker. This is his shop, ain't it? I'm to be the bookbinder."

"Nay, 'tis not," Smythe hollered. "'Tis in the next room, through that space in the wall. We're to have a door over it when the carpenter can make his way through this filthy storm. 'Tis part of the bargain."

Viola did not understand the drift of the conversation. Already weary, the day waxed long before her with nothing getting done. She was hungry and in need of a morning draught.

Of a sudden, the joiners, wood turner, and carpenters burst into the shop, dragging the Finches and rain with them. They made a hellish din. Viola smiled, for the toil would begin and soon she'd be to the clerking business.

Fifteen

More than a week later, Viola studied penmanship as she sat at a table with an ink pot, paper and quill. The shops had been put to rights with a door installed between, and even with it latched, she could hear the press at work. The constant drum of it calmed her, and her quill marched along the paper in tune with it.

The rain continued with a high wind for several days. She'd been told Whitehall was in a flood, the tides of the river swamping houses and buildings along the riverfront until all seemed quite drowned. It was extraordinary how she gained knowledge of the west side of London City and nearby liberties, not hearing a word of the Bridge or its environs. She truly felt the foreigner Knollys now called her, making her lonely indeed for her family.

The clerking people were to be her new family, but it was a sore, unhappy one. The boy, George Herbert, seemed a likeable fellow, but he was quiet as a mouse. Other than hearing him weep softly in the night, she had learned little about him. Smythe hired a new maid-servant, but she seemed a clumsy girl with very little knowledge of a kitchen. Simon Kirk, the prentice, gone since she'd come had still not returned.

Knollys scowled at the favoritism. "Where's Kirk? I ain't seen him a full month, now. Have you cast him out, Master Smythe?"

Smythe would only grumble, "Ain't none of thy business."

Above all, Lucy's illness fretted Smythe most heavily, putting him in high distemper. One day the girl would seem fine and the next she'd be sick abed.

Viola had no patience for Knollys, him being an exceedingly filthy, arch knave, but he seemed to be the rump of their master's misery. Smythe rattled him up every chance he got, clapping Knollys about the ears and hollering at the horrid quality of his work. It put the prentices in a froth of worry, George always with tears in his eyes. Everyone wondered which one of them would next to feel the master's displeasure. Viola kept her head down, and put as much effort as she could in the task at hand.

Smythe had her write in longhand from a book entitled: *Godlie Government in the Householde*, and a jolly book it was too, according to her master. It gave stern examples of how a wife must obey her husband. Their children must obey both parents in a God-fearing household, and it also told how to keep this same household a Godly place for the world entire to see.

She'd been writing from this book all week long, and it was wearying, the subject matter extraordinary horrid. On occasion, the master stopped by to pick up the papers filled with her hand, grunting over them, then placing them back on the table. She never knew what to think.

It would be wondrous better to write of world events. Viola knew the press next door printed out journals and the like filled with the changes in government. More and more folk were drinking openly to the King's return. Even Monck now boldly thumped the table in favor of the monarchy.

All heard the King was ragged and near starved from lack of food and coin. Sermons from pulpits praised the poor, unfortunate fellow still in exile over Netherlands way. Standing in church during one of these sermons, Viola watched Smythe instead of listening to the minister extolling the poor unfortunates in that dead flat country. Even though he frowned darkly, her master seemed resolved to the change. She knew her sister must be thrilled to the gut as the government moved toward all she desired.

Master Smythe walked up to her, carrying a book. "Scroope, I've noted thou hast a clean hand, and am of a mind to see how thee will do with shorthand." He handed her the book that was worn with use. "This will guide thee to becoming a valued clerk when thou art in the world."

Knowing great joy, Viola took the book. She was resolved to learn a perfect shorthand that would guide her in all things honorable when clerking. She held it before her to see it was by a well known shorthand person, but her happiness was dashed when Smythe said, "Take these papers you've been filling with longhand and make them small into shorthand."

Squinting at the papers before her with a blear eye, she had hoped for a different subject matter.

As soon as Smythe walked out of earshot, Knollys laughed. "Oiy there, Foreigner, the work not to your liking? Ha! Bet you're really a' thinking of frolicking with a saucy slut." His laughter fell into an ugly chuckle. "That's what I'll be doing soon as possible. Going to find me one as soon as I can."

Little George said, "Look. The rain stopped."

With the thumping of the press, Viola hadn't noticed. She turned to the windows to see a bit of sun poking through the grey veil. It cheered her heart, and she picked up the book of shorthand.

That afternoon, a door slammed and a clamor arose from the bookseller and print shop. It disturbed Viola's study of the intricate shorthand, and she looked toward the panel the two shops shared.

It burst opened with a thick, strong looking fellow filling the open space. Grinning at them, a satchel at his side, he cried, "Oiy, I'm back. How you all be?"

Knollys jumped up from his stool. "Kirk, where've you been? I've been here longer than thee, and should be going on adventures as the master sees fit, not you."

Viola stared at the lad, knowing him from somewhere. He looked familiar and not from too long ago, either. Her hairs burned with thinking on it. When could it have been?

Kirk sauntered into the shop. "I went instead of you due to me fine hand. All your papers are thick with ink spots, and where there ain't stains, 'tis hardly above a scratch. No one can read your hand." He stood with legs spread, arms akimbo. "I've the best hand since afore the old King was beheaded, now don't I?"

He grinned, and Viola remembered. He was the fellow from the Old Swan when her papa nearly drowned, the one who gave her the idea to become a prentice. The world was filled with strange things, and gazing at him, she smiled.

Simon Kirk turned his regard to her. "Now, who are you? A green one come to help with the load? With the King about to return, we'll be very busy a' clerking."

Smythe worked his way round the clerk tables. "That there is Dothgood Scroope, the new prentice, and with a hand near as good as thine. I'm glad thee hast returned. We've plenty of work not being done, and I'm to be paid for thy services to Mister Sharpe. Where is he?"

Viola stifled a gasp. Mister Sharpe? There seemed no end of men called Sharpe since she married Roger, and her mouth dropped when the man walked into the room. It was Mister *Horatio* Sharpe, tall and strong, and grinning from ear to ear. He held a purse of coin.

"Well now, howdy-do, Smythe. I've come to bring you payment for services rendered. Simon has a fine hand and even better shorthand. If I'd a mind to recite a fast ditty, he'd be keeping right up with me."

Smythe grunted. "Took thou time in the matter, thou did. Expected thee back a sennight ago. Simon must do proper clerking for me, not for thee."

Sharpe kept on grinning. "The journey to the Spanish Netherlands was rough, foul weather, forward and back, but now happily done. Me errand's complete. Your heartburning shall not dampen me joy with the changes of government swelling along the tides. Nay, it shall not."

Viola watched the man puff out his chest like a turkey-cock whilst her master growled.

Smythe screwed up his face and pursed his lips. "I'll not be victim to your rattling and rowling, Mister Sharpe. This here is me God fearing shop, with tender prentices listening to thy blather. I'll not have any of it, so out with you afore I say something unpleasant."

Sharpe shook his head. "You ruffle me brains, you do, for times are changing, and you know it. You share these here premises with Royalists. You sent one of your own with me to the King, now you bluster about what we did. You're a thick skulled fellow, you are."

"You'll not pick a hole in me coat, Mister Sharpe. I know the world is a' changing and must go along with it, aye, I will, for I must make a living or be cast to the streets. I don't like it, nay I do not, but I cannot think on it. Me daughter is abed and nigh unto death. 'Tis a great trouble to bear."

Simon's happy countenance dropped to one stricken. "Oiy, Lucy's ill? What happened? How is she? I must go to her."

"Nay, you shall not," Smythe roared as Simon dashed to the stairs.

Viola jerked with surprise, dropping the quill. She watched with dismay as ink splattered along a clean length of paper, and quickly dabbed it with her shirt sleeve.

The master barred the stairs with his body. "It ain't fitting for a lad to enter a lady's chamber, and you'll not do it."

But no one listened to him. Everything went still as one by one they turned to Lucy who stood pale and trembling on the landing.

"I'm feeling better now, Papa," and she slipped to her knees then rolled down the rest of the stairs.

Viola jumped to her feet as everyone cried out, and dashed to Lucy on the floor. The press from the other shop went silent. The Finches and Mister Hammer rushed in to see what was afoot.

Crowding around, everyone was staggered with concern for the girl who lay like one dead. Smythe stood rigid with his eyes wide, and did not move when Simon shouldered through to kneel at Lucy's side.

He shook her. "Lucy lass, wake up. You ain't to die. You cannot. I forbid it."

As she leaned through the tangle of folk, Viola noted the lad's face filled with fear, and she remembered when they spoke together back at the Old Swan. He was the randy coxcomb, bragging on the tossing of his master's daughter, and she regarded Lucy with a new eye.

The girl was dead pale but stirring, and Viola knew without a doubt the couple had had too much satisfaction in each others' company. Their frolics had gotten her with child.

Simon hollered, "Move aside, move aside. You're too close. It ain't healthy."

Watching a prentice take control of his own daughter, Smythe came to his senses. "Oiy, now see here. How dare thee command your betters when thee ain't but of low stature. By the God Almighty, it ain't right."

Smythe wrestled through the throng, and barked, "Make way, make way. Let me to her."

With a great deal of chatter everyone stepped back, giving Lucy space, but Simon remained at her side. He muttered softly as her eyes fluttered, and a smile etched across her lips.

Simon crooned, "Now, now there. All is well with the world, ain't it?"

Viola resolved to be bold. She stepped into the open space, and tapped Master Smythe on the arm. He disregarded her with a shrug. Again, she tapped him on the arm, this time with more insistence. He did not heed her.

Stepping ever so close, she said loudly, "Master Smythe, mayhap the mistress is weak with hunger, for she's been off food of late. A bit of cheese and bread might do her very well indeed."

He jerked and cried, "Oiy, what's it to thee? It ain't none of thy business. Out of me way."

He pushed Viola with such force she lost her footing and rollicked backwards across the shop. She landed against the wall with a thud, and her nose burst out bleeding. Bewildered by what she thought a good deed, and stunned by the violent act, Viola laid in a daze on the floor.

"Oiy there," a man shouted. "You didn't have to do that. He's only trying to help. What are you about, for mercy sakes?"

Horatio Sharpe bent down to her. Viola saw him close and kindly, and very pretty he was, too. His smile was wide, and with joy in her heart she saw he had all his teeth.

He said, "You aright? Nasty bleed, that. Anything broken?" He handed her a kerchief, then held out his hand. "You're new, ain't you?"

Viola took his hand, rose to her feet and pressed the kerchief to her nose. He seemed ever so nice, but then she looked into his eyes. They were deep blue, the same as her husband's, the filthy creature.

She could not think on it, and lowered her gaze.

Dabbing her nose, Viola said, "Aye, I've joined Master Smythe whilst you were on your journey. Dothgood Scroope at your service, sirrah."

He smiled. "And I am Mister Horatio Sharpe, owner of yonder bookseller shop." He took her hand and shook it. "How do you do, Mister Scroope."

Sixteen

A few days later, Horatio hurried up the stairs to Smythe's lodgings, wondering what the hullabaloo was about. The man was raising a hellish din. Horatio had been alerted by Knollys, a most troublesome prentice. He'd run into the booksellers shop cruelly stricken, railing something about murder, and Simon.

Vexed by the interruption, Horatio found it a bother to share his business with a rank Puritan, but all the world knew Providence Smythe put out the very best clerks in the City. Some of them became scriveners, or went off to other high positions with members of Parliament. One even found a place with the Lord Mayor of London, most fine.

With his bookshop, the press, and the clerk shop combined closer to Westminster City, they'd have a corner on the market when all broke loose in the government, and the King returned to England.

For the King would return. Aye, indeed he would, and soon, too.

Being an emissary between Royalist agents from the time of Cromwell's son, Tumbledown Dick, Horatio made several sea voyages to Brussels, and to the Netherlands. Over the months, he traveled to various places as the King moved about, and carried encouraging messages: All would soon be well; Do not despair; and, All would be done most kindly.

Lately with Simon in tow, he'd been to Breda with a packet of letters where the King said he'd heard rumors the Puritan cause had all but fallen to rack. With a smile and a bow, Horatio said, "Aye, indeed, Your Royal Majesty, 'tis going our way most joyously."

Already, the Fleet was working its way to Gravesend in anticipation to fetch the King, and would eventually set sail for the Netherlands. When all was aright, Horatio vowed to be there, as well.

It would be a most wondrous, historical event, and about time the Puritans were cast to fodder in the streets, but it wouldn't do to have Simon murdered. Nay, it would not. The lad was a very good clerk.

He and the troublesome prentice dashed into the kitchen. The ruckus was loud with all from the household staring at the drama afore the hearth. Smoke rose from a cauldron set above the coals, the air smelling of burnt porridge and hare.

"Stop thy blather, girl," Smythe hollered as he tried to strangle Simon. "What hast thou been about, rascal? Tell me, straight away."

Horatio saw the man was vexed to the gut and might well do murder as he rattled the lad whose eyes were closed, his mouth in a stern line of defiance. Breaking through the crowd, Horatio cried, "Oiy there, what are you doing Smythe, killing your best apprentice?"

Without turning away from sorely abusing the lad, Smythe cried, "Methinks strongly he's done something foul to me daughter, but cannot get a word out of either of them."

Horatio turned to those lollygagging, and snapped his fingers. "All you prentices off to the shop and to your business."

As everyone left, the troublesome prentice swiped the new lad across his back. "Down to the shop, Foreigner. This here's private, and you ain't needed."

Frowning, Horatio was stumped by the new prentice who seemed not quite right for a lad, and looked very familiar, but could not place where they had met. Those thoughts were dashed when Smythe cruelly clapped Simon across the head, sending Lucy into gales of tears.

It was time to put an end to this rowdy behavior afore poor Simon was tossed to his grave, and he pulled the boy out of Smythe's grasp. "Oiy, man, keep your temper. Don't want to kill the lad, now do you?"

He pushed Simon behind him then pulled Lucy out of harm's way as Smythe turned to pacing before the hearth. "And here I thought me daughter-dear was dying of the ague or something like her saintly ma did back in 'fifty-five. It near killed me, it did, thinking I was to lose Lucy, too. I was shattered, I tell you, shattered with it. Now, it all comes to play afore me."

He stopped to point an accusing finger at Lucy. "Thou ain't ill with the ague, but with child, ain't thee? Thou hast been the instrument of wickedness, enkindling vile incestuous behavior with Simon who's been more a son to me and a brother to you since he came into our house."

Smythe grabbed his hat off his head and threw it into the fire. Pulling at his hairs until his eyes bulged, he cried out as if he'd been stabbed with a hot poker straight to the heart. "What shall I do? Oh, what shall I do? I'm undone by the whoring and deceiving in me own house. God will strike us all to fiery pits of hell for this. I know it. I can see it afore me."

Lucy sobbed, and taking her in his arms, Simon declared, "Aye, 'tis the truth afore thee. I hold my true lady love, and am sore to the heart for the agony our coupling has caused."

Horatio said, "Smythe, sit down afore your eyes roll back in your head." Turning to the couple, he asked, "How did this come about, then? If we know all started in innocence, mayhap it can be gently solved."

"Gently solved?" Smythe cried. "'Tis incest, 'tis, and punishable by church courts."

Horatio disagreed. "Nay, not since Cromwell took control. Church courts were popish and suppressed, if you remember. The King has not returned, and so it remains."

"'Tis still incest, I tell thee. All the world will blame me for siring a bleating whore."

Raising his hands in protest, Horatio cried Smythe down. "Nay, we ain't to be sidetracked anymore by your banshees. We shall look to these here two and learn the truth of it. Lucy, stop crying."

Simon said, "Master Smythe, I did not betray thee. It all happened innocent like in the cold of winter. Me and Lucy here bundled together on the bed to keep warm."

Smythe turned an angry face to the lad. "Ach, don't give me that. Don't hark base falseness as if I fell off a turnip cart. 'Twas pure lust. Thou couldn't keep thy pole sheathed, and that's the truth of it."

"Nay, Papa," Lucy cried. "'Twas so very cold, and the coals burnt down, and the other maid did not stir them to fire or add more."

Horatio's brow hitched. The girl must think they were base stupid.

Smythe roared, "Curs, knave, whore!"

Simon stepped into the thick of it. "Alright then, I avow afore God I betrayed your trust. We bundled together in the night, and on Sabbath afternoons when you were off to extra services."

Lucy admitted, "We didn't do nothing forever the longest, and then one day it happened. Simon kissed me and hugged me, stirring me blood to boil, and then Simon put his long thing into me."

"Hell fire, mongrel bitch," Smythe screamed in a frightful manner, his hands outstretched as if to kill her.

Simon placed himself in front of Lucy as the man charged towards her. Horatio grabbed the crazed man by the collar and thrust him away before he did terrible damage he'd regret. "Nay, you shall not kill her. It took both of them to play the game, and now they're the sorrier for it."

But Smythe was blinded by the betrayal of it. He shouted, "Out of me house, now, and never come back. Thou art carnal curs, and thou art dead to me." He sank to the settle, buried his face in his hands, and wept piteously.

~ * ~

May 1660

As the press thumped and banged, and books were bound or printed sheets were hung to dry, Horatio stood staring at the closed door between the shops. The clerk's side had fallen under a pall of gloom. There was no mirth or even talking over there.

Simon and Lucy had been thrown into the lane without even a cloak to keep them warm. From the bookseller shop windows, Horatio watched Simon with slumped shoulders as Lucy bawled high, pounding on the portal that was forever locked to her.

Simon avowed to keep Lucy.

Horatio ordered his bookbinder, Daniel Hammer, after them as they trudged down the lane, and took them to his house on Tower Hill. It was far enough away so that Smythe would never cross paths with them, nor would he know Horatio housed them. There, they would be allowed to gain their feet.

With a letter from Horatio, it had not taken long for Simon to find work as a clerk in Fleet Prison, but it was a good distance from Tower Hill. It was sad work, Simon had said, but brought in enough coin to make a stand in this here hard world.

Horatio knew they would soon be able to have a place of their own, and had almost enough coin for the first six months' rent. Not that he wanted them gone, but to have the two of them filling his house was not in his best interest when he was a stud for a constant stream of *barren* women. No one but he needed to know this bit of private business which was becoming a lucrative sideline to his bookseller shop.

It troubled him there were so many men about London and suburbs who could not get their wives with child, and he wondered why. There was a group of fellows who met at Gresham College to discuss science and mathematics, and he considered giving one of their meetings a visit. Mayhap, one of those sharp brains would understand the woe of so many sterile men about town, but that would have to wait, for to his great joy, the Fleet was now at Deal, near ready to set sail for the Netherlands to fetch the King.

Since returning from Breda, Horatio was tasked with new responsibilities that were more pleasant than anything else in his whole life. He wrote letters, gathered ribbons and fabric to decorate the ships for the King's return voyage, and sent all of it by courier to the Fleet. He then received letters, packets of documents, coins sterling, and instructions for diverse worthy gentlemen that put him in high contentment with all that was new to the world.

The King's 'Declaration of Breda' (where King Charles II promised not to make the same mistakes as his father) had been recently read by Parliament and readily received by all and sundry. Bonfires sprang up all about the City and her environs. Good folk danced and drank in the streets whilst effigies of the King were fashioned, and hung on walls or placed on platforms all over town.

Horatio picked up a packet of documents that needed delivering to Parliament and strode out of the shop. As he stood on the lane, Smythe's new prentice stepped out of the clerk shop. The lad paused, looking at him all afeard like, and Horatio wondered again where he'd seen him.

He smiled. "Oiy, then, what are you about on this fine day? Got time away from old, sour Smythe and prenticing?" Hoping to reassure the lad, he asked, "Scroope, ain't it?"

The lad nodded. "Aye, Dothgood Scroope, at your service."

Horatio tried not to frown. Horrid name, that, and full Puritan. With all thought turning to royalty, the lad best change it. Scroope waited for him all respectful like, and Horatio asked, "What you about then?"

"Going to Paul's Yard where there's a game of skittles, the prentices against the lads of Paul's school. 'Tis a high gamble amongst them. Knollys is one of the players. Master Smythe's given us the afternoon off."

Horatio's brows furrowed. What was Smythe up to, giving the lads freedom midweek? Interesting, that. He nodded. "Would you like company to the end of the lane? I'm off to Parliament."

The lad's cheeks reddened, and he coughed. "Aye, as you please."

They walked together in silence, Horatio regarding the lad from the corner of his eye. There was something that nagged at him, but he could not reach what it was. They came to the end of Ave Maria Lane without another word and parted company, Scroope to Paul's Yard, and he to Parliament.

Later that afternoon, as he walked toward his shop with another packet of letters and documents, he knew more joy in his heart than ever a man could have. He'd been directed to personally take the packet to the Fleet, a frigate already awaiting him in Deptford. He was to depart the very next afternoon, for time was short.

He could not stop grinning as he rounded the bend to Paternoster Row, but his grins suddenly stopped. Bailiffs pounded heavily on Smythe's door. It took Horatio a moment to realize it looked as if the bailiffs were trying to break down the door.

Running down the lane, he hollered, "Oiy, what're you about?"

A man watching the bailiff kick in the door turned to him. "We're breaking down this here panel. There's a dirty rogue within, and we must take him to gaol."

The panel collapsed to pieces at the bailiffs' feet, and they scrambled into the shop, shouting and waving their cudgels. Horatio flew in after them, not knowing if Smythe was in or not, and afeard the men would tear the shop to bits.

The lower level was empty of lads but when everyone looked up the stairs, the new prentice stood at the balustrade looking all affright. He was pale, his eyes wide.

The bailiffs hollered, "Fetch thee down here, thou scurvy piece of dung. We arrest thee for riotous behavior in the streets. You shall come kindly or we're fain to wallop thee forthwith."

Knowing the lad could not have done anything of the sort, Horatio ran up the first few stairs. Nay, his brief view of the boy marked him as one who could never rise to such mischief as these men were crying about.

Horatio made a shield against the ruffians who would harm the lad. "What's he done, then?"

Smythe kicked the rubbish at the entry. "What's this all about? What villains laid me shop so ill?"

A bailiff swung around. "We're about to arrest this here lad for riotous behavior in the streets, a penal offense, if you care to know. We're to take him to gaol."

Smythe stepped over the debris then looked up at Scroope. "Dothgood, art thou a rascal to be cudgeled?"

Gazing over his shoulder, Horatio saw the lad pale as death, gulping and shaking his head. "Nay, Master Smythe, I ain't. They're looking for Knollys, and mistake me for him."

Smythe shouldered through the bailiffs, and shouted, "Thou ain't anymore near Knollys than ever before in this here world. He's dead ugly with spots about his face, and an injurious fellow, I tell thee. You've the wrong lad."

He poked a bailiff. "But thou doest me grave injury, breaking me door down under false pretenses. Cry off, I say, or I'll complain to the local alderman."

Just then Knollys ran into the shop as if the very demons of hell were at his heels. Crashing into the rubble on the threshold, he tripped and sprawled across the floor.

Smythe cried out, "There's the lad you seek, for he's a troublesome fellow right down to his corn cockles."

The bailiffs ran in circles around the shop, then descended onto Knollys with great fury, and soundly rattled him.

Knollys fought back. "Nay, I ain't done nothing. You've the wrong man. It weren't me, I say."

"Thou art a mean and lowly person, and we shall take you alive or dead to gaol if you ain't careful."

"Nay, I've done nothing. Thou art rude fellows, trussing me about this way. Ouch. That hurt!"

Smythe entered the fray. "Dog, rogue, cheat. Thy mother was a fornicator begetting thee to this here world. You'll not have a place here when all is finished. Nay, thou shalt not." He grabbed the lad's ear and wrenched it, sending Knollys into howling fits. "Get thee gone from me Godly shop and never return."

It took all the bailiffs and Smythe to hoist Knollys toward the door. Horatio's brow hitched. He sensed the new lad behind him and turned to see him watching the brawl.

Scroop's eyes were wide. "They're turning the shop to rubble."

"Aye, they are," Horatio agreed and pulled out his pistols. Trying to avoid an errant arm or fist, he cried, "Halt this very minute." He pointed a pistol at Knollys. "Stop thy ruffian behavior or I'll shoot you dead."

Knollys went still, and allowed the bailiffs to bring him to his feet and haul him out of the shop.

Smythe cast after them. "Oiy, what about me door? With it bashed in, we'll be knocked up by dirty thieves in the night. Come back, I say."

But his cries went unheeded.

Seventeen

The next day, as the maid-servant poured the morning draughts for those left in Smythe's family, Viola wondered what would happen next. No one missed Knollys, but within short order, the family had shrunk to a pittance.

Her master had turned all gloomy and skullduggery like, so far not replacing the lads he'd lost. Instead, he sulked about the shop, or left them alone for long hours and upon returning, never said where he'd been or what he'd been up to. He seemed to have lost interest in the business. The work had ground down to almost nothing.

Viola used the time to study shorthand. She wrote out texts from printed sheets lent to her from the bookseller next door, infinitely more interesting than books of moralizing verses. She practiced for hours at a time, becoming better at it than she could ever have imagined.

Smythe sat at the table in the kitchen, and stared at his drink with a sullen face. Viola watched him, and thought she saw a tear at the corner of his eye. It was all too horrid, his melancholy, and he even forgot to say first prayers. The small apprentice, George Herbert, shrank away from the discontent, while Viola hoped Smythe didn't become so hopeless as to give up having apprentices altogether. With his state of mind, she was afeard he'd throw them out to the streets.

Finally, the maid placed trenchers with food on the table, Viola and George tucking in while Smythe stared sightlessly at his. The house was quiet, the ticking clock loud on the mantel. It allowed Viola to hear a ruckus approach outside on the lane, and the door between the shops snap open.

Someone pounded up the stairs and Horatio Sharpe burst into the kitchen, seemingly transported with joy and grinning from ear to ear. At the same time, an outside clamor roused everyone. People were knocking on the large table wedged against the open space where the front door had been.

Smythe looked up from his food. "Oiy, what's afoot to disturb our peace?"

Horatio did not stop grinning. "We won't know until we move the table from the doorway, now will we?"

Viola and George thundered down to the shop, Horatio behind them with Smythe straggling behind.

A voice hollered from outside on the stoop. "Move this here barrier for we've important business with Mister Providence Smythe, master of this here shop."

The bookbinder from Horatio's shop ran to give a hand and helped move the heavy oak table, revealing the bailiffs from the day before. They tipped their hats in greeting.

Smythe said, "What's this here, then? Come to tear down me shop? I've had a good deal of plague with the lot of thee. Begone from me front door."

"Nay, we shall not," said a tall bailiff with brass buttons trailing down the front of his coat. "We've come to make amends for our haste yesterday."

"Oiy?" Smythe looked surprised.

"Aye," said the bailiff. "We're to repair your door, and here," he handed Smythe a rump of pork with flies buzzing around it and his person. "For your troubles."

Viola watched Smythe regard the meat with a smile. He nodded, and took the meat. "Well then, as you please, come in and do the repairs. Very nice." He turned toward the stairs and called, "Alice, come this very minute to get this haunch of pork. We'll have a fine feast this day."

Horatio interrupted. "Need to talk to you, Smythe. I'm to the Netherlands again, this time to The Hague. I'll need one of your prentices to accompany me."

Smythe frowned. "And who do you suggest? The little one is too young, and the new one is still learning. At this rate, I'll be shut out of me own shop. Find your own prentice. Paul's school will have one. Go there."

"Nay, for they're still under the old government."

While the bailiffs knocked up the door neat and tidy, Smythe roared, "And what am I, but a Puritan of the *old* government, righteous and proud. I shall not give you one of me prentices to ballyhoo with the demons of Royalty. Nay, I shall not. Look what happened when I gave you Simon. Me daughter turned to fornication and whoring."

Horatio's face went all stern. He hunched forward and shouted, "You shall give me the new lad, by God, and this very minute."

His ruckus startled Viola who hadn't expected such a rousing display of temper from Horatio. He seemed so nice, nothing like Roger, the filthy rascal, and it ruffled her they may be more alike than she thought.

Alice ventured tentatively near the two men who turned on her like scowling curs. With a yelp, the girl jumped back and out of harm's way. Viola watched the exchange with interest, for if Horatio got his way, she'd be happily on a new adventure.

Smythe snapped his mouth shut, and his teeth clanked. "Aye then, you may have him."

Horatio's jaw dropped, clearly expecting a high jangle over the matter. "What?"

Viola gaped in astonishment with her master completely turned around.

"I said thee may have him," Smythe repeated, and still holding the haunch, took himself slowly up to the living quarters. Alice followed behind him.

~ * ~

That very afternoon, Viola sat on a barge below the Bridge, waiting for it to push off into the current. It would take them down river to Gravesend where they were to board *The Lute* frigate.

Viola's initial reaction of longing, being so close to her family's house disappeared in the daring venture to a foreign land. She had never been outside London and its suburbs the entire of her life. This was so profound an activity, she couldn't get hold of it in her heart.

Then, she worried about seasickness, which would be very horrid and make her low in Horatio's eyes. Already, the rocking of the barge made her a mite queasy, and she stood to gulp the cool air.

Suddenly, they pushed off, and Viola lost her balance to fall hard to the bench. The sails unfurled, and with men at the oars, she held close to her chest the satchel with her goods as the current grabbed the vessel and took them downstream.

Horatio sat next to her, and her heart fluttered. She liked him very much, but knew she could never have him as she was still married to Roger, the horrid creature, and the fact she'd sworn off men afore the whole world forever more.

She could be friendly with him, though. She smiled when he turned her way. "How does it go?"

He grinned. "Fine and dandy, Scroope." He frowned. "But you'll have to change your name. Dothgood ain't a good name for what we're about to do. You must have a Royal name, now the King's to be returned."

"Me papa's name is James. Would that do, Mister Sharpe? I wouldn't mind having me papa's name."

He gazed at her for a long moment, his brow furrowing, and she wondered if she'd said something amiss. Thinking back to her words, she didn't reckon so, but his frown deepened instead of loosening, and she turned hot and jittery. "Is that not a good name, sirrah?"

Horatio's frown cleared. "Aye, the Duke of York is James. 'Tis a brave name." He clapped Viola across the back, almost sending her to the planks. "'Tis James, then."

She gave him a hollow smile and turned her gaze to the river. They were moving south past the Isle of Dogs toward Deptford. The wind was good, the sails billowed and snapped. The water was dark, and Viola watched as the barge skimmed through it with amazing speed. Even though she had really no clue, and unless it was terribly far away, she reckoned it wouldn't take long to reach Gravesend at this rate.

Horatio stood up and stretched. "I'm off to get a drink. Want to come with?"

Not knowing how to respond, and still tetchy over the name bit, she finally shook her head. "Nay, Mister Sharpe. I'm settled here fine."

Shrugging, he said, "Suit yourself." He fixed his hat firmly against the wind and strode forward through the benches where a man was loosening the bung of an ale barrel.

She watched as he stood against the wind, talking to the fellow who gave him two pots. Horatio nodded then turned away and retraced his steps back to her.

He handed her a pot. "Take this here ale. 'Tis said 'tis fine tasting," and he sat down beside her.

She smiled, and drank from the pot. It was full bodied and strong. Almost immediately, she felt it wind down to her belly and up to her head, making her woozy.

Horatio leaned toward her. "We should arrive to the frigate afore the sun sets. 'Tis good the days are longer and warmer. I can tell you, sea voyages during the summer months are much kinder than in the winter." He gazed at her with a grin. "The tossing of the ship during a winter gale is most troublesome."

The beer made her speak boldly. "I've never been beyond London town. Is it very nice in Holland? Are the folk hardy?"

Horatio said, "They are like us in many ways, but of a different language. The Frenchies, though, now they are most rude fellows. Don't take the least to foreigners clogging up their waterways and the like." He gazed at her. "They tell you to your face how they feel, make no mistake. Thicken your skin, me lad, if you plan to visit Frenchy soil."

Viola had no intention of going to such a popish, unfriendly place, and her thoughts rested back on the Dutch. She'd heard from Isaac Knollys the women there were saucy sluts. How he knew that, she couldn't guess for he was base stupid.

She said, "Heard the Dutch ladies kiss you right and smart, most impertinent." She stared at him with wide eyes.

"Aye," remarked Horatio with a grin.

Viola could not stop herself. "Once amongst the Dutch, will we have wicked meetings with fiddlers, and be witness to ribaldry? I've never afore seen in this world true ribaldry, and I've never afore had strong spirits."

Horatio threw his head back, laughing heartily. "Aye, if you so desire. We'll go to a brothel and see all the lewdness you want. What do you think of that? Simon had a most blessed time, although he railed against the guilt, and how he was in great want for a wife, his choice being Lucy."

He gave her a hard gaze. "Have you been with a woman, Scroope? A serious towsing will make thee a better man, put hairs aplenty on your cods and chest."

Viola choked on her beer, coughing and spewing. Her eyes watered. Horatio pounded her back until she was thrown off the bench to land on the planks.

He said from above her. "I take that for a nay."

~ * ~

The sun was near the horizon when Viola stretched her neck to see the rope ladder with flat, wooden rungs above her. The barge bobbed against the frigate, both vessels rolling to and fro in the water. The tide was about to turn, and they must be on deck ready to set sail when the currents ran to sea.

From the above, seamen hollered for her to leap to the step, and come aboard. Time was of essence, but Viola was afeard. She looked down between the vessels, the water plunking and splashing as they bobbed too far for her to reach the ladder.

Horatio growled behind her. "Art thou a mamby babe? Get thee up the step right this very minute."

Viola could not move.

Horatio took hold of her waist and lifted her up to where she could grab hold of the rungs, then she dragged herself upwards until a foot snagged a step. It was a harrowing climb as she scrambled over the rail of the frigate.

Shaking, she held onto the edge of the vessel, and gulped down her fear as she watched Horatio leap onto the deck. A man of imposing stature met him, shook his hand, then led him below decks.

Viola slumped against the rail wondering what to do. Very near tears, she could not think as a lad, or know how to act, what next step to take.

The ship was filled with men going about their business, running across rigging and setting sails. They cursed boisterously she was in the way, and Viola stepped this way and that to avoid getting run into. A rough and ready fellow finally pushed her against a stack of goods, but she still felt base stupid. Looking around, there was no place on deck to squeeze and be safe.

Horatio's head came into view. He shouted, "Scroope, come here. Don't get clapped by a rope tackle or swinging cargo. I've work for you right this very minute."

Relief filled her heart, and she scampered across the crowded deck to Horatio, following him below. Lanthorns swung on metal loops, casting moving shadows in the gloom as she trod down ladder steps and narrow passageways. Cabin doors came and fled in the swinging light.

The ship lurched as it set to sail, throwing her against Horatio's back. He turned and grabbed her, holding her to keep them both from tumbling headlong down a companionway.

His hands swept along her make-do breast band, and her breath caught. If he dragged his hand round to the front of her, he'd surely know she was a lass and overboard she'd go for a lying, troublesome woman.

She closed her eyes, and waited. They both steadied, and his hands stayed where they were.

He chuckled. "'Tis a good thing you've another shirt on, for it'll get a mite chilly once we're out to sea. The wind roars against you, and feels colder than it is." He moved away. "Our cabin is down yonder."

Viola stood still, trying to gather her wits and gave thanks she'd been saved from being thrown overboard.

Horatio turned to her. "Come along, then. We've much to do. Luckily, there's a table fastened to the planks so it won't skitter along with the movement of the ship."

"We're to *share* a cabin?" she cried loud. When at Master Smythe's, the lads—their brains filled with frolicking or other sundry things—never saw she wasn't what they thought. Being in the same cabin with Horatio would be her undoing.

"Aye, we are. The frigate is full of folk going to fetch the King with some of the cabins holding cloth for prettying the flagships. It's share a cabin or drag a bench into the galley for warmth in the night. Which would you prefer?"

She'd prefer anywhere but in a tight place with him.

The cabin was small, very small. There was a narrow berth and a table, as he had said. His portmanteau had already been brought aboard and placed along the short end of the room. She gazed at the narrow bed naked of curtains, realizing there was no room for her.

She would not share the narrow cot with the man, not evermore for the whole world to see. She looked at him and found him grinning.

He acknowledged, "Aye, where art thou to rest your head?" He pointed to the wall where a mass of fabric hung. "'Tis a hammock. You'll be stringing it across the cabin, and the piss pot is in yonder corner. Pray, do not splatter the wall when the ship tips in swells."

Viola was at a great loss how she'd make way through this trial. There was no barrier, and the man would have to be a thick skulled fellow not to eventually wonder why she didn't piss like a lad.

It was hopeless.

He opened the portmanteau and pulled out the Standish Smythe sent with them, placing it on the table. "We must to work, Scroope. Pull out the stool and get to it. I shall dictate a letter to the King."

Horatio seemed pleased with her hand, and when he dictated lists and tasks for the morrow, the shorthand she'd been practicing so rigorously let her keep up with him. It filled her with untold joy.

They worked until the bell rang for supper.

Standing and stretching, he stepped to the pot for a piss, sending Viola into a crouch over the table. Mortified, she studied her quill while listening to his stream hit the pot. It put her in a horrid pickle how she should take care of her needs on a ship filled with only men.

Straightening his breeches, Horatio clapped her across the shoulders. "You coming or not? I'm mighty peckish and could eat a bear."

Viola busied herself putting away the ink pot and quills into the Standish. "I'll be with you directly, Mister Sharpe."

He shrugged and reached for the latch. "Don't be long. The food will be gone afore you know it."

With the door shut tight, Viola collapsed onto the stool, troubled to the very heart. She must find a way to meet her needs right quick, or she'd suffer cruelly for it. Mayhap, at supper she'd learn of a place, and with a sigh left the cabin.

During supper, wherein she had a dish of pease and salted beef, Viola listened to the gentle talk about the table. It was with great pleasure she was allowed in the company of such high persons as the captain, and other like gentlemen. As wines and ales made their way around the table, talk became disjointed and loud, and she heard someone direct another to the privy that was located atop deck, and tucked under the bowsprit.

Her safety once again restored, Viola later returned to the cabin where she put the hammock to rights. Finding the hook, she stretched it to the wall. It filled most all the space and would be a horrid disturbance if Horatio fell over it, and her, in the dark. Climbing onto the swaying hammock, it sank with her weight. Her foot knocked against the table, and she knew once Horatio was abed, he'd not have room to get out again.

This was very close living. It made her all the more tetchy she'd be discovered a lass and thrown overboard.

Horatio entered the cabin, and the door banged against her. She yelped with surprise when he pulled up the fabric. With arms a' flailing, she rolled out of the hammock to the floor.

"Move aside, lad, so I can get to me berth."

She looked up at him, and said, "I need to be removing me shoes and stockings."

"Well, be quick about it, for me head's weary and ready for the pallet. We'll be onto the Downs and to sea afore sunrise."

Once done, she scrambled back into the hammock, making a fuss of trying to settle in as Horatio removed his clothes. Boots and skirt breeches came first, his linen stockings, coat and top shirt were off next, and then he bent to check the thickness of the blanket. Grunting most happily, he removed the rest of his clothing until he stood naked before her.

Viola could not stop staring at him. He was a wondrous beauty with firm chest and thighs, and his pole, even soft, was most joyous big with very nice cods underneath. She swallowed hard, thinking how lovely her privy parts would be with…

He clapped her so hard across the head she saw lights and stars, and she was cast off the hammock to the edge of the portmanteau. Gasping and in great pain, her cheeks went awash with tears, and she looked at him.

He stood above her and scowled in great distemper. "I ain't a stallion for your pleasures, lad, nor will I evermore be. Out with you, I don't care where, but out of me sight you shall go this very minute."

Whimpering, she pulled to her feet, and dragged herself from the cabin. At the open doorway, she looked out to the dim passageway.

"Oiy!"

Viola turned to see him vexed most terrible. He swept the hammock aside and thundering toward her, flung shoes and stockings at her. They slammed to the floor, then he threw the satchel which she caught in quick response. For a moment he stood there like a dead stone, then slammed the door in her face.

She stared at the closed panel as the lanthorns swayed with the movement of the ship, wondering where she should go, what she should do. She never had time to explore the below decks. She didn't know where the cabins with fabric for banners were, but she would look for those later, on the morrow. One of those cabins would be a safe haven, if she weren't caught. It would be so very much better than trying to locate a corner one of the seamen hadn't taken.

Until then, she must find somewhere to rest for the night. She was most melancholy, but reckoned everything would look better in the morning. Viola climbed the companionway to the upper deck and to the chamber with tables hard by the galley. She slumped onto a bench and laid her head on the table. She closed her eyes and let the sway of the ship lull her to sleep.

Hours later, her eyes snapped open with the men on deck, their feet a' stomping most loud. They were very busy, running around in great haste and hollering boisterously. She saw it was still dark as the ship slapped through high water. They must be to sea, and she suddenly felt ill.

Viola ran onto the deck and sought the privy. Water washed overboard as she sped forward, skittering around the working men. She reached a small alcove that held a flat board with holes in it and dashed in to do her business.

Once settled, she realized she was not sick. Her terms had come, and she groaned. Months and months had passed without them, and now here she was aboard a ship filled with men, and not a woman in sight to help her.

Her heart quite pulled down, she removed her top shirt and began ripping it to rags.

Eighteen

Horatio stayed in his berth having a think as the ship broke through heavy seas, the hammock still up a' swinging. He wondered of the prentice as water slammed against the ship, rivulets streaming through the rim of the closed porthole.

Very strange he was, and had been a puzzle from the beginning. For one thing, he could not shake having met him before. When he was near to breaking his brains over it, his thoughts drifted to times Scroope said or did something that had taken him by surprise, like calling his father papa. No lad called their da's such, at least not in his life for the whole world to see, and he wondered if the Knollys rogue had it aright, that Scroope was indeed a foreigner.

Though bright enough, the lad was of slight build, making one think he was prone to illness, and if not that, then mighty lassie-like.

It had been totally unexpected when he found the impertinent knave staring at his privy parts, then it vexed him to the gut. It would be a great woe if he'd invited an unnatural varlet onto the ship. His reaction of clapping him soundly about the head was immediate, and when he thought on it, aright.

It was a riddle, but in the end Horatio was resolved to understand it. Aye, indeed he would.

He forced himself out of the warmth of his bed and threw on his dressing gown. He must to the honorable employment of the day, for there was a multitude of businesses to attend to before they reached The Hague. By his reckoning, it would take about two days, and then after much celebration, they would bring home King Charles II.

He released the hammock and set it all to one hook afore opening the Standish, all the while the ship rolling and falling with the sea. One particular swell sent the lid of the box crashing to its latch, almost breaking it, and Horatio wondered if the sea was too rough for work.

He thought of Scroope, and opened the door where the lad sat crunched in a near ball against the passage wall. "What art thou about? You look pale."

Scroope frowned. "Are we to break our fast? The powdered beef last night made me plaguy thirsty."

Horatio was more used to the fare having been on several journeys, but after savoring fresher meat on shore, the salted beef always came as a shock. "Come in as I get meself shifted." He remembered the night before and glared at the lad. "Stay put. I'll be out when done," and he shut the door in Scroope's face.

The sea continued rough the whole morning as they crossed to the Netherlands, and though the lad was stark strange, Horatio was very pleased as Scroope continued clerking with great efficiency, even when putting quill to paper for others onboard. Under the circumstances, his hand was steady, and he seemed to take very well to the bouncing of the ship, grabbing hold the ink pot matter of fact just afore it tumbled off the table. It made Horatio smile.

As they were about to the noon meal, much harking came from above. A ship had been sighted and was bearing down on them at a fast rate. All rose to their feet and dashed to the deck, for the sea lanes were busy this time of year with both merchants and the King's return.

The frigate a' hoyed them, wanting to know if there was a Mister Horatio Sharpe aboard as they brought a packet from the King, and when complete were on to London, again. Horatio puffed out his chest most proud. It was wondrous exciting to be pointed out thus by the monarch. Someone tugged on his coat, and looking down he saw Scroope beside him.

"If they're to London afterwards, Mister Sharpe, wouldn't we want them to take the letters drafted this morn? It'd be most fast getting to Parliament folk and the like."

Horatio nodded. "Oiy, good thinking, Scroope. Go fetch them for transport. Be quick, for the ship is nigh unto us."

After the lad scampered off, he looked to the approaching ship, wondering what it was about. He'd followed all the King's instructions from the last trip. If there were more duties to perform, it'd have to wait until The Hague for he was hindered whilst aboard ship on these here rough seas.

The frigate dropped anchor as close as possible, and released a small boat. Men dashed down to it, and letting loose the ropes, rowed to *The Lute*.

A very serious gentleman came aboard. The captain said, "We're just sitting down to dinner. Would you join us?"

"Nay," the gentleman replied. "We're in a rush to make London so as to get all in readiness for the King's arrival. The City and environs must be scrubbed of the old regime forthwith. Is Mister Sharpe aboard?"

"Aye," Horatio answered. "What's this about? I'm fain ready to receive more instructions from my Royal Highness, if it be the case."

The gentleman smiled. "Nay, 'tis not the case." He turned to the captain. "Take us to the main chamber. I've an important message for this man from the King."

Horatio frowned. Why couldn't it have waited a day or two until he saw the King in person? And he was suddenly afeard he'd made a mistake on voyages to and fro, or in the long run during the past years, and hastily tasked his brains through the various actions of the more recent journeys.

Once in the great cabin, there were several men standing about, including Scroope. The gentleman from the ship rested his hand on his sword then dug into a purse. He pulled out a sealed letter.

Breaking the wax, he opened it and read: "To Mister Horatio Sharpe, for all thy kindness and fullness of heart during the past years whilst in the direst of circumstances, I hereby confer onto Sir Henry Rafferty, as my proxy until we meet again, the honor of knighting you, Sir Horatio

Sharpe, Knight Bachelor, for your full lifetime and until your death, by the powers bestowed onto me, so help me God."

Horatio stood stunned as the great chamber raised its roof with the cheering and clapping him on the back. He could not get his heart round what had just been said to him while Rafferty pulled the sword from his side and commanded, "Kneel, sirrah."

Overwhelmed with joy, Horatio fell to one knee, his eyes blearing as the sword pressed against one then the other shoulder, and he was declared Knight of the Realm.

As his senses cleared, he saw Scroope laughing and applauding. The prentice's eyes were bathed in tears which gave Horatio another dirty start, but with all the thunderous joy about him, he did not think more on it. The captain broke out a barrel of French wine, and releasing the bung, poured it into cups, pots, dishes, and the like, whilst all sang, "For he's a jolly good fellow," then cried, "Hurrah! Hurrah!" until his ears rang with the bliss of it.

~ * ~

Two days later, they joined the Fleet anchored off Scheveningen. Most astonishing, it was very crowded, for infinite ships bobbed in the rough seas.

Dragging Scroope, Horatio put them both to boat, and with the seas still running rough, everyone was near cruelly drowned before landing safe and sound on the sandy beach. Small boats from the many ships came and went, the shore filling with men and their portmanteaux.

With feet firm on the ground, Horatio noticed a boat filled with darkly clothed Puritans struggling in the rough water to shore. Now, what was this all about? It was no longer their time, and to have a pack of fanatic vipers amongst the folk of the new regime, and the King, caused his very hairs to burn under his hat.

Without thought, and leaving Scroope to gather their things, Horatio stomped down the beach toward the boat that floundered in the wild surf. He planned to give them all a hog high rant when they landed, but his breath caught in his throat when a wicked wave grabbed hold of the boat, tossing it like a toy at its crest, then plunged it with great force into the drink. Trunks went flying and men cried out mightily afore all dropped from the high waves to disappear in the water.

Scroope ran up to him. "We must save them or they will surely drown."

Horatio turned a gimlet eye upon the lad. "And how do you propose to do that? Can you swim at the best of times, let alone in this roaring surf?"

The lad drooped. "Nay, I cannot."

As men gathered at the edge of the water, watching for anyone's head to bob to the surface, one hollered, "There, a portmanteau, and it's coming upon us."

Indeed, it rode high on a wave as it swept toward them at great speed. As everyone scattered, and not knowing its weight, Horatio grabbed the lad by the waist, swinging them both out of harm's way. The trunk landed with a crash, and its lid bounced open. Contents spilled and were flung in a wide arc.

Pistols, swords, muskets, and Bibles fell to the sand as the broken trunk was caught in the tide going back out to sea. A man with a flouncing, feathered hat dragged it from the surf and gazed into it. When he looked up, his face was stark with shock.

Thinking nothing good was to come of it, Horatio strode to the fellow and the trunk. He gazed down, and could not believe his eyes. Inside, was a painted effigy, a very good likeness of the King as he was today, murdered, his head and neck bloodied red, his eyes open and sightless.

Horatio looked out into the surf and watched the boat and men, alive and dead, all tumble forward to shore. Waiting with the others, he hoped one of the live ones would be forthcoming as to why there was shameful regicide in the air.

The first man to wash in was dead, but one followed very closely who seemed alive. After landing, he rolled to his side, and retched water. The surf tried to pull him to sea again, but several men dragged him from the water to safety.

Horatio thought he knew the man, and stepping closer, pushed through the people. He looked down to see the man breathing heavily, an arm across his face. Horatio slowly bent down and moved the arm, and was astonished to recognize Wilds.

When Wilds met his eyes, Horatio fisted him hard across the skull. "Thou art a filthy rascal, and a damned fool. How could you do this to your wife? She doesn't deserve the likes of you." He stood up and hollered, "Someone, go fetch the constables of this here town. These men who art still alive are traitors and assassins to the Royal Crown. They will be hanged, their entrails gutted, and their heads stuck to pikes above London Bridge."

A Dutchman entered the fray. His English was heavily accented when he said, "But you don't know that for sure. You could be mistaken."

Horatio looked at the man and wondered where he got such gumption when he was a foreigner and not of the British world. He hollered, "Get thee to the portmanteau, then, and have a look-see what's in there. If you tell me these men ain't rank traitors, you shall go down with them, even if you art of this here foreign land."

He kicked sand on Wilds, turned on his heel, and stomped through the crowd of men. Making his way to Scroope, Horatio grabbed hold of the lad and pulled him to their boat, and their satchels. It was time to go into The Hague.

Nineteen

Grumbling, Horatio slogged through the dunes, expecting Scroope to stay alongside. "If it ain't a calamity of the times with such fanatics as these mucking up all that is finally good. To have me very own neighbor disembark at the same time as we, and betray his knavery for the whole world to see—an assassin with God on his lips. As a new knight of the realm, I shall defend me King to the very death. What do you think, lad, of this strange turn of events?"

When the lad did not respond, he looked to one side then the other, and found him nowhere in his midst. When he turned completely around, Horatio saw the lad struggling through the deep dunes. With the sand nearly to Scroope's knees, he'd slung his satchel over a shoulder with the Standish clasped tight under the other arm, vainly trying to keep up, his face screwed on most sternly.

Horatio was still cruelly vexed Wilds could be so base stupid. His actions were traitorous. He would be executed, and make Elizabeth a widow.

In a foul mood, Horatio hollered, "Well then, come along. Pick up your feet, lad, pick up your feet."

Scroope's head snapped up which caused him to lose his footing, and with a yelp, fell on his tail. Horatio clapped his teeth shut, retraced his steps to Scroope, and yanked him to his feet. Hoisting him up, he held the lad in a' dangle against him, and trudged through the sand to the road, the satchel and Standish dragging near the dirt.

Horatio could not let go of Wilds' base treachery. He released Scroope, walked up to a waiting coach, and yanked open the door. "Take us to your highest ranked magistrates of this here town."

He thrust Scroope into the carriage, and flung the satchels after, then climbed in. The coachman snapped the reins, and headed into The Hague, the city lanes very close to the sand dunes that bordered the sea. As the coach took them to City Center, Horatio calmed enough to remember this was the lad's first journey out of London. He watched as Scroope made himself comfortable at the window, and gaped at the houses, shops, and people with the rapt attention of a child.

The youth's obvious joy lessened the sting of Wilds' betrayal, and Horatio forced himself into a little contentment. "Can you speak Latin, lad? It'll help in conversing with these here foreign folk."

Still enrapt with the scenery, and not looking at him, Scroope replied, "Nay, I cannot Mister Sharpe. I shall be at a disadvantage whilst we travel in this foreign land, make no mistake."

The coach stopped in City Center, and they both got out. Horatio commanded the lad, "Stay here, then, whilst I go in and speak with the magistrates of the wicked knavery on the beach. I shall have the men clapped in irons until such time as our leaders can deal with their traitorous ways."

Later, Horatio felt much better as he strode out of the magistrates' building. The scurvy fanatics would be taken to Dutch gaol until the Navy officials from the Fleet could fetch them and return them to England for trial. It was a grievous moment, and could have marred the joyous return of the King who was expected to reach The Hague within the day.

As he and Scroope walked along the lanes of the town, not finding one free carriage to take them to an inn, Horatio regarded the lad and how very dismal Puritan he looked. It would not do.

Nudging Scroope, he said, "As soon as we find lodgings, we shall go to market for a suit of clothes and cast your Puritan coat and cap into the cesspit."

The lad looked up at him. "You mean me?"

"Aye, who else is here? It surely ain't me wearing such a dreary coat and breeches."

Scroope frowned. "I have but a farthing in me pocket, Mister Sharpe, and I think clearly a new suit of clothes will be infinite more dear than a farthing, especially pretty clothes to see the King in."

"You ain't to go in a flurry over it, for I shall pay. I'll not be giving the King mixed thoughts when looking at the both of us. I'll just take the extra coins you receive clerking for the gentlemen aboard ship," and his brow hitched when the lad scowled.

They found room in an inn that was already full to the brim. Horatio agreed with the keeper he'd share a bed in a chamber with several others.

The innkeeper said, "All the trundles are taken. We'll just pull a bench from the common room for your lad there, and all will be well, eh?"

Horatio noted the lad frowning most deeply, and he suddenly wondered greatly where he'd been during the past nights aboard ship. Scroope had made himself completely scarce once relieved of business, and Horatio hoped very dearly the strange lad hadn't introduced varlet behavior amongst the seamen. Being the captain's guest, and now a knight of the realm, it would vex him to the heart to know he'd brought a base, unseemly fellow aboard.

He'd have to watch the fellow closely now he'd shown his true colors. It made him want to clap the lad stupid until he came to right and true manly understanding.

~ * ~

Viola couldn't help but smile as Horatio dragged her with boyish eagerness to market for a proper suit of clothes. Everyone expected the King would come in from Delft with all his people, and Horatio was most joyous to be there when he came into town. As they walked to market, she noted all the people, the decorations hanging from the lampposts, and the maypoles at the front doors. She'd never seen a maypole, the practice being suppressed by the Commonwealth, and thought how very colorful everything was.

It was a bright afternoon, almost warm, and very pleasant after the foul, wild weather whilst at sea. Aboard ship and the first night in the chamber amongst the banners and ribbons to dress the royal ships, Viola thought she'd succumb to the sea sickness. She was forced to rise from her makeshift pallet and gulp air until all settled calm in her belly.

Then suddenly one night in the midst of the heaving and pulsing of the ship, the slapping of waves against its sides, and the drenching of water down the cabin walls, she slept most kindly all night long. Never having been alone in her whole life, sharing first with Paulina, Roger, and then the lads, it was really most wonderful to stretch, or snore, or rise as she saw fit without waking anyone.

She dreaded having to sleep with several men in a Dutch inn, and especially with Horatio in the bed next to hers. It could be her undoing, and in his strange state of joyous rapture, he could easily toss her in the gaol with those Puritan fellows.

Horatio stopped her at the outskirts of the market, his tall form stretching taller to locate a stall wherein they could purchase a proper suit of used clothes. She bit her bottom lip, hoping whatever they came up with weren't crawling with vermin, or stiff with dirt and sweat.

Moving through the stalls, she filled her sights with wondrous marvels, much more interesting than the London markets, the goods being so very foreign. Belgian lace, wood carvings, and pewter ware filled counters. Bolts of diverse cloths were piled high, and afore her on a pole of hooked nails, she saw truly lovely purses of many colors and hues decorated with small beads and the like.

They took her breath away.

Forgetting her purpose with Horatio, she removed a most brave blue taffeta purse from the others. It would be lovely with a gown, all flounce and lace, and her hair womanly again with combs and ribbons to match.

Horatio grabbed it away, crying out, "Art thou a stallion? I shalt not have it!"

Suddenly, tired of being a lad, she yanked it back from his hand. "Nay, I'm looking at this with me sister in mind," and without thinking, added, "Her name is Paulina."

"Paulina," he said with brows furled. "I've known one who is an impertinent jade and rambunctious. Is it she?"

"Well I wouldn't know, would I?" Turning all fretful like, she did not want him to remember Pall, nay she did not, for if he did, he'd remember her, wouldn't he?

"Give it to me," Horatio ordered with an outstretched hand. "It makes you look base strange to be holding a woman's purse so fondly."

When she didn't respond fast enough, he grabbed it from her hand and threw it to the vendor's cart. "Come along, and do not touch another thing that is lassie."

He sped away, forcing Viola to run after him. She fumed and hissed behind his back, vexed to the very heart he was such a rude fellow, and it dawned on her he was very much like his scurvy brother, Roger.

Horatio abruptly turned around, and she collided into him.

Grabbing her arms, he said, "I can hear thee hissing behind me. Annoyed, are we?"

She shrugged away from him and snapped, "Nay, I am not. Let's to the second clothes stall afore this whole damn market closes. I wish to retrieve the fancy frills soon as possible, then to bed."

He grinned. "You don't want to visit a brothel? Surely, I thought you'd want your first time a' scuttle-butting away with a saucy slut here in this very free country. The Dutch ain't so stiff as the Puritans in our England."

Horrified, Viola stared at him with wide eyes. It was the last thing she would do, or could think to do, and with him leading the way, well, it was just too horrid to contemplate. "Nay, I shall not scuttle-butt with you, not now or evermore."

At his fierce glare, she realized her mistake and stammered, "Uhm, don't want the clap, now do I?"

Horatio regarded her with a scowl, his eyes going all jittery like, as if he were trying to resolve a prickly riddle. It made her a' flitter, for as a lass trying to be a lad, she probably came across a mite strange. He turned away, walked to the stall with the seconds, and shuffled through the garments.

She ventured closer to him as he picked up one item and then another, looking for something that would suit her or the King, she knew not which. He tossed her breeches with falling lace at the base of the legs, a ribbon to make them very handsome, and a coat to match.

He did not look at her as he dove deeper into the pile. "Do you have a shirt, then?"

"Only what I'm wearing," Viola replied.

Pulling a shirt with laced cuffs from the others, he shook it. "Take off your coat."

"Why?" she cried out, suddenly all affright.

With his face screwed most annoyed, he hollered, "Because I said so, that's why."

Viola did not move, and clearly infuriated, Horatio grabbed her. He ripped the coat off her back. "Damn it, why do you trouble me so?"

He thrust the shirt over her head, forcing her arms through the sleeves. He brushed his hands down the length of her to straighten the fabric, and Viola froze when his hands stilled.

He stood straight and gazed at her, his face filled with disbelief. Her heart pounding erratically in her throat, Viola backed away.

Very quietly, Horatio asked, "What have you got under your shirt, Scroope? What art thou hiding?"

Viola shook her head, and stepped farther away. "Nothing."

"You will tell me what you are hiding or I'll force it from you, strip you 'til I see for meself."

Viola could not bear it. The very idea horrified her, and once he knew she was a lass, he'd cast her aside. At a complete loss, her heart filled with panic, she turned on her heel and ran.

Twenty

Horatio watched the lad weave through the people, his shirt billowing behind him. Scroope ran very poorly, and he realized what he had been missing.

The lad was a lassie.

He bolted after Scroope, intending to have it out with…whoever the bloody person was. It troubled him cruelly to have been so basely played, but he could not catch her.

Scroope was wily, weaving in and out of folk, stalls, carts and horses. It took all Horatio's effort to keep up, finally almost able to grasp the shirt as they dashed away from market and down a narrow lane.

Greatly vexed, he shouted like the devil, "Oiy there! Stop this very minute."

The lass breathed heavily. He knew she couldn't run much farther, but the lass did not slow down, and as a new knight of the realm, Horatio would be damned if he'd let a wisp of a girl outrun him. With a final burst of speed, he snatched the fluttering shirt, and yanked. "I said, halt!"

Gasping for breath, Scroope reeled to a stop, her eyes wide as Horatio seized her by the collar, and pushed her against a wall of a tall house. "I'm clapped by the heels thou art a lass, is this so?" and he shook the horrid thing for good measure. "Tell me the truth, by God, or you shall be the sorrier for it."

Snarling, Scroope's mouth was stiff as she wiggled against the wall. Horatio's nose hairs bristled with ire, and taking hold of the lassie's belt, he groped with his other hand under the shirts.

An eyebrow disappeared into his hat brim. "Well, well, me thinks this here apprentice is truly a lass."

He let her go, and she sank to a crouch, sobbing most piteously into the lacey shirt sleeves.

"Who art thou?"

Her face bathed in tears, she whimpered, "I am Viola, sister of Paulina Wilmot who you remember as an impertinent harpy."

She gazed at him with great, wet eyes, and of a sudden his rancor diminished. "Ah, I remember. You're the quiet one who cannot abide the eating of God," and he smiled. "Well, then, why don't we to the inn for the telling of this tale. Should be most entertaining."

Viola stood and glared at him. "Nay, it shall not be entertaining, and I ain't to be laughed at whilst I tell it, neither."

Horatio snapped his mouth shut, thinking she was a bold trout. She'd been false to everyone for the world to see, but he'd let it pass for the time being. He was itching to know why a girl would choose to be a lad if she didn't fancy women's tails.

He bowed and let her go afore him.

They walked back to the market where they met the owner of the shirt Viola was wearing. He wore a scowling face and carried a cudgel. Waving the club in high anger, he harked loudly in his foreign, Dutchy tongue.

Horatio raised his arms defensively, hoping to ward off any stout blows. "We shall wait to that inn, Mistress, and pay for that shirt you're a' wearing afore this here fellow clobbers us most cruelly," and he pulled out his purse to pay the man.

~ * ~

Later that evening in the common room of their inn, Viola swung a leg over a bench and sat down, laying her new suit of clothes on the table. Although very surprised after knowing who she was, Horatio still bought the lacy shirt for her, then purchased brocade breeches in a wondrous green color, a coat, and even a neck cloth, fine indeed for a lad to wear afore the King.

Horatio sat down across from her with a wink and a smile, making Viola edgy. Now that he knew who she was, would he take rude advantage? It near broke her brains to think on it, for it had been her main purpose to avoid such a thing when dressing as a lad.

Nevermore in her life would she turn slut for anyone. Roger, the beastly creature, treated her like a drudged whore, and he was her husband. She couldn't endure it with Horatio.

After the Dutchy maid set down two mugs of frothy beer and a platter of meats, bread and cheese, Viola asked, "What will you do with me?"

Wiggling his eyebrows, he grinned at her like a randy coxcomb. "What would you have me do with you, Mistress?"

Without warning, she was angered beyond reason. "If you play with me as if I were a low woman, you shall regret it, sirrah. I've gone great lengths to learn a' clerking, and to be treated right and true in this here business." She stood up, and leaning over the table, jabbed a finger at him. "I shall not be debauched, or treated cruelly, now or nevermore. You hear me?"

"Aye, as do all in this common room. 'Tis a good thing the folk in here are foreigners, and not able to understand proper English." He straightened his hat more firmly on his head and gave her a wry smile. "Let us speak more gently with one another, for I shall not cause you discontent. Tell me why you decided to be a lad."

She regarded him closely and sat down. She was in a sad pickle, ready for a dreadful fall. It would be good to tell him all for she'd been troubled by the deceit, always watching to make sure no one would see she was a woman, but she could not tell him the truth of Roger. Nay, she would not.

She took a deep breath. "It all began when me husband died..."

He listened well for she watched his eyes, waiting for them to go all shifty like, even admitting how her papa had gone so base strange with the wont for bringing dead heads back to life. His jaw dropped, and she halted in the telling. "What?"

"I saw you at Tower Stairs one day. It was near dark. A link boy pulled a head from an old man and threw it to the river. That was you and your father, weren't it?"

"And me sister, Paulina, too."

"This is a merry, droll telling."

Viola asked, "So, what will you do with me?"

Horatio leaned toward her and whispered, "We shall keep this cunning piece of trickery between us, you remaining a lad, won't we? 'Twill be safer all around. I ain't that good with me sword, you see. I'm better with pistols but haven't any with me at the moment." He winked.

She frowned, thinking he'd proved himself that day a wickeder rogue than Roger, and she sniffed.

He heard that, and turned very serious indeed. "You like the freedom of being a lad, methinks," and he cocked a brow.

He was right, for the men of the world had it far better than women, and now having the taste of such freedom as the breeches gave her, it would be a sore disappointment to be shelved again as ladies were. She nodded.

He continued, "And as I cannot goodly defend your honor whilst in the midst of randy men both aboard ship and on land, let us continue in it."

Viola grinned, deciding she again liked Horatio very much. "Aye, 'tis a very worthy freedom, larking about in a man's way of being so bold, and no one thinking you unworthy, especially during these new times, and bringing back the King."

He laughed, a thing so lovely especially with such pretty teeth. It near took her breath away.

~ * ~

Next morning, sipping her morning draught and nibbling from the fare, she waited in the common room for Horatio who was primping himself handsome for the King's entrance into town.

Horatio entered most joyous, filled with robust energy. She saw he could not stop grinning. "The King and all his people are to enter midday, a wondrous event. Let's to town center and find a place for the viewing of it. Mayhap, we shall be allowed into the grand salon for the King's greeting with the town's burghers."

Outside in the burgeoning crowd, the wind picked up, swooping down from the tall houses that lined the lane. Hats and kerchiefs went flying. Horatio looked down on her with a frown. "You haven't a hat. You ain't properly attired."

Instinctively Viola patted her head as the wind ruffled her hair. She'd known of it, but did not have enough face to ask him with her own purse flat.

He said, "And you ain't wearing gloves. That's against the rules of gentility when afore the King."

Viola gazed at her naked hands. Her fingers were black from ink, and she curled them out of sight.

"We shall get you these things, Scroope, and it shall be done forthwith afore the King comes trotting into town. Why didn't you say anything?"

She shrugged. "Didn't feel I had the right."

He frowned at her. "I shall not be chagrined by you when we are greeted by the King."

Looking up at him with a wide smile, she asked, "Will I also have the honor of meeting the King? Oh, that would be ever so lovely."

He pushed her away from him. "You shall not talk so. 'Tis far too lassie-like. Stop at once."

She did not care for his beastly behavior. With arms stiffly at her side, she cried, "And how would you have me speak then? I am a lass, and there ain't a thing you can do about it."

He stopped short to regard her, and a slow grin crept across his face. "Aye, then, so you are."

His gaze moved ever so casually over her body, resting for a moment where her breasts should be jutting out, then moving up to her lips. She shivered as her heart thumped heavily, and of a sudden wondered how he could be so very different than his horrid brother.

She said, "If you are caught looking at me like that, you'll be thought a stallion in search of a sweet lad." She gave him a jolly wink.

He scowled. "You make me into a most discontented ass, Scroope. One of these days, your bold tongue will give you much trouble."

She laughed. "Nay, it will not. Now, my sister, Paulina, there's another tale. She's most bold." She leaned forward and softly said, "Did you know she makes no bother of being married and taking another husband? If one becomes too bothersome, another will do."

Horatio laughed. "Indeed. Well, with the government switching back and forth, changing policies, and dismissing vicars as you please, no one knows if they are truly married these days. 'Tis a true pickle I hope not to encounter." He looked around. "Now, where is that market?"

They found it most convenient around the next row of houses, and to Viola's joy, he bought her a very fine, wide brimmed hat richly stocked with green and blue feathers. It fit well enough, but the gloves he gave her were too small.

She glared at him. "Do you consider me a child, Sir?"

"Nay, but thou art a small fellow to be sure." He waved his hand. "Pick out a pair that fits and let's be gone. The King will be soon into town."

Viola stepped up to the gloves table, searching for a pair that would fit. As she shifted through them, someone laughed nearby, someone with a chortling laugh very much like Roger's. Her gut roiling in dismay, she turned sharply and searched for the beastly rogue.

The market was too full of people. She could not see him.

Horatio snapped, "Quicken it up a bit, or we'll not see him at all."

Returning to the task, Viola picked up a pair of Spanish gloves, lovely with lace cuffs that were yanked out of her hand.

"These are ladies' gloves, you rank fool." Tossing gloves back onto the pile, he searched willy-nilly. Pulling up a pair, he pressed them against her hand in measurement and said to the merchant, "We'll take these. How much?"

The chortling laugh reached her ears again, and Viola turned quickly to see a man's broad back walk away through the crowds; a broad back very much like Roger's.

Of a sudden, the broad back turned around to face her, staring straight toward her. It was Roger, his twinkling eyes most wicked, but he did not recognize her. He wagged his head, then turned to disappear back into the crowd.

Her heart sank, thinking it a horrid crack in the world he should be in The Hague. She wondered at the cruel joke of it, never realizing until that moment she'd been hoping he had gone away, nevermore to be seen.

Horatio shook her. "For the love of God, what are you about? We must be away right this very minute. Follow me closely. I don't want the trouble of losing you."

They entered City Center, Viola holding onto Horatio's coat so she wouldn't lose him in the swarm of people. It was very strange how caring he was one moment and all grumbles the next. Afeard she'd get lost and stranded in a foreign land, she tightened her grip on his coat.

Through the multitude they wound their way until great shouting, trumpets, and the ringing of bells marked the entrance of Charles II into The Hague. Horatio took hold of her arm and pulled her through the people to a corner wherein a lamppost stood.

"You're too big to be sitting on me shoulders, lass, but up with you to the top. You'll soon see history in the making." He grabbed her backside and sent her up to the metal bits just below the lanthorn box.

Viola squawked loudly, never having liked being so high except when looking down to the water from London Bridge. She grabbed hold of the metal bits with all her might and hugged the post as if she'd soon be cast to death.

But not for long.

Taken up by the passion of the moment, she watched as all a' horse, the King and his retinue paraded down the street. People shouted, waving their hands, flags, and banners in the greatest of jubilation.

Viola forgot her fears as she watched the procession. The King wore shining, new clothes covered with silver and gold gilt. Lace and brocades of the brightest colors paraded toward her, very beautiful after the dismal years under the Commonwealth. The wind blew pennants and feathers as the horses' harnesses jingled down the lane.

The King with hat firmly on his head, sat straight in the saddle. He seemed very tall as he rode to where she clung to the lamppost. The horse that had to be a good nineteen hands looked almost too small for His Royal Highness. As he drew closer, his face was somber, almost sad. He looked fit, and as he approached, he turned his gaze to her.

Suddenly filled with elation, she pulled off her hat, waved it, and cried out with great joy at his return. "I shall not forsake thee, milord King, not ever in this world for all to see, this I promise you." She leaned dangerously forward, still waving her hat, and near touching him.

The King broke into a grin, and it wiped the sorrow from his face. Still gazing at her, he straightened his shoulders and nodded.

Viola abruptly burst into tears.

Twenty-one

Viola followed Horatio to a banquet chamber in the stateliest hall of town, and then to a trestle table close as possible to where the King would sit.

He pushed her to a bench. "Stay here. Don't move. I'm off to find us a plate of food to share." And off he went, leaving Viola to spread her arms along the bench, not allowing anyone to take Horatio's seat.

The King and his people dashed to places along the table on the center dais, some not finding space and moving down the tables toward her. One such brazen fellow gave her a smart look, cast her arm aside and sat down beside her. "What are you about, pretty lad, that you're so near the King's table? You're but a low person in His Royal Highness' midst."

She gave him a dirty glare. "I ain't of low stature and you're not to say such. Milord's a Sir recently knighted by the King this very journey to fetch him."

The beastly fellow sneered. "Oiy, and who might your new lordship be?"

"'Tis I, Harry, you old scoundrel. Get thee gone from me place," and Horatio gave the fellow a jolly punch to the arm. "What are you about, making sport with me clerk?"

Harry stood. "I ain't making sport with your clerk, dainty though he be. What are you about with the likes of him?"

Horatio snorted. "He's but a clerk, nothing else." He pulled Viola from the bench. "Get thee gone and find your own plate. Mister Harry Sattler and me are about to catch up since we last met."

"When was that?" Viola demanded.

"Thou art a bold cur. Not that it's any of your concern, but you may be interested to know 'twas the very night your da was saved from drowning. Now, off with you."

He sat down where she had been, completely disregarding her as his friend returned to the bench. "Take up your knife, Harry boy, and let's break into this fare. 'Tis cold, but not so as to lard up."

Viola wandered off, locating the banquet table set with prodigious and unusual dishes, very brave, for folk not good enough to be served with the King. There were no wooden bowls or trenchers left so she picked up a thick collop of beef, and returning as near to the King as she could, hunkered down to watch all the activity.

Spaniels darted amongst the royal feet as scraps of food fell in their midst, the King talking and laughing to those around him.

Then a fair lady asked, "Tell us of your adventures, Your Highness, afore you escaped to France."

The King grinned.

A flouncy coxcomb leaned forward, his neck lace sweeping across a plate of food. "Heard you were a fugitive after the battle of Worcester. It would be wondrous if Your Royal Majesty will take the time and tell us of it."

The King said, "I knew every officer by name, and together, we fought against Cromwell and his men. Our pistols were empty of powder. The fight was too close for swords and pikes. We could only fight with our fists and the butts of our guns."

Viola forgot all about the collop of beef in her hand until the lard warmed and grease started to drool down her fist. She licked it up before it reached her pretty lace cuff, and took a bite of the meat.

The King continued, "Amongst Worcester's lanes, I begged the men not to despair and to keep up the fight. I was willing to be shot dead rather than retreat, but in the end, I knew we must withdraw. There would be no victory."

He shook his head. "There had been too many killed. Too many. I was advised I must live to rule another day, so I looked for the best road to exile."

Finding a discarded kerchief, Viola wiped her greasy hands and crept closer to the King's table and his story. Many of the courtiers were clearly bored by the tale, but it grasped her imagination so that she could see most vivid the town bathed in blood. Dead bodies piled in heaps in the streets, at the base of buildings, and beyond to the battlefield.

The King stood up and started pacing along the edge of the dais. "Me armor already removed, me George was stripped from me neck and put into a pocket with a Roundhead cloak thrown over me shoulders. I was taken to a house carved out of the city wall where we stood quiet as a cannon ball thundered past the door to break another hole in a column of men…"

Viola sat enrapt as the King launched into his escape from England, a hunted man by Cromwell's army who would do him grave ill. It was an extraordinary good telling as she'd ever heard in her whole life, and most romantic.

Forgetting all time as the King talked, Viola jerked at a sudden noise. An unholy din barked at the entrance of the banquet hall, snapping her from the King's tale. She groaned. The ruckus worked its way to the great table where the King sat, his finger still pointed to the ceiling in the throes of the telling.

All the noise of the chamber and the King's words faded to nothing as everyone turned to see what was afoot.

A group of men clamored to the King, dragging a bound fellow. Horatio jumped into the tussle. Viola saw he looked most vexed with the trussed up man, his hair and black suit rank from the sea.

The banquet hall rang quiet as people stood or climbed on benches to watch this sudden mad stir. Everyone wondered what it was all about. Viola stepped closer to Horatio, for he looked ready to burst.

A man swept off his hat and cried most loudly, "Your Majesty, this here fanatic viper had murder in his heart when he landed on this here shore. We had the burgermeister throw him in the clink but now the local magistrates demand he be freed to do mischief as he sees fit. What shall we do with him?"

The King regarded the tethered up fellow. "Who was he to murder?"

Horatio bowed. "You, Your Majesty."

Turning to Horatio, the King asked, "How do you know this? What's his name?"

"His name is Robert Wilds, Your Majesty, a varlet neighbor of mine on Tower Hill. He's Presbyterian, and will not change with the times, but has since become greatly fanatical, and strange."

Wilds struggled against the bonds.

The King asked, "How do you know this? If indeed it's as you say, I am certain you'd not be the best of companions."

Horatio regarded the bound man with a smirk. "I could nevermore be this man's friend." His smirk broadened into a sneer. "His wife and I are jolly, good friends, though, Your Majesty," and Viola watched the man wrench toward Horatio, his eyes narrowing into slits.

"Aye," Horatio repeated. "We know each other very well, indeed."

All the people in the room knew what he meant, including Viola, and she gazed at Mister Horatio Sharpe with new eyes. He was no better than her filthy husband, but since he was Roger's brother, how could she have thought otherwise?

He'd gone quite low in value, and her heart sank most melancholy.

A man garbed in heavy black thrust himself through the crowd. Reaching the King, he did not bow or remove his hat, but cried out most boisterous, "I am of the Presbyterian delegation from London, Sire, come to dictate what we expect of you as our King. This man, here, ain't of our group. You must not think of him as one of us."

Regarding the churchman, the King went dead still.

A courtier stood with a rush. "Who do you think you are not removing your hat with due respect, and *dictating* what our King shall or shall not do?"

The King snapped his fingers, bringing the disorder to a halt. "Odds fish, this is too dull and foggy. Remove both these men. I shall not discuss order of business, nor shall I address traitorous deeds this joyous day."

A man in a dark coat with brass buttons cried, "But, Your Majesty, what of this villain who intended you bodily harm? What shall we do with him?"

A gentleman from the high table waved an arm. "To the lockup on one of the ships with him. We are celebrating now. We'll deal with him, later."

With much ado, both men were removed from the banquet chamber, leaving behind a jumble of rowdy conversation. Viola stood on her tiptoes, and watched Horatio leave with his friend, dragging Wilds betwixt them.

She found the whole affair most astonishing, and greatly disturbing. With her husband so beastly, and now Horatio bragging afore the whole world he'd taken his poor neighbor's wife, was there no honor amongst men for a lady to appreciate for evermore?

Following the men out of the hall, she lowered her head. She was resolved there was none.

Twenty-two

After everyone had gone away, with not another word on the King's adventures into exile, Viola wandered discontented from the banquet hall. Stepping outside, she braved a wind that blew most harsh. Hats and all manner of bits flew across the lanes that were full of men from the Fleet, and who were unable to gain their ships in the rough seas.

The Hague was busy with English folk and other cultures, for she heard infinite diverse languages. As she strolled towards the market, still up and running due to folks crowding the town, she realized her excitement of the place had been tainted with the wont to kill the King, and Horatio's baseness. He'd certainly showed what a damned rogue he could be, indeed he had.

Viola drifted through the market and came upon a stall with quills and ink pots, papers stacked high and weighted down to keep from flying away in the gusty winds. With clerking for more than just Horatio, she'd used up most of her supplies in fast order.

As she studied what she could purchase, Viola heard laughter. At first she knew it to be Roger's, but then she turned to see Horatio with his back to her, Harry Sattler at his side, rowling it up with a pretty Dutchy lass. Mighty bold she was, too, with her dimpled, pink cheeks, and her saucy blue eyes shining as Harry sidled up to her with a wink and a grin.

Viola was not liking men at the moment, and was about to walk away when Horatio said loudly and clearly enough for the whole world to hear, "Aye, there seems to be a glut of barren women in London town, and I'm in the business to get them all with child. 'Tis been a most satisfying affair, I can tell you. Me partner's the lady of the Mitre on Fenchurch Street."

With a gasp, Viola regarded the Dutchy lass to see if she understood his talk, but her face remained blank as she stared at Harry. He grabbed hold of the girl's waist and tugged her to him with a laugh. "Ain't that fine and dandy? Hope you're paid well for the task. 'Tis better than paying for it as I'm about to do." He bent down to kiss the lass. "Ain't that right, me pretty maid? Ready to frisk and hey about?"

Viola was astounded. Since Roger, she'd resolved men were absolute beasts. This afternoon had not changed her thoughts on it, nay, it had not. Would both men share the lass, and was Horatio's goal to get her with child? The very idea made a hell in her mind, and she stomped up to them with a fierce frown.

Arms akimbo, she glared at Horatio. "What's this all about then?"

Frowning, Harry asked, "Who's this, again?"

Horatio replied, "Me clerk, and a brazen filly she is, too."

Harry's eyes went wide. "A woman? Why, she's outfitted in lads' clothing. 'Tis all very strange, Horatio, and if I'm thinking a' right, then I've had you pegged all wrong these many years. You ain't a perverted fellow, are you?"

"Nay, you blockhead. I hired a lad from the shop to do me clerking. 'Twas only yesterday I found he was a she. Don't know if you're aware, but shipmen don't take to women being aboard. We're keeping her this way for safety's sake. Can't protect her every minute, now can I?"

Harry grinned. "Well then, relieved I am to hear it. Had me going, there, for a moment. Nasty trick that would have been." He hugged the Dutchy lass. "Well, Sir Sharpe, by the looks of your lassie, I reckon I'm to a better place than you. Come along, me Dutch-girl. Come along. 'Tis time to frolic."

Off they went jolly as you please, the Harry fellow roaring for a rattling tumble and toss. Viola stared after them, fuming. Men were base stupid, for the woman could be riddled with clap and he'd not know it until after the deed.

"Oiy there," Horatio hollered, snapping Viola away from the Sattler fellow and her dark thoughts.

Horatio turned her to face him. "What's this all about, then? Why should you give a tinker's damn what I or another fellow do? It ain't your call to stand all vexed like. Nay, 'tis not."

Viola stared at him for the debauched fellow he was, and before she could stop herself, she blurted, "You ain't any better than Roger, may the devil take him straight to hell. He's here in The Hague, should you be interested to know."

Horatio sucked in his breath. "What do you say?"

"I said Roger is here in The Hague."

He regarded the market booths, then turned full circle before taking hold of her and shaking her until her teeth rattled. "How do you know I had a brother, may the dirty cur's heart be pulled from the cold grave and staked to a pike for the whole world to see."

She wrenched free of him. "Because you are the same as he, a filthy, cheating dog who'd lay with any saucy slut just to satisfy your needs."

"That ain't no reason to know him."

Grabbing his neck cloth, Viola pulled him close so he could see every word coming from her mouth. "He ain't dead, *Sir* Sharpe, nay he is not, and you know how I know?" She stared into his eyes. "Because I'm married to the filthy rascal, that's why."

"What? You cannot be married to the dirty knave. I killed him, I did, after finding him with me wife."

"Your wife?"

Horatio's face went stark mad. "I cannot endure it. You are an impertinent harpy to remind me of that terrible time."

He turned away from her, and she watched him walk away, his back bent like a broken, old man's.

~ * ~

Horatio hated to be reminded of his wife and brother, and their treachery. Not that it mattered. The thoughts of it rarely left him. As he walked, he hardly noticed the noise of the marketplace drifting away and the town becoming quieter. Every night, unless completely drunk, he saw in his mind's eye how he'd been betrayed, and what he'd done about it.

He strode at a furious pace until the road ended, and slogged heavily through the sand, barely seeing the tide rush in as the memories blazed through his brains...

~ * ~

The whole day had been foul with a cold rain drenching him at every step. After a long time at his business and finally to home, Horatio was tired to the bone of the rain and wind, and was very much desiring a warm, cheery hearth.

It had been a spring of gales blowing up the Thames, and this one had been at it since before dawn. Houses were awash and people drowned. It was sad to be sure, but he could not think on such bad tidings. His wife was with child, and he was over the top joyous, hoping for a lad.

He rushed home from his bookseller's shop, the rhythm of the press still throbbing through him. Stepping to the front door, he dashed into his house to find it dark and quiet, most unusual. Even the maid, a noisome creature, wasn't to be heard. His wife's yellow cat slept all curled on the settle in the front entry, another thing most strange for his wife loved the cat and had it with her always.

Unease sliced through his gut. Afeard all might not be right with her and the babe, he ran up the stairs to the level with the bedchamber and burst into the room to see the bed rollicking most grievous with loud groans coming from inside the curtains.

A man's joyous bray and his wife's satiated scream pierced to the rafters and out the curtained bedstead.

Horatio stood like a dead man as his soul filled with the sounds and movement before him, and his heart broke to pieces.

In a sudden white rage, he swept aside the curtains to see his own brother, Roger, towsing his wife with the babe snug inside her. The shock of knowing the child more than likely was not his seared through Horatio, and with thunderous anger roaring in his brains, he ripped the curtains away from their anchors.

Not caring one bit of the harm he could do to the babe, he pulled his wife from the bed, she all the while shrieking. He clapped her hard and cast her to the wall.

Hissing and grinding his teeth like a madman, Horatio jerked out the dagger from its sheath to kill his brother.

~ * ~

As he stood in the water with the surf crashing against him, Horatio realized he'd soon drown if he didn't retreat to higher ground, and he struggled to a dune with blowing grasses on it. He was wet through, his new boots ruined. Whatever Viola had meant, Horatio knew he'd killed the filthy blighter. He had stabbed him in the heart while the man's cock was still hard and wet from his wife.

The man named Roger whom Viola had called her husband was not his brother, and he turned at a loud shout to see the lass walking towards him.

She called, "Art thou well?"

Even as the shock of it screamed through him, Horatio hollered, "He is dead for I stabbed him in the heart. I watched him breathe his last, and then dragged me wife up the stairs to the attic where I locked her in 'til she was dead."

The lass looked horrified. "Did you kill both of them?"

Cruelly rattled, he shook his head. "Nay, me wife died of smallpox. She had the beginnings of it when she and me brother…" And he stalled in the telling.

She sighed. "That's good."

Giving her a look askance, Horatio ground out, "There ain't nothing good about it."

Viola pulled him from the dune toward the town, and patted his hand. "You must know Roger had stab wounds about the chest all a' festered when I met him." She stopped him with a gesture. "I was nursemaid in a charity ward for the ill and lame. Besides the wounds," and she paused for a good while, "he had smallpox. He raged in his fevers, and we all thought what he cried out was his illness, nothing more."

She stopped to regard him. "But it was true, weren't it? He and your wife betrayed you for the whole world to see."

Horatio was spent. "Aye."

"Your brother still lives."

"Nay, he does not."

Viola tugged him through the last of the sand. "'Twas a grievous thing done to you."

Allowing her to pull him back to town, he swallowed hard the lump in his throat.

She patted him on the hand, again, like a poor, sad babe. "He is alive, and in The Hague, Sir. Let us hope the two of you do not run into each other."

Her persistence vexed him. "We shall not meet, for me brother is dead and burning in hell."

She said nothing but grunted most unladylike.

He said, "He was married, you know."

Scroope gasped. "Nay, he was not."

"Aye, to a lass called Betty."

"Is she still alive?"

Horatio shut his eyes for a moment against the possibility the filthy rascal still lived, and that he must kill him, again.

He finally said, "I know not."

Twenty-three

After several days, the wind finally died down, allowing them aboard ship again, but not *The Lute* as before. Horatio came aboard *The Naseby* as it was being made ready for the King due to being one of the first to be knighted by the returning monarch. Great, colorful sheets of fabric were slung across the bow with pretty ribbons unfurling and blowing in the winds. The name of the Commonwealth's ship was struck and in its place was painted *The Charles*.

Despite a mighty melancholy droop he could not shake, Horatio was pleased to be traveling back to England with the King.

The amount of folk coming aboard was astonishing though, and he was afeared the ship would sink with the weight of them, for it was not just people. They came bearing great chests and portmanteaux, dogs and horses. Hard by on another ship, he watched a carriage being hoisted on deck from a barge, and farther on, a yacht was being affixed to a ship, very brave.

The Charles was most populated, forcing him and his clerk to bunk with two other fellows whom he did not know. It made for tight quarters, and he was a mite tetchy the fellows would discover Scroope was a lass.

Horatio ordered, "You'll be most cautious when fitting yourself for wake and sleep times. I'll not have the men on this here ship discover who you are."

Scroope gave him a dirty regard. "I ain't so base stupid as you may think, sirrah. I shall be most discreet."

Horatio was vexed by her cheek. "You shall address me for the high person I am, Clerk Scroope. I'll not tolerate any cheeky behavior by a low person as yourself, or you'll be dunked into the sea for the whole world to see."

Her eyes widened but he reckoned it was for her own safety, and he refused to back down. >From the look on her face, he felt sure she realized he would do what he threatened, in front of the King or not, since she knew what he had done to his wife.

He said, "You shall address me 'Sir'."

The lass squinted up at him, her face vexed into stone. Horatio snorted with disgust. How could she have been so duped by his brother? Refusing to believe Roger was not dead, he shook himself to rid thoughts of the damned rascal, and turned them back to his lassie clerk.

Even though he spoke so base cruel to her, he had come to like Scroope. Now that he knew her to be a woman, she was fetching in a petite, flat-titted way.

It also came as a great surprise she could do so well in the business as Simon Kirk, one of the best clerks in London town. If he was willing to admit it—and he was not—she was even better than Kirk. The lass had a concentration and determination he'd not seen in any man.

An impertinent jade, she was filled with a quest for knowledge he admired. Her eyes were wide like a child's with all she saw in their adventures of the returning King. It was most enjoyable. It gave him pause for a hard think, but must leave it until later. There was too much hullabaloo around him to reckon on anything.

The King and his people came aboard. His family and courtiers spilled over the sides and onto the deck. The dowager Queen and Princess Royale were hoisted aboard and deposited atop a coil of hemp rope. They turned round in the small space, and gaped at all the people and goods stacked in their midst with hardly enough room to breathe.

Horatio smiled when the very happy Duke of York stepped into their midst. Even though his clothes were frayed and tired, he was trimmed in bright colors. The King was little better, but he made a brave effort to appear smart. As more of the court people came aboard attired in ragged splendor, it told a strong story of the privation they suffered during exile.

Horatio regarded his clerk watching the high folk come aboard. Her eyes told it all as she stared at the King's people with both interest and sadness. What England had done to their King was horrid hard, and Horatio was ashamed.

The King walked to the rail and waved at all the ships anchored nearby, everyone knowing he would be the center of focused glasses. When the guns from the Fleet boomed, the thunder of it rocked Horatio's brains until his head felt ready to burst.

But the King seemed glad. He was most kind to all with his subjects flocking to receive his blessing and kiss his ring. Gazing around him, he towered over all, the wind snatching at his feathered hat and long hair.

It was a grand day for the whole world to see. The King was returning to his land, a welcomed monarch.

~ * ~

In the afternoon whilst the guns continued to roar, and the ladies were back to shore, Horatio played cards on deck. Servants mixed with the high and low, and for a shilling each, Horatio enlisted his clerk to write letters for the gentlemen aboard. Her hand was good, and there were few blotches. She knew the way of a quill.

All was well with the world until he watched with astonishment as his brother, alive and well, came aboard. The dirty cur, laughing and larking about as if he'd never suffered a bad day all his life, was blazing drunk. He stumbled across the deck, demanding the privy and passed by the King without so much as a bow or removal of his hat.

It made Horatio stark mad to see it, and he stood in a rush, upsetting the card game. In his anger he fumbled with his dagger sheath, cursing mightily. With the frustration of the dagger not coming free, he was about to cast the table aside when Viola forcefully pulled him away to a quiet corner.

"Nay, you shall not, Sir. He is showing his knavery for all to see, and will be banned soon enough. Let the other gentlemen handle it."

And she was aright, for Horatio would by no means at anytime ever want his name associated with the damned rascal.

Growling, he turned to his clerk. "How could you have married the bastard? Were you so blind you could not see his arch rogue ways? I know you ain't that base stupid."

She stared at him as if he'd struck her, her eyes wide and her mouth in a deepening frown. If he didn't know better, the bloody clerk's heart was quite pulled down and she was about to burst into a fit of weeping. It would add to the calamity of the day.

He spat, "Nay, you shall not bathe the deck in tears. Thou art a clerk, and a lad, and it would be horrid wrong to cry like a babe afore all these men. I forbid it."

Tears welled over and fell onto her cheeks anyway, making her a damned plague to him.

She said, "I did not know he was married, milord. I was with child and me papa put a pistol to his head, forcing him into it."

He turned his back to her, watching his brother trip merrily toward the privy for a piss. Horatio knew if he were near, he'd tear the dirty cur to pieces and throw him bit by bit into the sea, this time truly dead.

Not able to endure it another moment, he was about to turn away when Roger made a sudden stop at the rail. Only a few feet from the King, and laughing all the while, he pulled out his pole to piss. It splattered in the wind, blowing back onto him and toward the King.

A great hue and cry bellowed to the tops of the masts, several gentlemen and seamen grabbing hold of Roger and throwing him overboard. He screamed in a frightful manner until he hit the water, people running to the rail. They watched, but Horatio did not. No one attempted a rescue.

He regarded his clerk with a stern eye. "I reckon that business is done. Mayhap, he'll drown. What do you think?"

Scroope sniffed. "I'm not sure I shall ever again be your friend, sirrah. Thou art a beastly creature." And she ran to the rail with the rest of them to watch Roger thrash in the sea.

Later that evening after supper, the King strode bareheaded into the ship's great chamber, a bottle of wine in one hand and a Venetian drinking glass in the other. Earlier, as everyone assembled in the dining chamber, he had been forced to remove his hat that knocked against every rafter and door lintel. Once removed, he seemed more like every other man aboard. His hair was fine indeed, thick and black.

Horatio watched his clerk moon and sigh, for all the women thought the King ever so handsome in a rugged, sad way. His adventures were romantic and daring, and by the looks of Scroope, she thought the same as every other simple female in the world.

The King sat on a stool, a smile spread across his face. He said, "Now, where was I in the tale?"

His words brought Scroope's face to shine most joyously. She crept closer to their monarch, and settled close.

Horatio walked out of the great chamber as the King sang of his adventures, and stood on deck listening to the surf pound the shore. The night was like pitch, the wind still blowing with flags and banners snapping above him. The Hague seemed to have disappeared, the only lights being lanthorns of the Fleet rocking about him.

Behind him, seamen went about their business, for all would soon set sail for England. The King would once again stand on his native soil after the complete trouncing by Cromwell back in 'fifty-one.

Everyone knew it was a miracle the King had safely escaped without injury, but Horatio had no need to be in the great chamber, having heard the story many times. His journeys to and fro over the past months placed him in the King's midst who had a tendency to regale anyone within earshot of his exile adventures. It made him glad to be near alone on deck, giving him time for a think.

He grabbed hold of the rail, and squeezed until his arms hurt. He was still shattered after seeing his brother, alive and well. At first, Horatio thought he'd seen a specter walk across deck, knowing he'd stabbed the damned fellow in the heart, but his ire must have steered wrong his hand.

He shook his head, knowing he'd have to kill him again. This time, he would hit the mark and be done with it.

A rush of voices came forth on deck, distracting him from his dark thoughts.

His clerk appeared afore him most lively. "Oh that was lovely," she said. "Truly lovely. The King's adventure was so romantic and dangerous, very fine. Did you know he hid in the boughs of a great oak a full day as a troop of horse searched high and low for him, straight away in the wood below wherein he was hid?"

Her great joy cruelly vexed him and he growled harshly, "Aye, I did. Keep thy voice down. Do you want those around us to see you ain't a lad?"

The lanthorn fires wavered in the wind, casting sharp shadows over the clerk's face. She looked discontented.

He cried out angrily, "How could you have not known the cunning deceit of Roger? Are you so base frivolous you could not see past the man's cock?"

Her eyes narrowed. "Now, who's talking so high, and a' hollering so all will think you're a stallion? I am still a lad to them, if in your heat you can recall."

Horatio felt his lips thin. "I shall strike you down for the impertinent jade you are, don't think I won't."

The clerk leaned forward and snapped her teeth. "I was also abused by the knave. Don't you dare touch me, ill or foul. I shall not, nevermore, be handled base by you, the filthy rogue's brother." She turned on her heel and walked away from him, and into the company surrounding the King.

Damned angry, he watched her act all mirthful with the high crowd, and he was resolved he'd had enough plague with her. She was a troublesome cheat, finding out after all this time she was a lass. Now, she went and told him of her base ignorance, marrying Roger.

He should cast her aside.

Every time he looked at her, he was reminded of the betrayal. It caused his head to cloud as a threshold covered with fleas, forbidding him to think farther than the closed door. Troubled to the heart, he was of a mind to stomp across deck to clap her soundly, anyway, but then good sense settled across his shoulders. It would not do to show a coxcomb manner in front of the King, especially now he was a knight of the realm.

Horatio turned around and grabbed hold the rail, squeezing it as if crushing the very life out of Roger, his wife, and the clerk. If he could, he'd happily tear the whole damned lot to pieces.

~ * ~

Viola, lying in a hammock slung across the cabin, was terrible miserable. During the night, the Fleet set sail for England, and near dawn, Viola could not sleep.

While the ship plowed through heavy seas, the swinging hammock rocked right over the men snoring in their beds, and then hit the wall where the porthole leaked water something horrid. She didn't mind the swinging so much as it was more a lullaby, but the hard fabric of the hammock squeezed her wretched. It would not allow her to turn to her side as on a bed or pallet.

Then Viola noticed the hammock seemed to be slipping its knots.

At first, she swung free and clear of the men, being lulled to sleep as the ropes creaked with the swells and dips of the sea. Awakening, she seemed lower to the floor, the hammock pitching full across the cabin. As the night dragged on, she'd either hit the wet wall or scraped her backside against the men as they snored on without awakening. It put her right off her hooks, and she tried very hard to separate herself from it.

Her tired brains drifted to Horatio.

Here she'd thought he was such a fine gentleman once he discovered she was a lass. She was guilty of being false on the apprentice contract, and due to the deceit of it, he could have cast her out but did not.

Then she thought of Roger being tossed overboard. By the time she'd reached the rail he was gone. All the ships moved and bobbed furiously in the water so there was no way of knowing if he'd drowned or not. She'd never known if he could swim. It would surely solve her troublesome brew if he sank like a rock to the bottom, never to return.

Viola had not known of a previous marriage. Did the dirty blighter have no honor? If the first wife was still alive, Roger was a bigamist. He could be sent off into slavery, or have his hand burned, or the like. It would serve him right, the filthy creature.

She smiled. Mayhap, he had drowned, and was finally and absolutely dead. She sighed. Her luck had never been that good.

Sorely vexed, Viola yanked herself around in the hammock. It swung most exceedingly, making her near sick in the belly, and she tried to sit.

Just as her hand reached the wall, a surge of water sprang from the closed porthole. The wet cascade surprised her so much, she flipped out of the hammock, landing hard on the floor.

Not a good start to the day.

Viola stood, no longer interested in trying to sleep. With the Fleet plowing through rough seas, and the winds mighty fierce, there was no point. At any rate, she wanted to be near when the very high gentlemen came out of their cabins for the new day.

The King would be amongst them with his spaniels on deck running amok. At first not realizing the dogs were his, she had been astonished at the mess they made with no one doing a thing about it. The men snickered and chuckled, thinking it all a lark, but Viola considered it horrid. The way was filthy across deck with piles of shit and torn rubbish, which sent her high value of the King tumbling most severe.

She shook her head, and pushed her feet into her shoes. She was off to the privy then to the rails to watch the Fleet cross the sea to England.

Twenty-four

June 1660

The barge sailed up the Thames toward London. Horatio was going home amidst the greatest of pleasure and the worst of pain.

The King already arrived in the City several days earlier with people harking and cheering along all the lanes to Whitehall. Having been with the Fleet to bring him back brought joy to Horatio's heart, but he was mightily shaken with his brother still alive.

He couldn't overcome seeing the hated rogue full of spit and vinegar saunter across the ship's deck whilst outside The Hague. Of all the ships out there, Roger had chosen the one he'd been aboard, shattering Horatio beyond all reckoning.

How could the damned rascal not be rotting in his grave? Horatio couldn't fathom it, thinking his high choler at the betrayal must've steered wrong his killing hand. It was all very strange, for the filthy knave certainly seemed dead, a' bleeding most grievously as he was dragged to the lane and dumped in the muck.

And his wife? Horatio shook his head. Her illness lasted only a short while, but had she lived, he would have cast her to the streets for the very whore she was, babe or no babe.

Horatio was not a forgiving man, and he hated exceedingly all things associated with Roger, which should include his clerk. Like a mad, weak simpleton, she had fallen for the dirty bugger, and then married him.

He snorted with derision.

She turned to him, her brows furrowed. "What's this about, then? We're almost home. You should be glad."

Grunting, he just shrugged and closed his eyes, trying to wrap his brains around something gentler.

Scroope moved on the bench, the rattle of her shoes on wood planks forcing his eyes opened. She asked, "Why are you so gloomy, then? What's burning your hairs so?"

He snarled at her insolence. "You may not talk to your betters in this manner, or I shall clap you soundly round the ears, woman or no."

Balling up a fist, she shook it in his face. "You best not, seeing as you're me brother-in-law. I shall call the bailiffs, I shall, make no mistake."

"I ain't your brother-in-law since the bastard was already married, and she's still alive."

"We don't know that, now, do we?"

The barge landed at Billingsgate stairs, keeping Horatio from hollering at her. Scroope scrambled off the boat, her satchel swinging.

As he climbed out after her, she said, "I'm off to me papa's to see how all is. 'Tis been a long stretch since I've seen him or me sister, and we've landed so close."

Horatio gave her a dark look. "You shall not travel alone through the City lanes. I forbid it."

She gasped. "And who are you to tell me what and what I cannot do, sirrah?"

"Thou art me sister-in-law, and I'm in charge of you until we sort out this troublesome brew with me brother."

"He's gone, and good riddance," she snapped.

"You don't know that, either. No one saw him drown like the rat he is."

Scroope pointed. "What about your portmanteau?"

Horatio cried out, "A pox on it. I shall go with you to the Bridge."

Slinging her satchel over her shoulder, Scroope's arms went akimbo. "I shall wait until you make arrangements for your trunk, then we'll go to me papa's."

Horatio gnashed his teeth, but did as she bade. After giving the porter a shilling, he turned to Scroope. "Take me to your da's house, then, and be quick about it. I want to sleep tidy in me own bed tonight."

She turned on her heel. "You best call me Mistress Sharpe whilst at me papa's."

"But Sharpe's my name."

Scroope laughed. "So it is."

They walked up the ramp to the Bridge, and it always amazed Horatio this busy community was so close to the City yet apart from it. He knew people were born and died here without stepping off the Bridge their whole lives. Astonishing.

He asked, "Where do you live?"

"Not far now," and Scroope walked, then went into a jolly skip as the road narrowed most grievously, houses all a' jumble surrounding them. It was suffocating.

He quickened his steps to catch up. Scroope of a sudden slowed down, then dragged her feet terrible. A crowd clamored at the door of a house. He wondered what it was about, and he walked into a wall of hideous stink. His thoughts stopped dead.

It made him want to retch, and his eyes burst to watering. "What the hell? 'Tis most horrid."

'Tis me papa's house," she said, and coughed.

Pulling a kerchief out of her pocket, she pressed it against her face and walked toward the crowd rattling round the door most dreadfully. Horatio did not like the looks of things, and stepping closer, he saw a red cross painted on the door.

Someone in the house had the dreaded plague.

"Oh nay, nay," Scroope cried and ran through the smell and the crowd. "Papa, Papa," she pounded on the door. "Are you in there? Are you aright? Where's Pall?" Beating hard against the panel, she let out a mighty cry, "Papa, come out of there this very minute."

A constable grabbed her. "Stop harking to wake the dead. We've come to take a look. This smell ain't right."

Her face bathed in tears, Scroope said, "It's probably the dead heads fetched from the river. Me papa is good and sound if you'll only open the door."

"Nay, I shall not. We must ask the nurse-keeper first to tell us what is amiss, or all will remain until the dead rot to bones in there."

Scroope turned her ear to the panel. "I hear someone or something. Quick, open the door."

"Nay, I shall not," the constable hammered back at her, most vexed. "I shall not allow the pestilence to fly out that door until the nurse-keeper says 'tis aright."

He knocked on the door. "Is that you, nurse-keeper? If so, holler for all to hear."

"Aye, 'tis I," said a disembodied voice from beyond the door. "The old man is dead, and dog heads a' rotting where they sit on the table. In the night, I'll take what I can and leave this place."

Scroope cried most vigorously, "You ain't taking away our goods. Where's Paulina? Tell me where Paulina is?"

The voice from inside said, "There ain't no one here but the dead man and that what's rotting on the table."

Horatio covered his nose and mouth with a kerchief, and shouldered through the crowd. "When'll you allow us to take the body to the grave?"

The constable cast an eye on him. "Oiy, and who are you?"

"I'm the lad here's employer."

Scroope grabbed his coat sleeve. "Where's Paulina? Has she died already? Is she already in the grave? I cannot abide it," and she broke into volleys of tears.

Despite himself, Horatio felt his heartstrings tug at this great grief. He patted her awkwardly on the shoulder, not sure how to appease her given the crowd around them knew her for a lad.

The constable pounded on the door. "Have you seen a Paulina, then?"

The nurse-keeper's voice rippled through the panel. "Nay, I have not."

He turned to Horatio. "Looks like there ain't no one by the name Paulina living or dead in there. We'll call the death cart to transport the poor, dead soul. Where'd you want him?"

"St. Magmumm—th—mmm…," Scroope snuffled against his coat.

Still patting her ungainly like, Horatio answered the constable, "Have him removed to St. Magnus the Martyr. We'll take it from there."

Scroope rubbed her wet face against his coat then stood up straight with a gasp. "I must be gone from here," and with that she ran off down the lane toward Southwark.

Standing as a foreigner amidst Bridge folk, befouled by a fearsome stink that was making him ill, and bewildered, Horatio watched her retreating back, not knowing if she'd ever return.

~ * ~

Viola's papa was gone, and she never had a chance to say goodbye. But where was Paulina? Where could she have gone?

Almost too late, she realized if any of the neighbors recognized her, they would find her most strange and depraved garbed as a lad. All she could think of doing was run away.

The events of the past month happened so fast, sweeping her to The Hague to fetch the King. She had never told Paulina where she had gone. The last time Viola had communicated in any form with her sister was to send a letter soon after going into Smythe's new place, but she'd heard nothing from Pall these long months.

At first, Viola hadn't thought much on it, knowing she could return to the Bridge when needed, but now she was afeared Pall had never received the letter. They might be lost to each other forevermore in this entire world.

Stopping mid Bridge Road and sobbing hard, she could not think what to do. Someone tugged on her arm, but she shook it off. Going weak in the knees, Viola began to sink to the cobbles.

The person grabbed her, holding her up. "Mistress Viola, ain't it?" a gentle voice asked.

Viola could not stop weeping.

"Come," the voice said. "We will make you more lassie like so there won't be unkindly talk amongst the neighbors, but we must hurry afore the death cart takes away your papa."

And taking hold of her, the gentle person took Viola into a house hard by, where amidst her sobbing, a heavy cape was thrown over her shoulders. Her lad's hat was removed to be replaced by a lady's hat, the ribbons tied under her chin.

Viola gazed at the gentle person through a veil of tears. "I thank thee."

"Oiy, it ain't nothing. Just being neighborly, is all. 'Tis the Christian thing to do."

"Who art thou?"

"I'm Mistress Barking. Remember Jimmy, my son? You played kittles, and hide and seek when bairns right here, in this here house, and along the road, you did."

Trying to think beyond her grievous pain, Viola could not fathom who this Jimmy was, only that should she remember him. They'd played a very long time ago, and she'd lost complete touch. It being most difficult to dredge up the memory, she shook her head.

Mistress Barking shrugged. "Well, he's been gone awhile, now. I won't be seeing him, again, in this here world I don't reckon."

Despite the harsh pain in her heart, Viola asked, "Why not?"

"A' cause he's gone off on a ship across the sea to keep his Puritan ways. He's gone off to a place called Plymouth in New England, and left his wife and two children here, with me, so I won't be losing me whole family."

It seemed mighty strange for a man to wander off on a ship nevermore to see his kin again. "Why would he leave you behind? Will he return?"

Mistress Barking's shoulders slumped. "Nay, he shall not. He could not accept the King coming back, and me daughter-in-law is for the King."

She shook herself and smoothed out the cloak. "This will be a mite warm, I reckon, but it hides your lad's garb. You must return to your house afore the death cart."

Opening the door, she pushed Viola out to the stoop. "No need bringing these things back. God bless, and ta-ha," and the door closed.

Twenty-five

Viola rounded the corner of a large building jutting into the already narrow Bridge Road and saw her papa's body being carried out of the house. "Oiy there, hold on. Wait for me."

Horatio's deep frown turned to a scowl. "Where the blazes have you been, leaving me here alone to attend this horrid mess that ain't none of me business? Thou art ungrateful and corrupt, thou art."

She snapped, "And how do you reckon that? I'm the one who's lost me family in entire, not you. I'm sad most grievous. As me brother-in-law, you should be taking care of me and me business."

For a moment, he looked contrite, but scrubbed it from his face all quick like. "Nay, you shall not put me in a rakish place, nay you shall not. You married the blighter. You deserve what you get."

She gasped. What a terrible mean thing to say, and her eyes again filled with tears.

Glowering, he turned away, and cried out exceedingly to the fellows with her papa, "Take the body to the church. We'll follow you."

Thinking Horatio was doing better towards her, Viola remembered the death watcher. "Oiy, what about our stuffs in the house. Don't want no old hag taking it away."

The constable growled. "'Tis how she's paid. She'll take what she can carry out of this here house, and there's the end of it."

Horatio patted the top of her hat. "You don't want what's in there, anyway. It'll always smell of death, never parting no matter how hard you scrub." He turned away. "We'll buy you anew."

Viola's tears washed again onto her cheeks, running down her chin. She couldn't think how he kept changing so quickly.

Sobbing, she burbled, "Thank thee."

As all dispersed, Mistress Barking again stood in the crowd, and beckoned towards her. She broke away, stepped up to Viola, and took her aside as if to talk all secret like. "You looking for Paulina?"

"Aye, do you know where she's gone?"

"Nay, but I do know she's run off with a trumpeter who has a position with a lord."

Viola was amazed. "When did she meet him?"

Mistress Barking shrugged. "I know not, but as the Fleet made ready to fetch the King, she went off with the trumpeter."

Horatio, who'd started to follow with her papa to the church, hollered, "Are you coming?"

Viola took hold of the older woman's arm. "Do you know his lord's name, or the trumpeter's name?"

She shook her head. "Nay, I do not."

Viola smiled. "I thank thee," and giving her arm a squeeze, she joined Horatio.

He grunted.

She snapped, "Don't be a goose's skull. She was telling where Paulina had gone."

He sniffed. "Where'd she go, then?"

"She did not know, but did know she'd run off with a lord's trumpeter."

"Then we'll find them at Whitehall, I reckon."

Viola nodded, not surprised Paulina would end up at Whitehall, and in the presence of the King.

~ * ~

Horatio bellowed, making the birds in the belfry squawk and scatter, "What do you mean there ain't no room for this here dead person? What do you expect us to do with him?"

Viola pointed toward the pews. "Our family sits along there."

The parish clerk sent a glance that way, and shook his head. "I say we've no more room. As you can see, there's no dirt outside the church to lay anyone, us being so close to the water works on the river and all. Underneath the tiles we're standing on are full of the dead. Everyone wants their dead persons near their pews." He shrugged. "What're we to do?"

Viola went all soggy around the heart. "Can't we make room, somehow?" She shook her purse. "I've got a little extra to give you."

The man went thoughtful, raising his eyes up to the ceiling then down to the floor. He shuffled his feet this way and that, then looked her in the eyes. "I reckon we can push the remains what's already under the tiles back toward the wall. It'll make room for your poor, dead da."

Viola understood his unsaid words: *And no one would be the wiser*. She nodded. "That'll do just fine."

The parish clerk bowed. "We have used coffins over here if you'd like to choose one." He turned on his heel and walked away, expecting them to follow.

Viola grimaced, for she wasn't too keen on her papa being laid in an already soiled coffin. "What happened to the other poor dead person using it?"

Horatio leaned close. "Removed to make room for another like your da, I reckon." He motioned to the floor. "They were bones more like, and see those flagstones? You can remove them, and there's space underneath. After the bones are pushed aside to make room for your da, the tiles will be knocked down, again, most tidy," and he gave her a grin.

The vision of infinite bones scattered round the caskets was most horrid. Viola did not respond, but followed the clerk.

They were led to a chamber once used as the sacristy, but was now storage for soiled caskets. "Pick the one you'd like. The painted ones are more dear due to their fancy bits."

"But they've already been used, and more than once by the looks of them," Viola said, her heart quite pulled down.

The clerk glared at her.

Viola frowned, and then nodded. "I'll take that there black one."

Horatio hollered, "They're all black."

She walked to the casket and stood. "This one. 'Tis not so banged up." She asked the clerk, "How many times has it been used?"

He shrugged, and walking to the doorway, snapped his fingers. "Oiy then, Oliver. Come over here to move one of these here coffins."

A scrawny boy shuffled up to him. "Heard from the constable there's a person in this here place dead of the plague. I ain't going near someone dead of the plague, nay, I ain't."

The parish clerk sucked in his breath. "You shall do as I say or you'll be knocked flat with me hand clapped about your ears, you will."

Stretching his narrow frame tall, the lad shouted back, "Nay, I ain't. I'll not touch a dirty plague person!" He squawked when the clerk pulled his nose, squeezing and yanking it most vicious.

Viola was astonished by the bold behavior in a church.

Horatio cried, "Oiy there, we'll have none of that. 'Tis been a long, sore day, what with the lassie's da dead and the stink of it. Find someone else to put the poor dead person in the coffin right this very minute."

Releasing the lad's nose, the clerk faced Horatio with a narrowed gaze. "There ain't no one else, sirrah. If you must have it done aright, you must help me finish the business." He gazed at the lad. "Oliver, take that there coffin into church."

Later, Viola, bathed in tears, dragged alongside Horatio. Her papa was so fouled, he was laid under the church tiles without proper ceremony. The clerk had sent the stubborn boy to fetch the parson, and with nary but a few words they shut the coffin tight. Her papa was bundled off to rest under the floor near their family pew, everyone holding kerchiefs tight against their faces.

She'd been tumbled to great sorrow by it, and then to hang it all, they walked out of church into a hard rain. Horatio stomped ahead toward his shop, the rain pouring in a cascade from the wide brim of his hat. Hunched forward, he slogged through the rubbish swimming in the lanes, not caring at all for or about her heartbreaking woe.

He shouted over his shoulder, "Come along then. I'm hungry and tired, and 'tis uncommon strange we haven't seen one damned hackney since coming along Lombard Street. How do you reckon?"

She did not know, and burst anew into loud sobs.

He jerked around, the cascade of water from his hat sloshing her heavy. "Stop your caterwauling. 'Tis the way of the world, and your da's in a better place." Just then a hackney came upon them, and he hailed, "Oiy there."

In short order, they arrived at his bookseller shop, the shutters still open for business. Viola gazed next door, but Smythe's place was shut tight.

As Horatio entered his side with her close at his heels, she wondered what was amiss with the clerk shop, and her master. It was high summer, the day not darkening until quite late, yet it looked like no one was there.

Viola heard the printing press thumping, and a sudden shout rang high with Mister and Mistress Finch coming to greet them. "Welcome back. 'Tis been quite the month here in the City and without. We've much business since the King has returned."

Mistress Finch gazed at Viola. "Who's this, then? Where's prentice Scroope?"

Horatio pulled off his hat and shook the water from it. "This here is Scroope, but not a lad. He's a she."

All agape, the Finches cast their eyes on her. "Is that so?"

"Aye," replied Horatio. "She was false on her prentice papers. I hate to see how Smythe will react."

Mister Finch shook his head. "Smythe ain't here."

Horatio and Viola exclaimed, "What?"

Viola demanded, "Where is he? What happened?"

Mistress Finch answered, "He was too sad woebegone, and could not abide it here any longer. He's gone off to the Colonies. Across the sea to a Puritan place called Salem."

Twenty-six

James Finch said, "Smythe's given the clerk shop to us."

Horatio didn't believe it. "Smythe's a wily creature. What did he ask for, and what did you give him?"

"He charged you thirty-five pounds, which you shall pay me forthwith. The money gave him enough to get settled yonder in that Salem place."

Horatio's brows rose. "Anyone left in the shop to clerk?"

"Only a small lad. We've given him tasks whilst you were gone. He's staying nights with his family."

Charlotte Finch asked, "What will you do with Scroope, then, now you know her for a lassie?"

Viola piped up, "I ain't Scroope but Sharpe. Viola Sharpe."

The Finches went dead still, their eyes wide, their mouths open. James cried, "Whoa there, Horatio, you gone and got married to this here lassie prentice?"

The impertinent jade's revelation struck Horatio cruelly to the heart. Calling herself Sharpe brought his brother to mind, and the betrayal, and he nevermore ever wanted to be reminded of that. The girl was a she-devil monster, borne of a man and a baboon, yet she had gone and blathered on as if it were the most natural thing in the world.

How could she have been so base stupid? It made a very hell in his mind, and he clamped his mouth shut to keep from giving her a hog high rant, or worse still, hitting her.

He took a deep breath. "Aye, 'tis very strange our names are the same," and clapping his eyes very strong on her, added, "Ain't it? We ain't relatives or anything like that." He clenched his teeth. "Are we?"

She gave him a hollow smile. "Nay, we ain't. 'Tis very strange, indeed."

The Finches gazed at him as if they did not believe a word of it. Charlotte said, "Right. Well then, what will you do with the lass now she ain't a lad?"

Horatio replied, "Since she ain't strong enough to work the printing press, we will teach her the way of the booksellers, or better yet, woodcutting for caricatures."

~ * ~

A week later, Horatio found himself a proud owner of both bookseller and clerk shops, and he'd gone and hired Simon Kirk away from Fleet Prison to take Smythe's place.

The lad was joyous to leave the employ of the prison, it being such a dark and foul place, and damp too. The fleas were thick around the doorways and in corners, attacking him fiercely so that his lower legs were scarred with bites.

Kirk said, "I thank thee," as he walked alongside, scratching and slapping his legs.

They strode through the lanes to Kirk's house to tell Lucy the good news, and Simon said, "Lucy will be happy. Our house is low and mean, not fit for the birth of a babe."

Horatio smiled. "How's she doing, then?" and he immediately thought of Elizabeth Wilds. He hadn't seen nor spoken with her since he'd returned. He had no idea how she was doing with her husband surely charged with treason.

Kirk said something, and Horatio asked, "What?"

"Lucy's doing fine and dandy, Sir. The babe's a lad, we can tell, for he kicks her mightily in the night."

Horatio laughed. "He'll rollick and roil round town, I think. Hopefully, not too much of a brawler, like Knollys. We wouldn't want him thrown in clink."

Kirk sniffed. "He shall never be as Knollys but a fine scrivener someday, as will I. With the King back, I shall learn the trade as I run the clerk shop." He gulped. "If that's aright with you, Sir."

Smiling, Horatio gave the lad a glance. He was heavy atop, more fit to row a wherry or barge, and unlike what anyone would consider the likes of a scrivener. It always surprised him to see how pretty a hand the fellow had. "Aye, as long as you see to the clerks. I'll not have you lollygagging away the working hours studying another business whilst I pay you for clerking."

Simon Kirk looked upon him with great joy. "Oiy, you shall have the perfect shop, Sir."

It had only taken the Kirks an afternoon to clear out of their small space near the prison and relocate back to Smythe's clerk shop. Lucy reclaimed her bedchamber, pulling Simon in and shutting the door. By the looks of the lad the following morning, all was aright with the world as he grinned the hours away.

Lucy was also a fine cook, with gravies and sauces running gentle over meats, far better than the cook shop hard by. Horatio had near busted a tooth on a piece of meat that was no longer fresh, all gristly and stringy. Most times cooked food from that ordinary gave all who ate it the trots. Most horrid.

Viola tapped him on the shoulder. "Sir, may I have a word?"

He gazed at her, a fetching thing now all in woman's clothes, but he could not forgive her for blathering she was a Sharpe. "What do you want, then? Be quick about it. I'm off to me house on Tower Hill."

She looked at him most curious. "Now that your shops are here in this part of the City, why live so far away?"

"That ain't none of your concern. State your business and be done with it."

"I'm wanting to Whitehall to look for me sister. Will you accompany me? I'd rather go as a lady than a lad."

"You shall not go as a lad. I forbid it."

The bold woman leaned forward, her eyes blazing ire. "You will not tell me what and what not to do, sirrah. I'm a married woman all alone in this here world, and have the right to do as I please."

He bent down so that their noses almost touched. "You are not alone, but cared for by me. You live in this house and as such, you shall do as I say. You will not go to Whitehall alone whether a woman or a lad."

She stared at him, most cross.

"Do you hear me?"

"Aye, as does this house and street entire."

He softened. After all, it wasn't her fault she had fallen for his filthy brother, she being a weak minded woman and all. "Well then, when would you like to go?"

Her face cleared, and she was all smiles again, very nice. "How about Sunday morn, then? Mayhap, we'll see her coming from church services since she likes the pomp so much."

Horatio grunted, distressed he'd softened so quickly. It had been a long time since he'd been with a woman, and reckoned this turnaround must be due to his sacks being so heavy. It was time to see Elizabeth, or go to the Mitre to get another woman with child.

He said, "Aye," and walked away from her and out the door.

~ * ~

The afternoon was very hot. The long days of high summer were upon them, a worrisome time. Plague often struck heavy during these months, only slowing upon the cooling of autumn and into frosty winter.

He'd seen some doors marked with red crosses showing plague there, but praise be to God, nowhere near his shops, or his house on Tower Hill. He agreed with Viola, though, his house was a good distance away and outside the City wall, a long ways to go to and fro each day.

He could lease it and find another near the shops since most of the activity took place at Whitehall these days. It may be a good idea when the seasons turned colder, the nights shorter.

But not just yet.

He'd had a month's mind of Elizabeth Wilds. He wondered how she was doing, if she were even at the house on his lane since her husband had turned to treachery. His pole stirred. Soon, he would see her, and mayhap, frolic with her.

He walked into the Mitre. Clarkson, the publican, stood near the door, and scowled. "What do you want here?"

Astounded, Horatio replied, "To have a mum beer, if that's aright with you. 'Tis a tavern, ain't it?"

"Aye, 'tis me inn and tavern, but you ain't welcome here, nevermore for the whole world to see."

Horatio was at a great loss to think what caused this. He was a Royalist as was the publican, so that couldn't be the problem, and then he thought the man might have learnt of the stud business. "Why am I not allowed to this here inn? What's this about, then?"

"You've made me wife upset. And when me wife's upset, I'm upset."

"What've I done to your wife?"

Mistress Clarkson came out of the kitchen, her face flushed with ire or heat of the oven, he knew not which. "It ain't what you did to me, but what you did to me sister."

Horatio's hairs started to burn. "Well, what then? What did I do to your sister?"

"I won't say whilst we have gentle company sitting round this here common room, but you ain't to come back here never again. Our business is done and gone, do you understand?"

"What?" Horatio cried, not understanding why they should rattle him up so, but he did understand what she was saying about the business. He'd not empty his cods in the upstairs hidey-hole, again.

The publican shoved him. "Out, and never darken our door again."

Being pushed to the stoop, Horatio cried, "Where is she then? It ain't right to accuse me of something and not know what it is. I can't defend meself."

Mistress Clarkson flung her cleaning rag at him. "Out this very moment or you shall see the oil of me husband's whip, you will." And he was summarily tossed out to the street.

It was very strange indeed. Brushing off his coat, and settling his hat more firmly on his head, Horatio was resolved to seek out Elizabeth. He must find out what the hullabaloo was about. Within a short time, he strode up his lane on Tower Hill, and was greatly stumbled by the high activity at the Wilds' house. Furniture, boxes and the like were scattered along the lane and up the stoop into the open doorway. A horse-drawn dray was being loaded by burly types.

Reaching the boxes in the lane, he was amazed and pleased to see Elizabeth walk out of the house. She was prodigious large with child, and looked most wondrous beautiful. Then, he saw her face, all pulled and sad, her eyes puffed as if she'd been a' weeping.

He said, "Oiy, Mistress Wilds, how art thou this hot, long day?"

She looked up, and when she saw him, her face went all pinched and snarly. She waddled to him. "How dare thee come to me like a turkey-cock as if I'd accept you in me heart after what you've done?"

Horatio could not comprehend what was amiss. "What are you talking about? What have I done? Your sister and her husband sent me packing from the Mitre. I ain't never to enter there, again."

"You've killed me husband, you have," and she burst into a swath of tears.

Most vexed, Horatio cried, "Nay, I have not killed thy husband."

She screamed and sobbed alike so that it was hard to tell what she was saying.

"Calm yourself," he exclaimed. "I can't understand you."

Taking a deep breath, she shook terrible. "You were part of taking hold of me husband whilst in Holland. He's to be hanged, then drawn and quartered for the whole world to see Tuesday next."

She raised her arm as if to strike him, and he took hold of it. "I was there, aye, but he would have gotten caught even if I weren't. Don't you see? He had gone there to kill the King."

She keened. "It put a dark mark on me and me family who art stout Royalists, and I'll never forgive you." Going limp against him, she sobbed on his shirt.

Trying to soothe her, he patted her shoulder. "There, there, now. 'Twill be aright, you shall see."

Elizabeth straightened her back and cried, "I shall never forgive you, never, ever. I'm forced out of London until the King and all forget this, and to the country where I must stay with country bumpkins, a most horrid thing for me and the birth of me babe." She pulled herself free and slapped him hard across the face. "'Tis worse than the gaol where you should be sent to rot!"

Horatio stood stunned afore her, his face stinging, and his eyes near to watering by the unprovoked, unfair attack upon his person.

She hissed. "Thou art a dog, and a knave, and I shall hope you disappear and are declared dead. This babe within me shall never know you. Thou art *dead* to me."

She turned on her heel and lumbered through the stacks of personal goods toward the house whilst he stood staring after her like a damned rock.

Suddenly, a man dashed down the stoop to the lane, his face filled with noble concern. He looked familiar, and Horatio started slowly toward the two of them. The man took hold of Elizabeth all gentle like, and helped her up the steps. Just afore stepping into the Wilds' house, the man swept off his hat and turned to Horatio. His eyes twinkled, and his mouth turned slowly to a broad grin.

Shattered to the core of his being, Horatio stared slack-mouthed at Roger, his brother, who had betrayed him with his wife, and now, again, with Elizabeth.

Twenty-seven

Blind rage surged through Horatio. He unsheathed his sword, and shrieking like a madman, dashed through the boxes and furniture to his brother. This time, he'd kill Roger once and for all. Someone hollered from a distance but he did not heed it. Swinging and slashing his sword, he attacked his filthy, bastard brother who should be burning in the bowels of hell instead of standing on the Wilds' stoop.

Men pounced on him from everywhere, the lane, the house. They jerked the sword from his hand and pulled him off the stoop. He couldn't breathe, couldn't think as he struggled and tried to yank free. Men shouted and soundly clapped him about the head and ears. They forced him to lie in the street, then they sat on him.

Horatio gasped for breath and watched Roger sidle up to him. The dirty rascal gazed at Horatio, grinning and chuckling. "Well, if it ain't me loving brother. How art thou this day?" He tsk-tsked. "Not so well, methinks, what with you all trussed up by these stout fellows. The muck of the lane giving your hairs a' jangle?"

Horatio struggled against the men. "Let me free, I say. Let me alone with him right this very minute."

"Nay, you ain't to do anything base stupid," a woman's voice ordered, and he noted Roger's face go wide with surprise.

He said all oily like, "Now, ain't this lovely—a bloody family reunion. How art thou, Wife?"

"You dare call me that when you are a whoring blackguard for the whole world to see?" She motioned to the men guarding Horatio. "Release this man from the dirt, if you please. He ain't done what any other wronged man or woman wouldn't do."

Roger feigned hurt. "Now, is that the way to treat your long lost husband who holds you forever dear to me heart?"

Viola snorted.

The men pulled Horatio to his feet. They held onto him as if he'd do dire harm to the wicked whoreson in front of them, and indeed he would if given the chance.

Elizabeth Wilds shuffled to them, waving her hand. "Get thee gone from me house, you and the lass. We've much to do afore the dray moves all me goods to the country." She gave Roger a sweet smile. "Art thou coming?"

Horatio tried to yank away from the men holding him, but Viola stepped in, pressing her hand to his chest. "Please don't. I dare say he'll be dealt with soon enough."

Gazing into her imploring eyes, he nodded and relaxed. It gave the men pause, and they slacked their hold. Horatio lunged out of their grasp to take hold of Roger's neck.

Squeezing with all his might, they fell to the street. Horatio straddled Roger who clawed at his hands and arms, and tried to wrench away the stranglehold grip, but Horatio would not let go. He squeezed tighter and tighter, wishing the filthy bastard should be garroted, his entrails pulled and flung into the river.

Horatio was out of his mind with anger and hate. He growled like a cur as he watched his brother's face go red then purple. Roger's eyes bulged before he collapsed limp.

~ * ~

Viola cried, "Stop him!" and before her eyes, one of the men hit Horatio with the butt of his pistol, knocking him unconscious to fall across Roger.

"There, that'll do it," said a fat man with grey stubbles across his chin. He woefully shook his head. "I ain't never by no means seen anyone so wicked full of hate as this here fellow. And against his own brother, too."

A wherriman by the looks of him, large atop with narrow legs asked, "Do you think they're dead?"

Viola fell to her knees to shake Horatio and Roger awake.

"Nay," said another fellow. "They're too wicked to be dead."

Horatio still breathed, but he was dead to the world, while Roger moaned beneath him. Viola sighed, for she would nevermore want Horatio thrown into gaol for disorderly conduct in the streets. As for Roger, he was not worth a rush, but a crooked, beastly fellow. As the lady with child told Horatio, Roger could also disappear and be declared dead for all she cared.

She stood. "Please help me take him to his house. 'Tis right down the lane, there."

"Nay," a young man with droopy eyes said. "We ain't being paid to haul a dead person away."

Viola stamped her foot. "He ain't dead. Look at him, breathing and all."

Roger moaned. "Get him off me. I can't move."

Mistress Wilds cried from the stoop, "Get the arch rogue away from me house and me goods."

Two men hoisted Horatio from atop Roger and hauled him down the lane, his boots dragging through the muck.

Viola ran ahead to Horatio's house. "This one, over here."

As the men lugged him like a limp sack, she dug in his coat pocket for the keys and ran up the stairs. She opened the door. The house was hot and dark, the main chamber stuffed with a bedstead, table and benches, discarded clothing, all pushed up close to the fireplace. Moving aside the bed curtains, she said, "Here, put him here." They did that, and not so very gentle like, either.

He did not stir, making Viola afeard he'd been struck too hard, and would go base strange like her papa. She shook him, and not hearing but a sigh, shook him, again. "You must awake, sirrah. Awake!"

He groaned. It cheered her heart. Taking hold of a wooden bowl with something fluid, she cast it at his head then grimaced. Whatever was in it was nasty horrid. It splattered his face and hair, and slathered down his neck. It stunk terrible.

He sputtered and coughed. "Ach, what is it?"

"I know not, but something quite pitifully gone bad."

Scraping a piece off his nose, he squinted at it. "'Tis me pottage."

Viola leaned closer, and goggled. "Your what?"

"Me pottage." He tried to sit, and groaning, fell again to the bed. "What's happened? I feel terrible."

"You've been near murdered, sirrah, knocked on the head with the butt of a pistol, and all a' cause of that horrid brother of yours. He ain't worth it, you know. 'Tis a pity you can't get over his villainy as I have."

An eye opened, focusing on her. "Oiy?"

She went all annoyed. "Your brother. Roger. You keep trying to kill him. Why don't you just leave off, and let someone else do it? His knavery will do him in sooner than later."

His eye closed, and he sighed shakily. "I don't feel right, and must rest."

Fear gathered round her heart. "Nay, you may not. If you go to sleep you may never come awake, and if you come awake, you'll be like me papa."

He muttered into the linens. "Go away."

"Nay, sit up and tell me you're better." She pulled on his arm. "Sit up, I say, or I shall vex you until you do." The smell of the spoilt pottage was horrid. "I must help you clean off the rotten bits, at any rate. Where's a rag? I must boil water."

~ * ~

It took every bit of cunning she knew to get that stubborn man and his linens cleared of the rotten bits and bobs. Then what did he do for her pains? He hollered hog high, "Out, out, and nevermore step so bold plain on me stairs, again."

He shut her from his home and locked the door.

She grunted. Ungrateful wretch, but he was awake, a good thing. Viola was no longer afeard he'd turn so very base strange as her papa. Nay, Horatio seemed all too well himself when he slammed the door in her face.

She shrugged, and walked down the lane toward Tower Hill Road, passing the house where Roger had taken up with the lady Horatio liked. The boxes and furniture were gone, as were the dray and horse. Looking at the house, it seemed empty, quiet.

'Twas a small world, what with Roger coming back, Horatio and the lady...

She swung around to gaze at his house, shut up and gloomy. She remembered the grand feast at The Hague, and the traitor being taken bound to the King's table, Horatio being all smug, proclaiming to have dallied with the poor wretch's wife.

She swung back around to stare at the quiet house where Roger had lain. Horatio had been with the lady. He had frolicked with her until...

And standing quite still in the middle of the lane, Viola knew without a doubt the child in the woman's belly was Horatio's.

Twenty-eight

Viola stood at Horatio's door, letting the clapper drop again and again. He hadn't been to the shops in days, and she was afeard the knock on his head had caused terrible damage to his brains.

She heard movement, and dropped the clapper again.

He hollered, "A pox on it, get thee away from here. I ain't seeing anyone."

Viola pounded on the door with her fists. "Let me in to see if you're aright in the head. Why haven't you come to the shops? Everyone's afeard something dire happened to you."

She grabbed hold of the clapper, raising and dropping it until like a wild man, he thrust open the door. His appearance took her breath away, his clear anger forcing her back a step.

"What do you want?" he cried out mightily. "Can't you leave a poor man alone? Get thee from me house."

He slammed the door shut.

His tone made her plaguy mad, and she stomped up the stair to pound the door with one fist whilst dropping the clapper with the other.

He opened the door, his eyes full of ire, his breathing coming in heavy puffs.

Viola shouted at his face, "I shall not go away, and if you put one finger against me, I shall cry up the bailiffs for the lazy rogue you are." She gazed at him with wonder. "You look horrid."

He near collapsed on the threshold, his shoulders drooping almost to the ground before he turned his back to her. Shuffling to a straight chair with arms, he fell into it, and sighed. "What do you want, then?"

"I wanted to see if you were right in the head, and not base strange as me papa went." She frowned. "'Tis dark as pitch in here, and hot. You'll come down with the plague if you ain't careful."

She looked for a window, and finding a wall of them, opened all, then released the shutters. Light flowed in, driving them both to hide their eyes in their hands. A breeze rolled through the chamber. Viola breathed in the better air, and lowered her hands.

"Ooo me, your house is shattered with filth."

Bent low, his face buried in his hands, he moaned.

His melancholy vexed her. "You shall not crouch, sirrah. Life gives bitter tonics now and again, but you must not allow it to put you low."

He shook his head in his hands. "You do not understand."

"Aye, I do, sirrah."

He sat up. "Nay, you do not."

"Aye. I do."

Horatio frowned. "How do you know? No one knows but me."

"Ah, methinks more folk than you, sirrah." She waved a hand. "The lady heavy with child, her husband who will very soon be swinging from the gibbet, and aye, Roger."

He rolled his eyes. "You are forgetting Mistress Clarkson of the Mitre."

Viola smiled. "Aye, and Mistress Clarkson of the Mitre." She dragged a stool to the table, and sat on it. "Have you seen any of them since the other day?"

His face turned mulish. "Why did you follow me? Thou art an interfering trout."

He was winding her up, he was. She snapped, "You forgot the purse from the day's business. I was bringing it to you."

"How did it take you so long to reach me?"

She shouted, "A' cause your damned legs are too long, that's why. I was fain killed by the run as it was. Then you go and get yourself clobbered 'bout the head hard enough to break your skull into your brains." She stood with a rush, and the stool fell to the floor. "You've gotten right up me nose, you have. Thou art an ungrateful rascal."

"Well, well, have I come into a family all a' jangling?" Roger sang, and sauntered through the open doorway. Horatio sprang to his feet.

Roger shook his head. "Nay, do not stand for me."

He gazed around the chamber, and motioning to the bed, he asked, "Is that the one from upstairs?"

Horatio snarled, but Viola dashed between them afore they fell onto each other with fury. She demanded, "Thou shall not go head-to-head, again, either of you. Roger, what do you want?"

He shrugged. "Just a gentle conversation, 'tis all. Is it too much to ask?"

Viola pushed Horatio to his armchair. "You must sit before you fall down. Roger, you may have only a moment."

Horatio snarled. "Nay, he may not."

"Oiy, I do," countered Roger. He pulled two pistols from his coat and cocked them ready to fire. "And I shall stay until I've been heard."

Viola gasped, and took a step out of harm's way.

Horatio looked as if he'd like to tear Roger to pieces. He said, "I hate you exceedingly for what you've done to me and mine. Because of you, me wife and child are dead."

Roger smirked. "That babe was mine, not yours. We'd been going at it for months afore you found out. She loved me, you know, and was going to leave you."

Gripping the arms of the chair, Horatio leaned forward, hissing.

Roger laughed. "Life is so very fickle. Do you want to hear a wee tale?"

Horatio and Viola cried as one, "Nay!"

Still pointing the pistols at Horatio's heart, Roger kicked a stool and sat on it. "I was in The Hague to fetch the King and fell into a bit of bother. Thrown off a ship, you see, but before all failed, I was pulled from the drink near drowned and flung in a lockup with the most villainous of characters."

Horatio's face pinched sour.

"Ah, you knew of the wicked fellows, did you?" Shrugging, Roger continued, "Wilds was there, and in his hour of need, he rattled me up about a whoreson claiming to be the father of his wife's babe." Gazing at Horatio, he laughed. "After landing, and the poor man was dragged away in chains to dungeon, I came straight away to his grieving wife."

He clapped his eyes most serious upon Horatio. "I shall marry the lady and take the child as mine."

Viola was stopped dead by the pure hatred pouring out of Horatio.

Roger gazed thoughtfully at the ceiling. "Strange I hadn't seen her whilst visiting your wife, the two houses so close and all. It would have been quite the opportunity, I should think."

Viola could not endure it. She hollered, "Stop it this moment. Thou art a filthy varlet. Get thee out of this house once and for all."

In her ire, she yanked away one of the pistols, surprising Roger so much, he jerked and fell from the stool. His pistol fired off to the ceiling.

Holding the other, Viola pointed it at his heart. "'Tis cocked, and ready to fire, husband. I should very much like to see a bullet go through that cold heart of yours."

His eyes went wide as he blubbered and spat. "Nay, nay, you must not. 'Twould be most unseemly for a wife to kill her husband. You'll be hanged for it."

"Nay, she would not," said Horatio with a grim smile. "It would be best for both of us if you were finally dead and gone to hell. The thought gives me great joy."

Viola began to squeeze the trigger. It was very stiff. Holding the pistol with both hands, she found the trigger less stiff.

She smiled. "I think I shall kill you now, Roger. I think I'd like that very much." She squeezed, feeling it move ever so slightly.

Horatio yanked it out of her grasp, the pistol not firing at all.

She screamed. "Let me kill him. I must. He's a horrid, beastly man. Let me do to him as he deserves."

"Nay, you shall not," and Horatio pushed her behind him. He waved the pistol at his brother. "Get thee gone from me house, or I shall do as she wants."

Roger scrabbled to his feet and fled.

~ * ~

Horatio turned away from the empty doorway. He set the gun down on the table, staring blindly at it. It was a beautiful thing if treated kindly. Deadly too. Why didn't he do it? Kill him, and forevermore never see him again in this here world. Viola knew it aright, but for some reason…

He heard weeping and focused towards it. Viola was bathed in tears. Slow to understand, he asked, "What's this about, then?"

Her hands were hard fists at her sides. "I hate the sight of him, and for his base carriage towards us. Why did you let him go?"

Walking to the open windows, he sighed. "I know not. Mayhap, I didn't want to see you hanged for murder. It would have been a bother to stand at the foul, rat ridden bench whilst you were tried, and me possibly implicated in the murder along with you. It would also vex me businesses."

She snorted. "That's a jolly tale. You've gone missing from your businesses these several days, now, all droopy, and all in the shops think you for a lazy, corrupt rogue. Why would my trial make any difference?"

He did not want to talk about it, couldn't bear thinking of his damned brother another moment. It would drive him mad.

He completely turned the subject. "Why don't we to a coffeehouse at the 'Change? I could do with a drink."

He heard her suck in her breath, and her face was still pinched and drowned from weeping. She stared at him for a long moment, then shook her head. "Nay, you're stale as they come, and still marked with the spoilt brew I threw upon you the other day."

"I shall shift into a fresher shirt, then," and he set to undo the buttons. "I haven't eaten today but a bit of cheese and bread. We can go to a cook shop for a jowl of ling. That would be right and dandy with the coffee."

She gave him a strange look. "You've gone rackety mad, I think. How can you think of eating after what just happened?"

His life was in despair with the cunning villainies of his brother. He must climb back on the horse and into the world again, or truly go mad.

Ruffling his hairs until they spiked about his head, he said. "These past days with him and his deceits have near broke my brains, and I'm tired of it. If I let him stop me from going forth, he wins the game." He pulled the shirt over this head. "You ken?"

She sighed. "Aye, I ken."

~ * ~

Horatio decided to keep Roger's pistols, and would never again be caught unawares by his filthy brother. Besides, what with his poor swordsmanship, it would be good to have them whilst traversing the City lanes. It had been a long time since he wore pistols, though, and he'd forgotten how uncomfortable they were as they rode unhappily in his belt.

He led Viola down the lane toward the Royal Exchange just off Threadneedle Street. "Come along, then, we'll into this here cook shop and choose what we'll take away for dinner."

"A jowl of ling does sound jolly good," Viola said.

Regarding the counter of available fare, Horatio saw no cod fixed ready to eat. "Nay, it does not seem to be on the menu."

Viola sniffed. "Nay, it does not. What are you up for, then?"

A man of the shop brought out a steaming kettle and plunked it onto the counter. It smelt wonderfully good.

Trying to regard the contents through the steam, Horatio asked, "What's this here, then?"

The man gazed at him as a froth of sweat dripped down his face from the heat of the kitchen. "'Tis sheep's feet soaked in wine sauce, very brave, and very fresh. Animal was killed this very morning just out back."

That's why Horatio liked this shop. Very seldom would the meat turn afore sold. "Ah then, we'll have a pot of your jolly sheep's feet to take away."

Smelling the richness of it made his stomach growl. After giving the man a Dutch groat, he walked out to the lane, knowing Viola followed.

He shook his head. Now, she was a lass for certain, and his cods tightened. Viola wasn't a prating wench as some who never gave a man a moment to think. She adapted well to all sorts of environments, even as a laddie, and he chuckled.

"What's causing all this mirth?" she asked as she near ran alongside. "Slow down, if you please. You walk too fast."

"I want to get us to the coffeehouse, don't I?" he said but slowed his step.

He was near dead from starvation, realizing he really hadn't a good meal since before the scuffle with Roger in the street. The thought if a dish of coffee with the warm sheep's feet, mayhap a bit of news from the world while at it, made his mouth water.

"Come along. 'Tis just up here hard by. We shall have this good food, and listen to news and gossip."

Viola tugged his coat. "'Tis a man's world, coffee shops. I ain't allowed, am I?"

"Aye, you shall be," he said, vexed she should bring that up, for indeed, 'twas a man's world they were about to enter. Not many females marched through a door of a coffeehouse.

"How will I be allowed in then?"

Not willing to cruelly cast her away after the recent bit with Roger, he knew how to fix it. Not liking it one bit, though, and near stomping to the front of the establishment, he swung around. "You shall be my wife. No one will throw you out whilst you're me wife." He beetled his brows and clapped stern eyes on her. "And there's an end to it."

Twenty-nine

Still as a stone, Viola stared at him with her mouth open. "You are mad. I ain't your wife nor ever shall be. I'm already married, even though it seems of no matter to anyone, at all, in this here world."

He grimaced. "You are a Sharpe. I am a Sharpe. You are with me as a wife, should anyone be so brazen to ask. 'Tis to keep you from being thrown out on your ear."

"But if we're heard calling each other 'Husband' or 'Wife', then we shall be married, won't we?"

Horatio became vexed to the gut. He hollered, "We won't be calling each other that, you ken? The last thing I want is another piece of frippery who'll go off a lollygagging with me brother, so don't get all nettled over the matter."

He tore away from her, and opened the door. Forcing a dirty smile, he bowed. "Art thou ready for a dish of coffee?"

She snorted and walked ever so bold into the coffeehouse, wagging her tail so that every man within gawped. The place was loud with folk shouting across the room. Pamphlets, and newssheets littered the tables.

As Horatio followed her, he saw a table and stools. "Oiy, over here. We shall eat and drink, here."

Setting down the bucket of sheep's feet atop a pile of pamphlets, he turned to the counter where the coffee roasted very kindly with a specially built jack. A lad turned the crank slowly, the basket of beans cooking above the coals ever so nice, bringing a very pretty scent. It always made Horatio wonder how the smell was very fine yet the brew was always so damned bitter.

Viola stood beside him where the coffee roasted, her eyes wide as a child's with the new sights. Pointing to the basket rolling above the coals, she asked, "Is that the coffee, then? They look to be very big, indeed. How do you drink them?"

The caretaker of the place, his cheeks and nose bright pink, grinned. "Why you powder them, don't you?" Pointing to the lad, he said, "When the beans are roasted to perfection, we take the basket off the jack and let them cool, then we ground them to powder with mortar and pestle, only a task for a strong lad such as we have, here."

The lad's eyes went bright with the compliment.

Viola coaxed, "And then?"

"Why, we put the grounded powder into the caldrons with water and boil them, don't we? Makes a mighty fine brew."

Horatio was hungry. Even though he enjoyed watching Viola's excitement over a new adventure, he was in a hurry to eat. "What have you for the lady fair here and meself to drink?"

The keeper crooked his finger, forcing him closer. "'Tis unusual to have a wench in the establishment, sirrah. What's this about, then?"

Lowering his voice, Horatio said, "Well, me wife, here, is in a most anxious way, if you get me drift, and was fain drowning in tears to see a coffeehouse. Knowing this here to be the best, and cleanest, I brought her here, thinking you'd make an exception."

With a wink, Horatio smiled. He also noted from the corner of his eye Viola glaring at him with a teeth-gritting-grin.

The man humphed and grunted, then shrugged. "Well I reckon it'll be aright this one time. I've a wife like her, and no amount of cajoling will fix the tears when they're pouring out of her."

He straightened. "We've coffee boiled dark, hot chocolate bitter, but when mixed with a bit of cream and sugar, 'tis most fine, and," he paused for effect, "We've the new china tea from East India Company."

Horatio wondered if that would be better than coffee. "What's china tea, then?"

"I shall give both you and the lady a sip freshly brewed." He ladled some in a dish, and gave it to Horatio, who blew away the steam and took a sip.

His eyes widened and he smiled. "That's ever so good."

He handed the dish to Viola, who took a sip. Her eyes closed. She ran her tongue over her lips, causing his cods to tighten evermore. "Hmmm, that's nice." She opened her eyes. "But I think I shall have a dish of hot chocolate."

Horatio said, "And I shall have a dish of this here china tea."

Later, after they had sucked the meat and gristle from the sheep's feet, the wine sauce drizzling down their chins, Horatio picked his teeth with his knife tip, reading a news book. It was most amusing, and he thought his bookseller shop might do well going into the newsprint business. But he'd have to talk to Finch about it, for his press was already going topnotch speed most days.

Still gazing at the news book he said, "There are disputes on who shall have a living in this new government; the Puritans or Anglicans. What do you think?"

Sucking a tooth, Viola answered, "Anglicans, I expect. Can't imagine the King allowing the Puritans to clog up the businesses."

He smiled. "Nay, I should think not."

She said, "Look at this here advert. There's to be a King's anointing of the Evil. Tomorrow. If we go to Whitehall in the morning instead of Sunday, mayhap, we'll find Paulina."

She gave him a look of wide-eyed appeal. "This would be a pomp she'd like, you reckon? I have a great need to know how she fares, and if she knows papa is gone and put to his grave."

It had been too long since he'd attended to business, but he had promised. Horatio sighed. "Aye."

~ * ~

Viola awoke to a soggy day, the rain splashing most severe on the outside tiles of the house. She had taken Smythe's old chamber and slowly but surely filled it with mementos from her trip to fetch the King, and afterwards from stalls at Newgate Market and shops round Paul's Yard. Her new chamber was more comfortable than the one on the ship with all the ribbons, or the ones she'd shared with Roger and Paulina. It was all her own, and very nice, indeed.

But the poor folk who had the King's Evil would nevermore be as fortunate as she. They'd be standing outside in the rain. If the King decided not to come out into it, they'd be waiting in vain.

From the advert in the coffeehouse, she learned once prayers were said over the poor persons, the King would touch them to cure the scrofula that clustered along their necks. Each of them would be given a touch piece, wherein they were to hang the coin round their necks as an added protection and blessing.

It would be most wondrous to see such a miracle, for the King's Evil was a dreadful sight. No one wanted to touch a person with it, in great fear of getting the same, what with the large open knots of sores hanging under the chin most ugly.

Viola shivered, and straightened the bed curtains. Even though rain heavily drenched the City, mayhap, Whitehall would be better since it was outside the walls and seemingly far away. She'd never been in the west suburbs, and only heard of Whitehall and Westminster from Horatio and Simon Kirk, who ran the clerk's shop so well. He was a happier man than Smythe could ever have been, and being quite the droll, he often made the whole shop laugh.

Viola went off to the kitchen for her morning draught, knowing with Lucy back, the maid wasn't so beastly lazy, anymore. Lucy seemed happy returned, too, even though her papa had gone away, forever. The house was in good order and nevermore so gloomy as before.

Since the King came back, the clerk shop was infinite with work, doing all manner of important businesses. In Westminster and London City, chairs turned at a swift pace with men all needing documents for their new places as knights and whatnot. Day and night folk came through the door, their titles being new, or lords faithful to the King during the sad times being brought up to new heights.

The shop was a' buzz with preambles for knighthood patents and the like, and once signed by the King and done up proper by the Attorney General, all were to be engrossed. It was brisk every hour 'til late, all wanting everything done right and proper, and immediately. To serve them better, Simon Kirk had brought in more apprentices, and even pulled Viola away from the press business though everyone knew her for a lass.

Horatio had assured Simon Kirk she had a good hand, which brought her great joy. She'd worked hard for Horatio and now Simon Kirk, and he seemed to regard her kindly.

Viola walked into the kitchen, and sat down amidst the lads, thinking how lovely it would be to have a dish of hot chocolate, but there was none of that. The maid, Alice, put down a pitcher of small beer and a trencher of bread and cheeses, whilst Lucy dished out porridge and boiled hares.

The lads tucked into the fare, but Viola sat quietly, nibbling on bread and cheese.

She thought most serious on these full days of the clerking business.

One of the papers being worked in their shop was the beginning to the preamble for Horatio's knighthood. To go along with the title, he had purchased a baronetcy for six hundred pounds, an enormous amount, considering the going rate under the old King was nearer three hundred pounds.

From her remembrance when he was knighted, Horatio could carry his title until death, but not afterwards for any heirs. He seemed resolved to change that bit and bob, though, hoping the final document would be approved by sleight of hand when there were so many in the pile to be signed. Viola shook her head. He was a corrupt rogue, he was, but of a gentler heart than Roger, the filthy creature.

Horatio sat down on the bench beside her, taking up a dish of porridge. "You don't look too happy, Mistress Sharpe."

"Nay, I am not. Me thoughts had sunk to that rascal, may he be skinned alive and his casing be tacked to a church door."

Horatio tsk-tsked. "Very cruel, but nicely thought. I must to Westminster Hall this morning with the preamble to me patent."

She turned to him with a frown. "But what about me sister?"

He sipped from his pot of small beer, and said, "I shall leave you at Whitehall once we find Paulina, have no fear. You'll be better off than getting in me way as I go through me businesses at the Hall." He dunked a spoon full of honey into his porridge and stirred most fervently. "We shall leave forthwith after we sup."

~ * ~

She pulled a shawl over her head and shoulders, and pushed her feet into pattens. It still rained heavy, and Viola was afeard her pretty, new dress would get all sodden afore they ever reached Whitehall.

She looked out the door. Nay, she'd be drenched by the end of the street.

Hearing Horatio behind her, she said, "'Tis raining very strong. We'll be wet through, and your papers drowned."

"They're safe in me new leather portfolio, and I've sent one of the prentices to fetch a hackney. We shall to Whitehall in a coach."

As they headed to Whitehall, the coach meandered through the lanes from Ludgate out of the City and into the suburbs. The rain drummed at a furious pace against the roof. Viola scooted close to Horatio to keep from getting awash as it hit the window covers, slopping down the insides of the carriage, which brought him to snicker at her.

"What's that about?" she cried out.

With a lusty grin, he responded, "If you get any closer, you'll be sitting in me lap. Art thou of a mood to frolic?"

His base words cut her most cruel. With a snort, she leapt to the bench seat across from him, he all the while chortling like a debauched coxcomb. She regarded him most cautious, but he still grinned at her, and she wondered what he was about. Viola suddenly reckoned he wanted a scuttle-butt, and shaking her head, could not ken why men always wanted such things at the most inconvenient of times. It seemed such a bother.

The coach entered into Whitehall premises, and Horatio said, "Here we are. Let's into the palace while the rain ain't splashing so hard."

Inside, he directed her to a pretty chamber overlooking the garden. He wagged a finger, and left her with a stern warning, "Stay put. Do not leave. I'll be right back."

She stared out the window to where the poor sodden folk needing the King's touch waited for their monarch. She could not imagine that the King would by no means go out there whilst it rained so hard. She turned away from the window to see Horatio returning, still carrying the leather portfolio wherein all his baronetcy papers were hopefully tucked dry.

"Ah good," he said. "Was afeard you'd gone off a' wandering through these endless hallways and chambers. I'd lose you for certain, and never find you, again."

Viola glared at him, still miffed at his bold behavior towards her in the coach. "I have not seen me sister."

"Nor will you standing here. The King is to touch all those poor folk in the Banqueting House. We shall go there and watch for your sister." He turned and walked away.

Viola protested loudly. "Nay, you shall not, sirrah."

He swung around, and scowled, "Aye, what did you say? Thou art an impertinent jade, and I'll not have it."

She softened. "Your legs are too long, and you walk too fast. I shall go lost if you race through this maze of a palace. I won't be able to keep up."

His shoulders relaxed. "Aye, all these uneven passageways and chambers running into each other are a mystery. I shall be more gentle with you."

Viola smiled. He could be ever so nice when he wanted to be. "Thanks to you, sirrah."

He held out his arm, and she took it.

Thirty

They wandered through the halls, up and down stairways, looking for the Banqueting House. Horatio said, "'Tis the same place where King Charles I was beheaded."

Viola thought that quite horrid. "God's teeth, was he put away on the same spot where those poor folk needing the King's touch will be standing? Where *we* will be standing?"

"Nay, he was beheaded outside. 'Twas a spectacle for the whole world to see. Men beyond our shores know us for rogues and regicides. 'Twill be a long time for that stain to be removed from their minds."

She began to see why Paulina cried foul against the old government, what with men killing men for wicked and ill, in the name of God.

She said, "Then, we must look to the outer edges of this here place. The Banqueting House must have easy reach for the people."

Indeed, it was. They had already skirted by it when they ran through the rain and into the palace. Stopping at a doorway, they stared into the very large chamber, filling with folk of all sorts, middling and upper aristocracy along with those with the King's Evil.

Viola blinked as she watched the people file into the chamber from across the hall, the doors flung open. "Aye, look-see, sirrah, we've walked right passed where those doors are now wide."

Horatio shook his head. "How is it we did not see them? Seems we've walked for miles, touching the very place we're to be, but not seeing it."

Viola laughed hearty, thinking how very droll it all was. Then she heard a gasp, and turning around, stood face-to-face with Paulina, all dressed in finery with lace, ribbons, and feathers in her hair. On her neck was a string of pearls entwined most beauteous.

Regarding her sister whom she had not seen in such a very long time, her eyes filled with tears. Of a sudden, they were sobbing against each other's ear, holding tight as if to let go, the other would fade away to nothing.

Viola slobbered and wept most boisterously. "Where have you been?"

"I've been right here," her sister answered with loud snuffles. "I'd thought you'd forever gone away after you left that morning. Where you said to apprentice was empty when I went in search of you."

"Didn't you get my letter?" Viola asked.

"Nay." Paulina wept against her neck.

Viola pulled away. "We've much to say. Is there a place we can go?"

"Aye," her sister said, her wet eyes shining. "We've apartments right here in this here palace."

"Who is we?" Horatio asked. He bent close, and looked very curious.

Paulina stared up at him. "Who are you?"

"Part of what we must catch up on," Viola said. "Come, show us your apartments."

They were very pretty although it took awhile for Viola to see them, all out of breath and completely lost after the march through the rambling palace. When Pall closed the door, Viola asked, "Where are we?"

Pall laughed. "Why, right here in Whitehall, you silly bee."

Viola did not think so. They seemed to have trod a very long way. The fact they were still inside and out of the rain said they were in a building, but not Whitehall. "Nay, we are not."

Pall grinned. "Aye, it took me a good while to understand this place. 'Tis several buildings all a' jumble, you see."

"Nay, I do not. Did you know papa's dead and gone?"

Pall wilted. She dropped to a straight chair. "Aye, I reckoned."

Viola asked, "What happened?"

Sitting very still, Pall's eyes took on a vacant look. Her tone was soft, as from far away: "I met Percy in church. The Puritans were fading away with the news of the King's return, and more of the City parishes fell to the old religion. Parsons and Anglican priests were being let out of Fleet Prison. 'Twas a most happy time."

Still staring ahead, she smiled. "Percy is a lovely man, and kind, too. What began with meeting for church services ended with sharing a dish after, and then taking long walks, laughing, talking."

Pall hugged herself. "One thing lead to another, and one afternoon, he took me to a man's lodgings where we frolicked the afternoon away." She blinked and regarded Viola. "I didn't know he was married."

Viola wasn't too sure she wanted Horatio listening to this very personal discourse. She asked, "What happened to papa?"

"It started as a lovely day. All the town was rejoicing due to the King's return. Percy and I were to watch the procession into the City. We were to meet at the Mitre beforehand, but he did not come. I was afeared something had happened to him. I went to our special place, but someone different came to the door. It was not Percy's lodgings. He had paid the fellow to use it.

"Very vexed I was, I can tell you. He lied to me, and then he'd gone away not to be found. I had no idea where he was, if he were ill or no." Pall paused, and bit her lip. "You know of life and its fickle ways. He could have been injured or worse, and I'd not know."

Viola pressed her. "What about papa?"

"I came home to see papa shivering most terrible. When I touched him, he cried out most hard with horror as if I did something dire to him."

Leaning forward, Viola asked, "What then?"

"He was shaking very badly, couldn't talk then fell to whimpering, saying how much it hurt. I cried, 'What hurts, papa? What?'

"And then I saw it, a token behind his ear. I opened his shirt, and his underarms were swelled with them." She gazed at Viola with trembling horror. "I knew then he'd been stricken with the plague."

Horrified, Viola cried out, "Was it the dead heads? Do you think they caused it? There were two of them, you know. The nurse-keeper said so."

Pall shivered. "They were dog heads, and I don't know if they caused the plague. Mightily afeard of being shut up 'til we were both dead, I rushed right out of the house, ran and ran, and coming off the Bridge, crashed right into Percy." She smiled ever so gently. "He took me here, to these apartments in the palace, and I've a very nice allowance to do with as I please."

"But what about papa? Did you leave him there a' dying with the door wide open?"

"Aye, I did," Pall said, her face all stubborn like. "What would you have done, stayed behind with the nurse-keeper and the doors and windows locked 'til we were all dead to this here world?"

Viola stared most astonished at Pall, but now she thought on it, she'd probably do the same. It would be horrid locked up until all died with the nurse-keeper.

Pall shook her head. "But Percy took care of everything. He went to the Bridge the very next day, and with the constable made sure the house was shut and padlocked with a red cross painted on the door. He paid a watchman to carry and fetch for papa from the market, and a lad to fume the house with brimstone, saltpeter and amber."

Horatio shuffled his feet. "Ach, horrid smelling stuff. What happened then?"

Pall's gaze cleared. "The lad put the brimstone and whatnot at the door, trying to wave it all in with a large fan so the smoke went under the door and around its edges. He could not go in, or must stay in until he, too, were dead." Standing up, she paced in front of Viola and Horatio. "Took a great deal of coin from his purse, I can tell thee, but he said I was worth it." Tears filled her eyes.

"What of the heads, Pall? Couldn't you smell those horrid dead heads?"

Pall's face crumpled as she turned to the window. Burying her face in her hands, she wept. She shook her head in her hands. "I don't remember!"

Viola went to her sister, and hugged her. "Nay, do not weep. He's gone and buried now in St. Magnus right at our pew. All is well and better, now."

Sniffling, Pall scoured her nose with the back of her hand. "Well, that's done, ain't it? Where have you been all this time?"

Viola laughed through her tears. "Off apprenticing. Me master, Mister Smythe, took us across the City to a new place the very day I went into the business. I sent a letter telling you of it, but now you say you never received it."

Pall shook her head. "Nay, I did not." She gazed at Horatio. "Who are you, again?"

Viola said, "He's the one who took us to the Mitre that one Sunday, remember?" When she saw Pall's eyes widen with recognition, she finished, "He's me brother-in-law."

Pall gave him a hard look. "Nay."

Horatio nodded. "Roger's me brother, the damned rascal."

Regarding him a good while, Pall finally said, "Oh my, it seems we do, indeed, have much to say. I shall ring for the servant."

She motioned them to a settee covered with turkey cloth then rang the pull bell. "Please, sit down."

A servant swept through with a tray of drinks and pasties, setting them down on a table. She curtsied, waiting, and Viola was astonished at how far her sister had come up in the world.

Pall said, "You may leave us."

Wide eyed, Viola asked, "Goodness, Pall, what's this about?"

"I'm the mistress of the King's trumpeter, very exalted." She smiled and spread her arms. "This is all mine for as long as I please him. He lives round the corner with his wife."

"Nay," said Viola.

"Aye," Pall responded. "And he's to leave her. He promised, for you see, I'm with child. His child."

For the first time since reuniting with her sister, Viola regarded her very strong. She was not yet showing. "When are you due?"

"Sometime in February, I should think."

Paulina looked very healthy. She would probably go full term, and in a sudden droop, Viola slumped against the settee.

Thirty-one

Horatio stood. He knew where this was going. He'd already lived and breathed the adventure Viola was about to tell her sister.

He said, "I'm off to work out the details of the preamble to me patent. I'll come fetch you anon." Bowing, he tipped his hat. "Very fine seeing you again, Mistress Paulina. I'll see meself out."

Walking up and down hallways, he searched for the route to the outside. He trod through passages that intersected, their curtains cast open or closed tight. Doors to chambers popped and slammed, and fancy dressed ladies and gentlemen dashed in and out, boisterously laughing and chattering.

Large chambers led to small chambers. He found himself in and out of them, down unknown, narrow halls. Too often, he bypassed nooks and crannies with folks a' frolicking. It was strange indeed to see how different it was from when the Roundheads were in control. Such sluttish, bold behavior would never have been tolerated.

Finally, Horatio found the Banqueting House and filled with great joy, he joined the push of people to the street.

The King's touch to cure the scrofula must've been done. He saw coins clutched in fists, the strings dangling while others had slung their coins around their necks. It was a memento, a thing to touch as remembrance and removal of the King's Evil.

As he walked round to Westminster he saw the rain had thinned, very nice. He walked at a fast pace to where he'd meet with a classical scholar who had a corner table with a quill and ink pot. Even if his scheme to have the King sign the bill to include Horatio's heirs failed, he still must get the patent or there'd be no record of his knighthood. It was a costly travail. He'd already bought silver plate worth ten pounds for the attorney general, and there were seven silver pieces in his purse for the scholar.

So far, Horatio had been traipsing back and forth over the City and now into Westminster, putting all to rights on the damned business. He was gladdened all was falling into place, for he was one of many, and small compared to some of those who were getting great titles. Monck, who was once full with Cromwell and the Commonwealth, who sat in Scotland for all those weeks while rumps of beef were roasting in the streets, was made Duke of Albemarle.

Horatio sniffed.

Once the preamble was perfect, he would hand over the warrant for his baronetcy to the attorney general who prepared the patents for the King. It was a bold move, for Horatio could be cast to dirt if found out. He was off to church afterward where he'd pray the King wouldn't notice the change as he signed the bill.

Horatio was very high on the matter, and was willing to take the risk. His knighthood must carry on to his heirs.

He frowned. He'd spread his seed amongst many women, some of whom sprouted true, Elizabeth for one, yet he could not raise one of the babes to his heir. If the purchase of the baronetcy solved the problem of the knighthood for more than his lifetime, he would be in a great need of a wife. She must be young, but certainly of age, and broad enough to produce a son without dying.

That meant a legal marriage with a binding contract, banns or license. An ordained minister must have the ceremony done in the parish church—with the Book of Common Prayer, old or new version—during the canonical hours of eight o'clock of the morning and noon, a lengthy, expensive endeavor. He must also locate a tract of land in the country with a manor house on it, a requirement for a gentleman lord.

Did it mean he'd have to give up his bookseller shop? Would he be allowed to be a gentleman and remain a middling businessman? He shook his head, knowing he'd learn soon enough how knighthood went.

Reaching Westminster, Horatio stepped lively into the place with the intent to seek out Mister Walter Barrington, a classical scholar of large repute. Horatio needed this scholar to write the preamble in Latin for the patent to his knighthood. He tried to make an appointment with the man, sending him a letter, but had no reply. He'd been assured; however, Mister Barrington was always seen in his corner, crouched over his table writing in large tomes. Business had been brisk.

But he was not at his table. There were no occupied corners this day, sorely vexing Horatio. There was nothing more for it at the moment, and he turned on his heel back to Whitehall.

The rain stopped with the sun peeking through the clouds. Viola would be pleased, and his cods tightened.

What was he thinking? She was his sister-in-law for God's sake. To think of her in any other manner, to touch her at all, would be incest. He must be going rackety mad, and he blamed it on his brother, the dirty sod.

The only way into Whitehall wherein he could navigate at all was through the main gate at the Banquet House, and in it he walked. Trying to recall the route he'd taken from Paulina's apartments, he squared his shoulders and dug in, trotting down passageways he thought looked familiar.

Long minutes into it, he walked down some stairs and through a curtain into a dim hallway. After his eyes adjusted to the darkness, he saw a man pressing against a whimpering woman, far along with child. He was fondling her breasts then chuckling. He crushed his hands into them, and she cried mightily out.

Withdrawing his sword, Horatio hollered, "You damned rascal, remove your hands from her this very minute."

He grabbed the man, and forced him around. It was Roger. Sudden fury blazed through his heart, and he began to lose control. Horatio fought hard against the rage that near crushed him, knowing it would stop all mindful thoughts.

It was a hard thing to do.

The dirty cur burst out laughing. "Well, well, ain't it mighty strange we're meeting so often of late?"

Taking a deep breath, Horatio motioned to the woman. "Take your leave, Mistress, and pray, stay out of dark corners. Only evil creatures lurk in the shadows."

Roger's lips curved in a pout. "And we were having such a lovely time of it."

Abruptly, Horatio's rage turned to deadly calm, allowing all thoughts to flash clearly. Staring at his brother anew, it was if he were regarding a dead man, and Horatio knew he'd be the force to rid the world of the damned whoreson.

He asked, "Have you already tired of Elizabeth, then?"

"Nay, she's too far along. Won't let me near her. I came here instead, to the new bawdy house resolved to tumble a saucy slut, with child or no." He wagged his brows. "Ain't that why you're here, brother?"

"Why do you call the King's palace a bawdy house?"

Roger gave him a look of surprise. "Why, due to the King a' rollicking with one mistress or another. There's the beginning of a gambling den down yonder on the ground floor, and if you get your nose out of the air for one minute, you'll see all the doors of this place a' swinging open and closed with ladies and gentlemen shifting their clothes to hide their privy parts.".

Horatio did not care about the palace folk frisking and haying about. "Do you have apartments here?"

"Nay, I can't leave Elizabeth alone in the country for long, her being fretful and all, and being out of the City now Wilds is dead. She hates you for it, you know." He laughed.

Horatio smiled. He was getting an idea. "Have you married the lady?"

"Aye," he remarked with a grin. "And soon she'll be having our babe, a strong bairn who'll look much like his new da."

Horatio nodded. He had him, now. Aye, indeed, he had enough to destroy his brother."

Thirty-two

Viola stared at Paulina with wide eyes, astonished her sister had turned so very bold. Her manner was not the least bit gentle, and Viola knew if she didn't put on a more honorable face, Pall'd end up in the streets.

Her married lover would never countenance such slutty behavior. So brazen, the wife would soon learn of it. Viola asked, "What happens when his wife learns of your affair? She will, you know."

"She already knows, and is fine and dandy with it." Paulina laughed, a nice sound, like bells tinkling, and Viola smiled.

Horatio burst in. "Get your cloak. We're off to the City."

"What's the hullabaloo?" Viola cried, rising to her feet. His abruptness took her by surprise. He was all a' ruffle with irritation and tapping foot. Fretful, too. His eyes were wild.

"What was your marriage ceremony like?" he shot, which dropped her back onto the chair.

"Why do you want to know?"

"Were you married by a true parson, or not?"

"Aye." She frowned. "I think."

"*You think?*" he hollered high enough for the King in his bed to hear. "You damned, silly girl, how could you not know if you were married by a true parson? Thou art a base, foolish woman."

Pall snapped, "Why art thou attacking me sister so dirty harsh when her marriage ain't none of your concern?"

"But it is my concern, Mistress, when she married me brother who was married afore to a lass named Betty."

"That ain't so," declared Pall with wide eyes, then she frowned. "He said he came to us never married."

"Ha!" Horatio cried to the rafters. "There you have it. A filthy rascal married to a bumpkin."

Viola remembered Horatio telling her Roger had been married, but she'd put no mind to it, hoping he'd drowned in the seas hard by The Hague. "Who is this Betty? Is she still alive?"

Horatio growled. "I know not. Only met her once, afore I was married and gone off to Tower Hill." He shook his head. "But no matter. I shall open me purse to a straw man, and he'll tell it aright to the judge."

"What are you about?" demanded Viola who felt there was evil afoot, and she'd be dragged into it.

"We shall not discuss it another moment," he stated and snapped his fingers. "Get thy cloak. We're leaving."

Paulina gasped. "Well, I never. You're a wicked varlet, Mister Sharpe, and rude beyond telling."

But Horatio did not heed her. He turned on his heel and trod out of the chamber. "I shall await thee at the entrance of this here place."

Viola snorted. "You don't have to get in a distemper of heat over it. I'm the one who's been cast to dust by the man, not you."

He turned on her. "You think not? He's taken the women I've loved right from under me nose. I've tried to kill him twice and failed. It's enough to drive me nose hairs blazing into me brains." He gazed at her furious hard, then said, "But I've a plan, and aye, you shall be part of it."

She didn't like the sound of that. "Nay, I shall not, for it'll turn on me most grievous."

Walking toward the doors, he laughed. "Nay, it shall not. We'll come out of it most joyous."

Viola gave Pall a swift hug. "I must go or be lost between here and the City. We must see each other soon. Promise?"

Pall kissed her cheeks. "Aye, very soon. You'll be an auntie afore you know it, and must be part of his life, our lives, Percy and mine."

Horatio hollered, "Art thou coming?"

Viola was near tears. "Alright then. Soon," and she dashed out the doors of Pall's apartments.

Holding her cloak and pattens, Viola tripped after Horatio as he near ran through the passageways of the palace. "Slow down. The floors are too uneven. I shall fall."

He ignored her and kept walking.

Stark mad, Viola stopped where she was, in a nook and cranny between intersecting hallways. It was dark. Gnashing her teeth, she watched Horatio's back retreat in the dimness.

Suddenly, she heard a deep chuckle and a simpering giggle. The manly voice was rich and full, and she realized it had been a long time since the feel of a strong pole against her privy parts. She sighed.

The man chuckled again, and Viola wondered at the sound that was cruelly akin to Roger's. Quietly gliding through the passageway, she moved a curtain aside to see him leaning heavily against a woman, kneading her naked breasts and kissing her neck.

The mere sight of Roger brought back memories of his body against hers after he'd turned into a beastly creature. It dashed her needs to dirt.

She said, "If you think he'll treat you kindly in the bed, Mistress, you are mistaken. He likes to rut like a dog."

With surprise, Roger pulled away as the woman gasped. He cried out, "What the blazes are you doing here?"

Viola laughed. "To be touched by the King. I've the King's Evil, which I got from you, Husband."

With horror, the woman pulled away from Roger, her eyes casting about for the telltale sores on his neck.

He growled, "That ain't true. I've not got the King's Evil, and you do me grave harm by harking it out to the whole world."

Viola gave him a wicked smile. "But 'tis true. You gave me the clap, *and* the Evil. I'm soiled beyond words because of you."

The woman cried out as if in great pain, slapping Roger away from her. "Nay, you shall not touch me. Get thee from me this very moment."

Roger pulled away from her, allowing her to dash away down the hall, straightening her gown to cover her breasts as she went.

Roger grabbed Viola. "Now, look what you've done, you draggle-tailed bitch. I was about to towse her good and proper. If you're poxed, it ain't from me. Who've you been frolicking with?"

Viola shrugged away from him. She was clean but she'd never let him know it. "Leave off. Who's this Betty creature you're married to?"

His eyebrows shot into his hat brim. "What do you know about Betty?"

"That you married the lass afore me, making me an adulterous woman, and you a filthy beast."

His voice went all snake-like. "I would never marry another but you, darlin' sweetie. How could you even think such a thing?" He grabbed her and pushed her into the nook, pressing against her. Her cloak and pattens dropped to the floor. His hand groped under her skirts, pinching her inner legs and privy puss.

Struggling against him, she turned her face away as he planted a wet and sloppy kiss, catching her jaw. "Get off me, you damned filthy rogue."

"Come and kiss me, Wife. You know you love it this way, a' frolicking rough in a dark corner."

Kicking out, she tried to dismantle him but missed. "I hope your cock shrivels to a stick and falls to dust. Leave off, I say," and she swung her leg, kicking him hard.

He dropped to his knees, squealing like the pig he was. Viola kicked him again, and scooping up her things, ran down the dark hallway wherein Horatio had gone.

~ * ~

Horatio watched her sink onto a stool in his bookseller shop. He was ashamed at his treatment of her, and wondered at her appearance. Her pretty dress was askew, her hair falling out of their pins. "What's afoot? You look all done in."

With dull eyes, she asked, "What's your plan? Will it kill him? I shall follow you in it."

He said, "Let us to my closet. I've new biscuits and some china tea from the coffeehouse hard by, very nice."

Taking her hand, he led her to his office near the printing press. Behind closed doors, the throbbing din of the press softened most kindly. Leading her to a straight chair, he took her cloak and pattens, setting them away, then poured tea into a dish.

He started slowly. "Here. The china tea is still warm, and dusted with sugar. It will give you contentment." Watching her take a sip, he continued, "I could not find the scholar for me preamble but have put something together I'd like you to look at, you being so good at this sort of business. Once it's in Latin, 'twill be difficult to read." He smiled.

The china tea seemed to perk her up, so he handed over a biscuit. "Dunk it into the tea. 'Tis ever so nice."

He watched her do as he bid, and taking a bite, her eyes brightened. Taking courage, he said, "I most humbly apologize for leaving you behind this day. Will you forgive me?"

She looked at him. "Aye. Thou art a man, after all, and cannot help but be cruel to a woman. 'Tis the way of things, ain't it?"

"Nay, it should not be," he professed, then added, "I do not like being cruel. That's what Roger does."

"Aye." She nodded over her tea. "He's a rake shamed rogue for sure."

He sat behind his desk, spreading his hands over the top of it. "Do you remember your marriage vows?"

"I think so."

He leaned forward. "Are you sure you're married?

"Aye, why?"

"Did he say 'I shall take thee,' or 'I take thee'?"

Viola blinked. "What's the difference?"

"A' cause if he said 'I shall take thee to my wife' or 'I will take thee', it ain't bound and legal. If he said 'I do take thee,' then it's surely legal and bound."

Shaking her head, she said, "I still do not understand."

Hoping she'd see the way of it, Horatio said very slowly, "To say 'I shall or I will' means a promise for the future. To say 'I take thee' means you vow afore all and sundry this very moment. You ken?"

Her eyes widened. "Oh, aye, I ken." Then her brows crinkled together. "I cannot remember what was said, everything being in such a flurry, and all. Me papa stood next to Roger with a pistol pointed at his head whilst the parson said his words, and Paulina bemoaned most horrid the maid went missing. She was forced to blow on the fire or it go out as it was such a blustery, frosty day."

Horatio bit down a laugh, for it sounded like she'd had a most troublesome time of it. He cleared his throat. "What happened, then?"

She shrugged, "Emmm, the usual. We both said 'I do', then the parson shut his book and demanded a pint of rum."

"Where did the marriage take place?"

"In me papa's house on the Bridge."

"Did you follow the canonical laws?"

"Oiy? What do you mean?"

"Was the marriage done between eight o'clock of the morning and noontime?"

"Aye."

"Were the banns read?"

Viola shook her head. "Nay."

"Was the marriage recorded with your parish?"

"I know not."

"Did you receive any sort of paper signed by the parson?"

Viola nodded. "Oh, aye. The paper was old and near falling to pieces, but we signed our names across it."

"Where is the paper?"

"I know not. Probably at me papa's house."

Horatio frowned. "We ain't going back there, what with the plague and all. If we did, the house is more than likely stripped of all its goods, anyway." He then asked, "Were there witnesses?"

"Aye."

"How many?"

Closing her eyes, her fingers moving, Viola said, "Me papa, Pall, and two of our neighbors, Tom and Nell Morgan."

"Did you fling the stocking with the guests watching whilst in your bed?"

"Aye, Roger did that."

Horatio frowned. "Your marriage was done clandestine. It seems most of what is necessary was done."

"'Tis for certain then, ain't it?"

Horatio nodded. "Aye, to fling the stocking means to consummate the marriage vows, making it all the more legal and bound."

Viola placed the empty tea dish on his desk. "Is this good or bad?"

He put his hands behind his neck and stared at the ceiling. Horatio smiled. "We shall make it a good thing."

Thirty-three

Horatio went back to Westminster with his preamble, which must be done right and proper for the patent, and in good order, or there'd be no record of his knighthood. The preamble was to be done in Latin, and by a knowledgeable person. Horatio had finally received a reply from Mister Walter Barrington, the classical scholar, who said he'd be within at his table this very morning.

Into the Hall from New Palace Yard, Horatio cast his eyes across the remodeling and scaffolding to a table wherein Mister Barrington usually sat. He was not there, but in the great din of excavation and hammering, he saw a man walk toward him, tall and thin with bushy, white hair all a' froth beneath his hat. His arms were filled with books. Horatio felt relief, for he recognized Mister Barrington.

Horatio hollered over the noise, "Oiy, Barrington, what are you about when we have a meeting for me preamble?"

Startled, Barrington dropped the books, and looking mighty cross, cried out, "Now, look what you've made me do. Help me pick these up. I'm off to a new cubby-hole in the Exchequer where 'tis far quieter. The King will have a new Hall for his coronation, but me brains are near frizzled with the hullabaloo."

Bending down to pick up books, Horatio said, "Looks like King's Bench is being torn away. Will it be replaced somewhere else?"

Barrington looked over his shoulder then back at his books. "Aye, to the south end of this here building."

"Ah," Horatio replied, very joyous since the King's Bench was where he'd need to put down Roger once and for all. He said, "Me arms are full, now, with nary a one on the floor. Let us to your new place of business to get me preamble done."

Later, after putting before the scholar all he wanted, Horatio returned to the Hall. He was in search of a straw man—all liars and cheats—to bring down Roger. Easily recognized by straws sticking out of their shoes, they huddled in Westminster Hall where the courts were held. Knowing their cozener reputation, he'd have to be careful and not give a full purse until the business was done.

Horatio saw one leaning against the wall, smoking a pipe, and watching the goings-on of the workers tearing down rickety court benches. He strode up to him. "Oiy, there, don't you have a sister named Betty who's been done low by a runoff husband?"

The man gazed at him, sizing him up for a good return on his services. He sucked on his pipe then blew smoke from his nose. "Maybe, what've you in mind?"

Horatio said, "I'll need your sister, too. There's good coin in it, make no mistake. I've had a bit of bother with a cunning rogue who needs a lesson taught to. I'll need testimony against him from you and your sister."

"When's this to take place? I'm a busy man, you see, and me sister has been done cruel by the filthy fellow."

Horatio smiled. "Did he get her with child afore running off? That would be a most horrid shame.

The man nodded. "Aye, that it is, and the poor lad's most discontented with his lot, being forced to steal from the markets and all just to keep food in his belly. His ma ain't doin' so well, neither."

Amazed, Horatio asked, "That old, is he? Why I'd a thought he couldn't be more than four or five. 'Tis a bit early to go a' thievin', poor lad."

The man pulled on his pipe. Smoke came from his mouth when he said, "Oiy, that other poor lad was from another husband, God rest his weary soul. His brother, now, a laddie of four or five is in the poorest of shape, skin and bones, always sickly a' cause there ain't enough food to go around. You might be talkin' of that poor child, I reckon."

Horatio nodded and smiled. "Aye, that's the one. Ain't this a calamity, someone showing his falseness afore the whole world? Shouldn't be allowed, that's what I say. I'm off to hire both a solicitor and barrister for the unhappy situation. I hope to see you thereafter wherein we can discuss this troublesome brew. Where will I find you?"

"Unless I'm needed at the Bench by another, I'll be right here a' watching the destruction of this here place being made ready for the King's crowning."

Looking around at the unholy racket of the remodel, Horatio said, "It'll take awhile to put this Hall to rights, I imagine, plenty of time to take care of this horrid business done to your sister."

The man cocked his hat brim. "Aye, it surely is."

~ * ~

The next morning Horatio left his bookseller shop resolved to finish with the patent once and for all. He'd been through a great deal of trouble with it, including the mounting cost, most dire.

His gut ground grievous when he'd purchased the baronetcy for six hundred pounds. He'd handed over a chest nearly full of coins from England, Holland, and France, an honorable mix of silver and gold.

Then, everyone had their hands out for the damned title, from Viola (two pieces) who fixed the preamble nice and pretty afore Mister Barrington (seven pieces) took it over, to purchasing plate (twenty pounds) for the secretary of state who held the grant of title, to the attorney general (ten pieces) who was to prepare the patent entire, except, of course, the preamble. It was a horrid pickle but worth the purse if he could make the knighthood continue to his heirs.

Grinding his teeth, he knew he should have the son Elizabeth would bear instead of his brother, another betrayal by the filthy rascal. With cruel thoughts filling his brains, he pursed his lips. By the grace of God, his plan to finish Roger would work, or he'd forever be a weak, simple man, never overcoming the villainy of anyone.

Leaving the City from Ludgate, he saw a sedan chair ahead of him, waiting to enter the City. Suddenly, an arm came out of the curtains, a gloved hand waving. The carriers lowered the chair then one of them helped out a lady. She was ungainly, and looked very strange like

Elizabeth, but it couldn't be, she being safely in the country awaiting the birth of his child.

The lady was a' weeping most extraordinary, pressing a hand against her lower back. As Horatio gained ground toward the chair and the woman, he saw it *was* Elizabeth.

He said, "What are you about? I thought you were in the country. What's wrong? Are you well?"

Her face awash with tears, she cried, "I'm searching for me husband, should you be so bold to know. Have you seen him?"

"I saw him not two days ago in Whitehall. Why did you marry him? He ain't any good, you know."

Elizabeth bawled high for the whole world to hear as she jerked to a walk, lumbering most awkward away from Ludgate, and toward Whitehall. The fellows followed with the sedan chair.

Horatio walked alongside her. "I had nothing to do with the death of thy husband. You must know this. The child is mine and I intend to have him."

"Nay, you shall not. I hate you exceedingly for what you've done."

Taking her arm, Horatio forced her to a stop. "What have I done? 'Tis only fair you should tell me. I have the right to defend meself, don't I?"

"You told Wilds I was an adulteress in front of the King and the whole world of The Hague. You said I'd go a' frolicking most reckless with any man at the Mitre." Losing strength, she near collapsed into his arms. "How could you have done this? I thought you cared about me."

Astonished by her words, he felt deadly anger grip his guts. "Nay, I never said this. I told the King you and I were very good friends, 'tis all. Roger has filled you with lies."

As if she could no longer stand straight, she pressed the top of her head against his chest. "Roger said he was there, that you confessed afore all I was a whore."

Trying very hard not to shake the base stupidity from her, he cried, "Nay. After what we meant to each other all those months, how could you believe a knave like my brother, someone you've only just met?"

He could not understand how women dropped to their knees whenever his brother walked into a chamber. Roger had the ability to snap his fingers, and women would believe anything he said, always false. His heart and soul were filled with villainy. All he cared for was to satisfy his carnal needs.

He'd never seen anything like it his whole life. Horatio could meet a woman and be true to her, then Roger would walk by, and the woman would forsake him as if he had never existed. She would believe everything the ratter said, accept everything he did, wretched or not. Even under the worst of conditions, the woman would follow his brother anywhere.

Since the betrayal with his wife, his mind had been in a delirium of trying to understand it, and shaking his head, he realized he never would. He'd never be able to hold onto a woman whilst his brother was still alive to take her away.

Putting her at arm's length, he said, "The filthy coxcomb will only forsake you when he's got what he wants. He'll leave you and our babe in the dirt." Abruptly realizing he no longer cared what she did, he added, "You must know I will never let that happen to our babe. You can go to the gutter for all I care, but I shall have our babe afore Roger's finished with you."

Her gloved hand went to her mouth. She gasped, her eyes wide. "Nay, you shall not have the babe. Roger will be his father, not you. Never you."

He laughed. It sounded cruel to his ears. "Nay, Elizabeth, I shall never allow Roger to be near my son. You can run and hide, but I shall find you and snatch the child from between your legs if I must, don't think I won't."

He waved to the carriers of the sedan chair. "Come, take this woman to Whitehall. Her husband is there."

He turned away from her, his mind finally free and clear of her. He'd get rid of Roger, then take his child from Elizabeth. As before with his wife, he didn't care anymore if Elizabeth lived or died.

In truth, he hoped the birthing would kill her.

Thirty-four

Viola divided her time between the clerk shop and the bookseller shop, doing an infinite amount of business since the King returned. Her strongbox was more than half full with silver and gold pieces, very nice, and the value to her name exceedingly higher than ever before in her whole life, near thirty pounds.

Even though she was a lass, and looked upon very strange by the men coming into the shops, both Horatio and Simon Kirk stood by her work, declaring her hand good and firm. It gave her great joy to be so kindly thought of in a time when men ruled the world entire.

Men, old and young, rushed hither and thither, all mad to get their patents sealed and their new titles registered. Even Horatio ran about in a fury, trying to put to order all for his appointment. He was gone full days, from breaking his fast in the kitchen to late at night, rarely attending to his businesses.

Since he was her brother-in-law, Viola pulled and tugged for him, hoping the Finches did not see his lax attention to the shops. In the mornings, afore everyone set to work, she and Simon directed the prentices to put the clerk shop in order, from sweeping the floors, polishing the tables, and wiping moisture from the windows to setting paper in orderly piles and filling ink pots.

Afterward, she'd direct a prentice or two into the bookseller shop, setting it to rights for the day. She'd point and demand, "Remove the dried, printed sheets from the drying lines and lay them flat on a table."

As the lads rushed to do her bidding, she turned to a new prentice with yellow hair. "Organize and straighten typefaces for the day, if you please."

And while he went to work, she'd command another fellow new to the shop, "Off you go, prepare press ink, and wipe moisture from the windows."

Later in the day, Viola directed one of the older prentices to dampen sheets for the next day's printing, a most grave important task.

It was a full day of pushing and heaving, and by its end, she was exhausted beyond words—but very grateful not to be with child as she could have done when the idea of turning prentice came to her. It took her breath away, thinking how close she'd come to calamity. As a prentice with a babe growing in her, she'd have for certain ended up in gaol.

Lucy was near the birthing time, and had slowed down to what seemed a painful waddle. She complained bitterly of swollen feet and legs, not able to wear her shoes any longer, but must stuff her feet into an old pair of Simon's or traipse around in slippers the whole day.

Viola was forced to market and butchers' shops for vittles and the like, and lately, she cooked most times, and knew she couldn't hold a bare stick to Lucy when it came to cooking. Just the other night whilst holding a pan of scrambled eggs and fried bread when the prentices and men came striding into the kitchen, they groaned piteously.

She placed the hot pan on the table and said, "It'll only be another week or so and the babe will be with us. I know she's much better than I am in the kitchen."

Thinking the next day on their discord to her sweat and bother over the hearth, she turned most cross, and cried, "You get right up me nose, you do. Off you go then, to a tavern or ordinary. I'll not slave over a hot hearth and you grumble over it. Nay, I shall not."

It made them grumble all the more, for when eating off the premises, they were forced to pay for their own food and drink. Viola did not mind. It gave her more time to learn the way of the printing press. Clerking was fine and dandy but not near as exciting as typesetting for the press. She watched Mistress Finch at it day in and day out, wondering at her quick hand and memory.

As time moved on, Mistress Finch beckoned to her. "Come along then, Viola. Let me teach you the way of it."

With their heads together Viola learned how to set type. In the end, she and Mistress Finch—Charlotte—became great friends.

The friendship was lovely, as was the lady.

Viola thought about when she'd first met Charlotte at the Mitre, and how bold she was with her face painted, but then how pretty she was with kindly eyes. Now, they worked together, putting to rights careless script by authors, and typesetting all of it. They chattered away on all subjects, ill and fine, from Cromwell to the King, from bright colored fashions to the great change of England for the whole world to see. They discussed how the new china tea was so much better than bitter coffee, and which did they love most, Rhenish or Canary wines.

Today, the bookseller and clerk shops were opened, but the printing press was silent. Horatio was absent, as were the Finches. She could hear Hammer at the bookbinding, but the morning was growing old. Viola was a' flutter something terrible wrong was afoot. She didn't give much mind to Horatio, his brains being scattered of late, but the Finches were always at the shop.

She went to the door, opened it and walked out to the lane, regarding it up and down. Folk were about, but she could not see the Finches.

Viola was greatly bothered by it. The morning drifted into the afternoon, and as the prentices cried for small beer and bread, mayhap a chine of beef, she became more fretful. It was not like the Finches to not be at the shop. They were as punctual as daylight and nighttime.

She turned to Simon Kirk. "I am most afeard something dire has happened to the Finches. Do you know where they live?"

"Aye," he said, and out of habit gazed at the opened door between the shops. Every time the bell rang to the shop, he'd look there whilst Viola went to wait on the customer.

She said, "They've moved closer to the shops, you see, and ain't near Cornhill any longer."

Simon nodded. "Aye, I know. They're on Pie Corner."

Viola took his arm and shook it. "Something's horrid wrong."

"Aye, you've said that. Will you have a prentice go round to their house, then? It's at the church."

"Nay, I must see for meself. I cannot bear it another moment." She pulled off her apron and thrust it at him. "I shall return anon."

Viola dashed out of the shops onto Paternoster Row and over to Ivy Lane. Picking up her skirts, she walked fast through Newgate Market which brought her thoughts of dinner for the lads. The market was active, but she did not stop. Viola jogged out of the City through Newgate and up Snow Hill, from thence skirting around Gilford Street to Pie Corner, hard by St. Sepulcher Church.

Their house was a pretty one that she reckoned would show curtains over the windows when the shutters were opened. Today, the shutters were closed, the house quiet. Dead quiet. Clapped by the heels something worse than worse was afoot, Viola ran up to their front door. There were no noises from inside. She pounded on the door.

Pulling the door wide, James Finch raised his hand in warning. "Must you be so damned loud? What's the hard fuss?"

Trying to look over and around him, Viola said, "I was much afeard something terrible horrid had happened. 'Tis deep in the afternoon and neither you nor Charlotte have come to the shop. Art thou well? Where is Charlotte?"

He pulled her inside and shut the door. It was very dark. "Thou art very high and demanding. What's it to you if we take a day off now and again?"

But Viola wasn't having any of it. She walked passed him into the house, trying to make out objects in the deep gloom.

"Where is Charlotte?" she asked and grabbed a candle lanthorn from the table. "I shall search until I find her, don't think I won't."

"Nay, you will not..."

She heard groaning, and raising the lanthorn high, Viola sent weak light across the lower chamber. It was in disarray. She raised the lanthorn higher, searching every corner. There was a very handsome cupboard of plate that glowed as the candlelight passed over it. She saw a chair with a turkey cushion, clothing flung across the back of it, and a bed naked of curtains.

Charlotte lay on the bed, curled in the fetal position and moaning most piteously. Her face was sheeny bright, her hair in lank strands against her forehead and pillow. As she pulled the covers up to her neck, she shivered grievously.

Viola was stricken most unhappy, not having seen anyone so ill in a long while. She cried out, "What is wrong with her? Will she die?"

James grabbed the lanthorn from her. "Nay, she will not. You do us grave injury to blather so."

Viola would not be pushed in a corner. "How do you know she won't die?"

"Don't be a stark ass. Can't you see she's right here before our very eyes, listening to our every word?"

"What's wrong with her?" and remembering her papa, she turned to him with a falling, fearful gut. "Is it the plague? When did she come down with it? Why ain't there a red cross painted over your door and someone guarding it with a pistol?"

James flung the lanthorn to the floor, and the light to winked out. Grabbing Viola, he shook her. "In troth, I never saw in my life anywhere anyone so base stupid as to blather to the world my Charlotte has the plague." He shook Viola again, making her teeth rattle. "Shut it, I say. Shut it this very minute."

Viola was afeard her head would snap off. "Alright! Stop shaking me."

James dropped his hands from her. He picked up the lanthorn and walked to the table where he lit the candle.

As if in prayer, he mumbled and slumped onto a stool, then ran his hands through his hair. "How can anyone be so base stupid as to blather afore the whole world me Charlotte has the plague. It ain't right, I tell you, it just ain't right."

He lowered his head into his hands and wept.

Feeling ashamed she'd thought so very much for her own hide and so little for Charlotte, Viola took the lanthorn from the table. If there was plague in the house, being there and at great risk, she may as well check to make for certain what caused her friend so ill.

After all, afore she met Roger, the filthy creature, she'd worked in a charity ward and saw all manner of illnesses. Whatever ailed Charlotte may not be the plague. Setting the lanthorn on the chair, she stilled her fluttery gut, and climbed onto the bed.

Leaning in, she said, "Come Charlotte, me darlin'. Let us open your gown for a look-see. We must fix our saddles straight so we can set a cure."

Burning hot, Charlotte whimpered as Viola pressed her onto her back and unbuttoned her bed gown. "Shhh,

Charlotte," she crooned, "'Twill be aright. I shall swab you down with a wet cloth, and you'll be right as rain in no time."

Tears washed the sides of Charlotte's face. "Is this aright? I don't have the plague?"

"Shhh, let's just see, shall we?" and Viola lifted the lanthorn. Being as tender as she could, she moved the fabric of Charlotte's gown and felt gently along Charlotte's neck, and under her arms for the telltale buboes.

There were no lumps, very good, nor did Charlotte shoot out of the bed in agonizing pain as Viola softly prodded the underarms. Moving the light over Charlotte's chest, Viola saw spots, and looking closer, they rose up her neck to her jaw and face.

Standing up, Viola said, "Nay, me girl. You do not have the plague, at least not now."

James gasped, and rose quickly from the table. "What? No plague? God be praised!"

Viola moved closer to James. "Fill a pitcher with cool water, sirrah. We must reduce her heat."

"Aye, I've already a cool pitcher. The water-boy came just yesterday." With a sudden quickness, he poured water on a kerchief. "Here. Bathe her gently."

Not moving, Viola said, "This you must do, James. She'll need you in the coming days."

"What's this? You sound so dire. How can this be when me Charlotte does not have the plague?"

Suppressing a groan, Viola said, "Because Charlotte has been stricken with smallpox."

Thirty-five

"How do you know? When will she be well, again?" James swung away from her. He bent over as if he would be sick, and wept anew.

Viola watched him, thinking how fortunate it was for Charlotte to be loved so fully by her husband. It was an extraordinary thing, and with a sigh, she realized it was something she'd never experience.

She said, "I know not, since she's in the fever portion of it with not many spots showing. I took care of me husband when he had the smallpox, and he came out well." She gave him a weak smile.

He stood straight, and wiping his face with his sleeve, commanded, "You shall stay here until me Charlotte is well, again. What will you have me do?"

Regarding the inside of the house, she had not expected it to be so crowded with stuffs, or so dim dark.

She said, "To begin with, you must open the shutters and windows. 'Tis awful stale in here. Then, we could do with a broth and small beer. Is there an upper floor in this here house? Why ain't the bed up there?" Viola wiped her sodden forehead with her hand, then continued, "She must have got the sickness a' cause of these overcrowded, stuffy conditions. We must change all of that right this very minute."

She was astonished at how quickly he jumped to do her bidding, grabbing goods until his arms were full. It brought her to a real smile, which she doused quickly, considering the sad state of affairs. Charlotte wasn't near out of danger. She could very well die during the height of fever, the Lord protect them all.

~ * ~

Three days later, the house was freshly laundered with breezes wafting through the lower level. The bed was happily installed in its proper place on the second level, and no longer naked. Curtains surrounded it, and the bedchamber window was closed. It wouldn't do to have too much air swirling about the place.

Once Charlotte lived through the first night, and then the second, Viola had a look around. The house was not settled after the Finches moved from Cornhill, which still did not explain why the joiners put the bed together on the lower level. It took a good bit of haggling for them to return, dismantle it, and re-join it up the stairs.

When they came to the back door, she cried out most fierce, "Thou art all knaves for a dirty job poorly done, and you shall not get another coin for the business."

With hats in their hands, they shuffled their feet on the stoop.

Viola opened the door wide. "Get on in, and get it done right this very minute."

In a brisk frolic, they dashed to finish putting the bed to rights, and all the while Charlotte rested on a pallet near the kitchen fire.

This house boasted a range in the kitchen, something Viola knew about but never seen work, and had come to love it most wonderful extraordinarily. It was so much better than cooking from caldrons over the fire, very hot. The range was hot, as well, but it did not put out open fire, being all encased ever so nicely. It took longer for the metal to cool, making it lovely for baking bread, and keeping a dinner warm for hours until it went quite coddled to dirt.

Viola was determined to have one at the shops for Lucy to cook over. Once she'd seen and worked on a range, nothing in the kitchen would ever be the same, and Viola lovingly caressed the now cooled iron...

Someone pounded on the kitchen door, and at first Viola was afeard word had gotten out plague may be within, but then she heard Horatio.

He cried out mightily, "Viola, art thou in there? Come out, I say, or I shall pull the door from its hinges. I've been searching high and low for you." He rattled the latch and clapped the bell. "Come out I say. Open this door at once."

Viola yanked it open. "What's this all about then? Don't you know Charlotte is ill, and may die this very moment?"

He snapped, "Well, if it ain't the wayward girl? Why didn't you tell me you'd hied off and away from the shops? I've come to depend on you as one resourceful and keeping the place fine and dandy." He sniffed. "You could have said something."

Viola laughed. "I couldn't leave Charlotte to suffer alone, now could I? What is it you want?"

Gazing at her all squinty-eyed, he asked, "No one answered from the front, so I came round back. May I come in?"

"Oiy, come in," she replied and moved so he could enter the kitchen. She crooned, "Look at this here range. Ain't it the most marvelous creation? We should get one for Lucy."

Gazing sightless around him with his eyes all glassy, Viola knew he hadn't heard a word she said. She sighed. "What do you want, then? Out with it."

"It's time to put our plan into action."

"What plan? I know nothing of a plan, only that you want to do Roger ill."

"I'm going to tell you of it, ain't I?" He gazed around. "Have you anything to drink? Rhenish wine would be very nice." He wagged his eyebrows.

Viola pulled a pewter cup from a shelf. "There's a cask in the far corner, but I must warn you, 'tis gone sour. Been too long in the warm kitchen, I reckon."

Nonetheless, he poured himself a drink. He sipped from the cup, winced, and said, "We're to destroy Roger. I've a lovely plan, and you're to be part of it."

"I will not leave Charlotte. She's become a great friend, and I'll not desert her."

Frowning, he gazed at the cup then took another tentative sip. "This is rotten. I shall to a tavern hard by and bring back a pitcher. We've much to celebrate."

"'Tis poor timing to celebrate when Charlotte may keel over any moment."

"Whilst I'm out, I shall bring back a physician. He'll know what to do. Why hasn't James done so?"

He settled his hat firmly round his ears and trod toward the still opened door. "Me paper's come through with the King's signature. I'll be able to pass me title down to me son."

Viola was astonished. "But you have no son."

He turned to her with a stone hard look. "Aye, I do. Elizabeth's about due and I shall have the babe to raise. I will call him Charles Henry Sharpe, after the King, and me da."

Viola felt her mouth drop. "Has she said you may have the child?"

Horatio strode out the door to the alley and away. With his back to her, he hollered, "Nay."

She could not believe it, and snapped her mouth shut. The man was most brazen to announce to the whole world he'd take a newborn child from the arms of his mother. No woman would give up a child so easily unless she was dead in the street. Nay, it would never happen.

~ * ~

With James Finch standing by her side, Viola watched Horatio march into the house holding a cask of wine on his shoulder. Behind him trailed a tall, dour man, carrying a satchel.

Horatio strode into the kitchen with the cask. "This here is the physician. Let him up to see Charlotte."

Viola led the way up the stairway, the physician and James following. "She's up here, abed three days now. She seems less fitful, but spots have sprung up all along her chest, neck and face. 'Tis most unsightly."

The man said, "Me name's Reed. You may call me thus." Sprinkling pomander of cinnamon and ashes as he climbed behind her, he sneezed. James sneezed.

Viola regarded Reed as he reached the top stair. He was an old man all gray, his hair, his face, and even his eyes. He looked more dead than alive.

She said, "Mistress Finch is in here."

As she started to walk into the bedchamber, Reed said, "Both of you stay put," and he walked in, shutting them out and alone in the hall above the stair.

James said, "What's happening? Why has he shut me out?"

Viola did not know. "Let us await his word. She seems better today."

His eyes brightened. "Aye. She does at that."

Horatio cried most loud from below. "Viola, come down this very minute. We have much to discuss. James can attend to his wife."

James smiled and gently ran his knuckles down her cheek. "You've been a great friend. I thank thee, and Charlotte thanks thee. I'll stay until he comes out, good news or bad."

Horatio hollered most peevish boisterous. "Mistress, attend me at once."

Viola sighed. He could be the most beastly of creatures. "Will thou hush thy voice? We have a near dead person in our midst."

James gasped, and she immediately felt grievous sad over her choice of words. She touched his arm. "I am most sorry. I meant nothing."

Horatio sounded vexed when he cried up the stairs. "Nay, I shall not be forever quiet. You must share a drink with me as I tell you the plan."

"Go, mistress," James said and pushed her gentle like. "I will let thee know Charlotte's condition as soon as I learn of it."

Viola went down the stairs, vexed to the blood over Horatio's lack of sympathy for poor Charlotte who might not have another hour to live. God only knew what the physician would give her, poison most likely, and then bleed her terrible 'til she fell to the floor in a faint or finally, completely dead.

When she reached Horatio, he handed her a cup of wine. "Take this and drink. We've much to discuss."

Very cross, she said through clenched teeth, "I should love to scream at you in a frightful manner, Mister Sharpe, but I ain't a bold hard woman." She took a sip of wine. It was Rhenish and of a proper age. "Charlotte is up there, near dying, and all you can think of is revenge on Roger, the filthy beast. Can't you, at least, act like you give a tinker's damn she gets well? She is, after all, your partner's wife."

He had the decency to look aggrieved, and removed his hat. "I apologize, Mistress, for me rude behavior. Now, let us discuss what's been eating away at me this whole day."

Before he could speak of what was so strong on his mind, James Finch ran hollering down the stairs. "Me Charlotte ain't going to die. She ain't going to die."

He ran to them laughing near hysterical, and grabbed the cup out of Horatio's hand. "Ain't that just fine and dandy? Me wife's to live most wonderful. All she has is the chickenpox." And he drank from the cup, emptying in one gulp.

Thirty-six

September 1660

Horatio dragged Viola farther into the City where she'd never been before, to Cheapside and St. Mary le Bow Church. It vexed her, for with all the bustle over Charlotte, he never did tell her the plan to ruin Roger.

He ranted most high, "Don't dally. We must to the Court of Arches."

"What's the Court of Arches? We're heading for what looks to be a church."

"'Tis where we'll bring suit against Roger. This is an Ecclesiastical Court."

"Nay, 'tis a church."

He snapped, "Do stop thy mouth from so much clamor. The court is held here. See the arches of this here church? 'Tis where we must be. What is your parish church?"

"'Tis where we buried me papa, St. Magnus at the Bridge. Why?"

He jogged to the entrance. "Never thee mind. Thou art a woman and will never understand."

Into the church they went.

Horatio pulled her along until her skirts caught between her legs, near casting her to the ground. She cried, "Slow down this very minute. I'm about to go a' sprawling with you running so."

Grumbling, he slowed down, and he walked at a better pace towards a portion of the church with offices. Viola followed and was astonished to see how busy it was. People milled about, men of cloth and clerks, along with laity, men and women alike. Horatio headed straight for a scruffy man and a dirty woman holding the hand of a child.

"Who's that woman?"

"'Tis Betty, Roger's first wife."

Viola did not believe it. Even after being with Roger for as short a time as she had, she knew he had better taste in women than the one before her. The woman looked like a sodded calf.

Horatio and the man nodded to one another, Horatio asking, "How's it, then?"

The man shook his head all woeful like. "'Tis not so good. Me sister here is pining. Her lad there is a' dying."

Swinging her gaze to the lad, Viola frowned. He did not look so poorly as one to be near crossing the veil. If he looked as Charlotte had been, there'd be another story to tell. Besides, the lad would be all droopy like and in bed, wouldn't he?

A proud, saucy man walked up to them. "Keep thy voices down if you will. This is a church, if you can remember."

Horatio said, "We're looking for the Dean. Art thou the Dean of Arches?"

"Nay. What do you want with him?"

"A case of bigamy."

The saucy fellow clicked his tongue. "Tsk, tsk, shameful that." He spread his arms. "As you can see the Court is hopeless, what with Cromwell shutting us down all those years ago as being Papist. We're still trying to get it aright after the return of the King. Come back when we're up and running, again." The man wagged his head back and forth. "Tsk, tsk. In any case, you must to criminal court for sodomy."

"Not buggery," Horatio snapped. "'Tis bigamy why we're here."

The man looked horrified. "Please, sirrah. Your language is most foul."

Horatio said, "It's most controlled. Where is the Dean?"

The churchman replied, "We're in hopeless condition and you must go right away. Our Dean of Arches is a busy man, not to be trifled with by the likes of you."

Viola watched as a frail, old man of distinction walked up to them. He asked, "What's this then?"

"Sodomy," the other said all frowny like.

Horatio clanked his teeth together, growling. "Nay, thou twitter pated dolt. 'Tis bigamy we seek justice for." And swinging his hand to show Viola and the other wench, he added, "Look at these poor, sad women taken in by a scoundrel of the worst order. We must put this to rights."

The frail, old fellow raised his finger as if to speak, but Horatio blathered on, "The King is back and the right church restored to order. This must be done proper for the whole world to see a' cause of the filth the Commonwealth left behind."

The saucy man, who wanted them to go away, waved his hand for Horatio to stop, but he would not. Horatio continued, "Because our rightful church was shut down, hardly any poor persons know if they're married or not, and others are damned predators, taking advantage just to frolic."

The proud churchman gasped. "Please, your language. We are in a church, and mixed afore us are frail women and a child."

Horatio barked, "I intend to see justice done in this regard, with or without this court."

The frail gentleman raised a hand. "Nay, we shall listen more to this." Regarding the young churchman, he said, "Go fetch our friend Giles Sweete."

He ushered them into an office. "Please take a chair or stool, whatever works for you." He shuffled weak like to sit behind a great desk, and said, "I am Richard Zaks, Dean of Arches, Barrister and Judge. Who are you?"

Viola watched as Horatio stood and bowed. "I am Sir Horatio Sharpe, Baronet, at your service, your Right Worshipful. Me brother, Roger Sharpe, has committed bigamy."

He motioned to Viola. "This here is me sister-in-law who's requested I speak in her behalf for the injurious harm done to her poor soul. And there," he motioned to the other woman, "Is Betty Sharpe, first wife of Roger, whom he abandoned most grievous once he learned she was with child."

The straw man stretched most indignant. "Betty's been on and off the streets, ever since."

The Dean of Arches asked, "Who are you?"

"I'm Betty's brother, ain't I?"

Viola gasped, then covered it with a cough. The men were spouting buckets of lies smooth as you please, nor did she believe for a minute the woman to be Roger's first wife. She wanted Roger smashed into dirt as much as Horatio, but he could have warned her what he was about, for bloody sakes. Viola did not want to ruin what he'd started, though, and settled in to hear the rest. She pressed her lips together to prevent any other shocked noises coming from her.

The Dean of Arches gazed at Horatio for what seemed a very long time, and she wondered if he saw the lies as clearly as she did. He looked at the other woman. "Is this true?"

'Betty Sharpe' lowered her eyes. "Aye, Your Majesty."

Suppressing a smile, the old man said, "Nay, I ain't the King, but the judge of this here Arches." He cleared his throat. "For awhile, at any rate."

The prideful churchman directed a tall, robust man into the office then closed the door. The new fellow bowed, showing a lusty leg. "You wanted to see me, Sir?"

The Dean of Arches said, "Hello, Sweete, come in and have a listen. These here poor sad fellows are in need of the type justice you're so good at."

~ * ~

Viola did not like the Sweete person. His eyes were filled with avarice, as were the scruffy man and woman, but Horatio said that was good for their plan.

She asked, "What is our plan? Don't you think I have a right to know? I will not be thrust afore those important types, making a fool of meself. It'll put all in jeopardy."

Horatio gave her a strange look as if her head had fallen off her shoulders. "I wanted to tell you the other day, Mistress Sharpe. You shall learn of it right this very minute."

He turned suddenly round a corner and headed for a tavern. Down a long passage from the street, they entered the Nag's Head, a large place. He said, "There are plenty of hidey-holes in this here inn to put our heads together and not be heard. I spent much time here during the dangerous times whilst taking letters and documents to the King."

Upon entering, Viola gazed around. There were several hearths, a sign of prosperity. She followed him between tables to a small one with benches in an alcove near a mullioned window.

She took a seat on the bench opposite him. "I could do with a pasty and a pot of ale, if you're buying." She smiled.

"Gore, if this business ain't killing me purse," and he waved to the maid.

While they waited, Viola said, "If you're going to use that woman and lad, you might as well clean them up a bit. They look all done in, covered with lice and the like. Makes me want to fight off a fit of itching just to look at them."

After ordering, Horatio rubbed his hands together. "We'll destroy Roger, be done with him forever more. I've been hugging this business quite awhile, now, and know it will work. He's been married three times, whilst all are still living and breathing. I know not if there are more." His eyebrows shot into his hat. "I could get forged documents to show more." Looking at her, he asked, "What do you think?"

Viola was becoming vexed. "Think what? I still do not know what you are working toward, except to ruin Roger, the filthy beast. How will taking him to court ruin him? If he ain't sent into slavery, all they'll do is burn a hand."

"If we show probable cause he's a cunning cheat with several wives deserted, he could be executed, or if we ain't lucky enough for that, he won't just have his hand burned, I've made certain of that. He'll be sent into slavery." He grinned ugly.

"Who's the third?" Viola asked. "I've heard of Betty, and know of meself. Who's the other?"

His face went dark. "Why, Elizabeth, of course."

And remembering how he felt about the betrayal by his wife, Viola did not reckon he held good thoughts for Elizabeth. As his face went darker, his eyes colder, she shivered. She hoped never to be part of a betrayal against Sir Horatio Sharpe, for it would do her very serious ill.

He cried out, "How could you have married the dirty blighter? It seems any woman who sees him, hears him, fall to their knees, and beg to be culled. He's the very devil, but women wouldn't know it. It burns at my very gut that your type are so base stupid."

She opened her mouth to give him a hog high rant when the maid brought them their food and drink. The maid's cheeks were pink, and she giggled merrily. Her neckerchief was askew, and her hair was coming out of her cap.

Both she and Horatio heard Roger's voice chuckling and braying from the kitchen. "Come along back, sweet mistress. I've a great thing awaiting thee."

The maid near dropped the tray of food and drink on the table, all the while giggling and a' gasping. Without further ado, she swirled her skirts around and trotted back to the kitchen.

Watching Horatio's face burn with fury, Viola said softly, "Aye, let's do him in right and proper. I've a few ideas you may appreciate.

Thirty-seven

Viola watched as Charlotte Finch, who may God defend, was back to robust health again, patiently guided a new apprentice. Very good at the business, Charlotte coached the lad to be a compositor, extraordinary brave work, as he set letterforms for the press.

Once the type was set (this for a jolly cookbook), she showed him how to beat the type with ink. It always astonished Viola when leather filled balls with handles, and slathered with ink, were pounded over the metal bits, covering it entire before going off to the printer. If the first page was aright and no changes to the type were made, several sets of pages would be printed.

During this time, Viola would begin with the next page, setting the type for the paper full. The columns did not make any sense due to the arrangement of the pages until bound by Mister Hammer. Working the press business was lovely, and made her feel ever so good and accomplished.

Horatio trod very quickly into the bookseller shop, spurs on his boots a' jangling most extraordinary, his sword snagging against all things. Irritably, Charlotte clicked her tongue, her arms akimbo.

Viola thought no good was afoot, and asked, "What's the hullabaloo?"

He leaned toward her and said quietly, "We've got him cornered. I've bailiffs ready to arrest him, but you'll have to declare his villainy." He stood straight. "I shall await thee at the front of this here shop whilst you get your hat and gloves."

Looking at her hands that were all ink laden, she frowned, for the gloves would soon be sore filthy.

Horatio slapped his leg. "Get thee shifted for this gracious event this very minute."

Viola ran to get ready. They had planned very hard strong, and now it was upon them, the beastly creature's ruin.

~ * ~

The bailiffs, Horatio, and Viola made a great din as they marched up to a house hard by St. Paul's in the City. Passersby and folk living in the area ran after them to see what the ruckus was all about. The bailiffs made a grand show of it, spreading their arms for everyone to halt as they prepared for a difficult tug. They flexed their shoulders, and cracked their knuckles, but it only took a mere tick to pull the door off its hinges.

A bailiff with great jowls stared at it with alarm. "'Tis a ratty door, 'tis. Could have knocked it flat with a feather, and the hinge bolts needs a good oiling. Whose house is this?"

With a mournful shake of his head, Horatio said, "A veryest slut and drudge."

Viola smirked. It was a good plan they had.

Neighbors clamored round, shouting down the Godless debauchery of the persons inside the house. Whilst the authorities were at it, they cried, "Pull the tiles off the roof and push the windows out their sockets. 'Tis the Godly thing to do."

The bailiffs went a' storming into the house, the neighbors trotting in behind, and without so much as a pardon me, cast Roger from the bed where he'd been a' rollicking and a' rowling most boisterous. Standing naked before infinite people, he stared like a wild man, his cock still wet, and his breathing heavy.

Horatio dragged Viola nearer to the bed, her heels skittering dangerously over the flagstone floor.

The slut who'd been with Roger wrapped bed linen around her, and slipped off the bed. She gaped at the ever thickening crowd.

Watching all this, Viola wanted to laugh.

A bailiff pointed at Roger. "Thou art a base, carnal person. You heard us coming up the street. Why didn't you get into thy breeches?"

Still gasping, Roger grinned. "Didn't know you were coming here, now did I? And so near the end, wasn't of a mind to stop. Needed to squeeze out the last drop, didn't I?"

The people rose up a cry to rattle dust from the rafters. It was the duty of a Christian to be steadfast in all things, not dance with lust on the bed in the afternoon and naked, to boot.

The bailiffs shouted down the crowd, and one asked the woman, "What's your name?"

She replied, "Betty Sharpe. This here is me husband."

Viola screamed out frightfully, tearing off her hat and throwing it to the floor. "Nay, he is not. I am his wife. Roger is me husband, not yours."

The crowd groaned, knowing a terrible crime had been committed.

Roger stared with shock at Viola, and then Horatio. His eyes narrowed. "You damned, buggered fellow."

Horatio sneered. "Officers, this here man is a bigamist. These women are both married to him, and I know of another." His voice was filled with venom when he added, "There are probably many more."

Crying out most horrid, the crowd lunged at Roger, and pulled him naked from the house. The bailiffs had lost control, and Viola was afeard in her heart they'd hang him from the nearest lamppost. Horatio stood like a stone, his eyes glazed over, staring after the pack of folk. He no longer saw what was afore him.

She shook him and hollered, "He could be killed. Do something."

As people hauled Roger down the lane, he quietly said, "This might be the best way. We'll really know he's gone forever, then, won't we?"

Viola could not believe it. After they had near broke their brains with scheming and plotting, she would not allow him this folly. She cried, "All will go to rack if you don't do something. Save him afore you lose your babe, forever."

Horatio's eyes cleared. Taking a deep breath, he ran after the crowd to shout them down.

~ * ~

Viola smiled as she walked into Westminster Hall and to King's Bench. She was to meet Horatio there, for today was the day of Roger's trial. The judge was to be Sweete, replacing Zaks who of a sudden had become too ill to preside. Horatio was pleased. Full truth did not seem a matter to Mister Sweete, along with the straw man and his woman who was to swear against Roger.

Viola accepted this as part of the game. She helped Horatio with a few things he'd never thought of, such as demanding Betty be shifted into more respectable clothes, and to not act sluttish but gentle, showing no baseness or dishonor. Viola demanded the straw man be out of sight at all times, for he looked the rogue, and Roger was the rogue they wanted to expose. After she said that, Horatio gave her a mighty strange look as if he'd seen her for the first time in his life.

It was a very pleasant feeling, and while she had his attention, added, "You must bring Elizabeth from the country, babe or no babe."

He'd said, "She is very near her time."

"Aye, better yet. If I am still about, as is Betty, than marrying Elizabeth 'tis even more clear how he shows base falseness for the whole world to see. Does she know of Roger's other wives?"

Horatio'd shaken his head. "I know not."

Viola smiled. "She should know of this as soon as possible. She should be at the trial."

He'd looked at her with the greatest of admiration in his eyes, and said, "In troth you are as pleasant smart as I ever saw in my life anywhere in a woman."

Viola stopped thinking of the planning, and gazed around the Hall. The place was all a' jumble with scaffolding. It would be difficult to locate Horatio.

Pounding and banging from the remodel was an unpleasant distraction. Workers were tearing down and dragging heavy objects across the place hither and yon. It was loud as Viola skirted round the activity.

The King's Bench was in the process of being moved from one wall to another, and in total disarray. She wasn't sure where Horatio would be. With all the chaos, she could not tell which way was south. The Hall was as busy as a bucketful of slithering lampreys. Even if she were at the place he wanted her, she'd never see him.

"Oiy there, Mistress Sharpe. Are you looking for me?"

She turned to face a very respectable gentleman. "Who are you?"

"I'm Betty's brother, poor soul. Her life has turned most foul since her husband deserted her and the babe." He shook his head woefully. "Most foul."

Viola was astonished. It was the same scruffy straw man who blew smoke from his nose and mouth. Looking at him most hard, he was completely changed, all humble looking and clean as a pin.

Rocking back on her heels, she exclaimed, "Well, I never."

He grinned, and offered her his arm. "Shall we go?"

With a smile, she did.

~ * ~

Horatio watched Viola and the straw man walk toward him arm-in-arm, and for some reason it vexed him. He crossed his arms over his chest, and scowled. The straw man had scrubbed up better than expected, and he reckoned Viola would go all a' swoon over the poxed animal.

When they got close enough so he didn't have to holler, he said, "We're to meet in another chamber fixed temporary to Bench. The barrister and solicitor are awaiting us prior to going in there. They have a few questions for us."

Viola frowned. "What sort of questions? I thought all was arranged, and all the questions fixed good and proper."

Horatio gazed at her, and liked what he saw. She was an honorable woman, and more like him than he wanted to admit. Betrayal caused her gut to twist as it did his, and with the conspiring against Roger, he'd come to admire her brain. Her eyes were mighty pretty, too.

But she'd tossed and frolicked with his brother, something he'd not be able to overcome.

She asked, "Well? Where are they, then?"

He cleared his throat. "Over here and away from the workers."

Leading them to a dim nook with a curtain, he swept it aside for them to enter. Betty was already there, sitting quiet on a stool. Viola's thought on making the girl less sluttish was extraordinary good, and he again thought how much he approved of his sister-in-law.

Two men stood ready, one tall and thin, the other short and stout. Horatio said to the tall and thin, "Mistress Viola Sharpe, please meet Mister John Gant, solicitor," and motioning to the short and stout, "and Sir Edgar Wills, barrister. Honorable sirs, Mistress Sharpe has brought due cause against me brother."

They both nodded to her, then without further ado, Mister Gant, solicitor, quirked up a lip most disdainfully. Holding a large, leather folder, he opened it showing a loose stack of papers, and handed one to the barrister.

Sir Edgar Wills sniffed high haughty, and squinting, gazed at the paper. With a rumbling clearing of his throat, he said, "This case holds many named Sharpe. It'll be most confusing."

With his lip still curled scornfully, the solicitor whispered in Sir Edgar Wills ear. The barrister asked Viola, "Didst thou know of thy husband's villainy afore the stocking was cast across the marriage bed?"

"Nay, Sir."

He gazed at Betty. "And you? Were you knowing of Mister Sharpe's intemperance when you were a' married to him?"

She gazed at Sir Edgar Wills with blank eyes, and the solicitor whispered in the barrister's ear. Sir Edgar Wills cleared his throat officiously, and asked, "Girl, did you know the man you married was a rogue?"

With wide eyes, she shook her head.

Someone knocked on the panel outside the curtain. "Uhm, sirs, I've got a poor, sad lady out here who could do with a chair or stool right this very minute."

He opened the curtain, and moved so that the Clarksons filled the opening. They protected Elizabeth, full with child near to bursting as she waddled into the chamber. Horatio's heart bled at the cruel turn of events that had brought her there and how he'd never be able to forgive her.

Sir Wills humphed. "Well, this is most extraordinary. Who are you?"

The solicitor whispered in his ear, causing the barrister to gaze pointedly at the woman. He barked, "Another Sharpe person. I say, this Roger fellow is quite the blighter, ain't he? Well, this will soon be put to rest, I can assure you. We shall see him stripped of all he holds dear, I can promise you that. Aye, indeed."

The solicitor whispered in his ear, and Sir Wills shook his head, his throat rattling imperiously. "Busy man, that. Busy man."

Men in robes and all formal looking entered the chamber. With noses in the air, they cried, "You are hereby called to the Bench. The Right Worshipful Sweete is ready to his chair."

Suddenly with his heart all a' flurry, Horatio took a deep breath, and followed everyone out of the chamber.

Thirty-eight

They were led out and about to a large, drafty chamber that held a platform with two tables facing each other, and a large chair between, wherein would sit the Dean of Arches, His Right Worshipful Sweete. At the tables in the ready men sat facing each other, three at one, and two at another.

This was the Ecclesiastical Court of Arches to try Roger Sharpe for bigamy, an offense that could result in dissolution of the marriages. Knowing this was not enough to punish his brother, Horatio was very glad the trial was being held at King's Bench, a civil court of the people.

To wreak revenge, he'd made sure this would be declared a felony which could end with execution, although Horatio knew that probably would not happen. Most bigamists, if at all caught, could have their hand burned, or sent to slavery in the growing colonies across the sea. He hoped Roger would be sent to slavery, forever, until he died and his flesh rotted, and his soul be cast to hell. Horatio had done everything in his power to make

Roger burn for his ill treatment of all he knew and professed to love.

Horatio also intended to take the babe from Elizabeth.

As she was assisted to a chair by her sister and brother-in-law, Elizabeth looked most grievously troubled. It was very strange, his feeling of disengagement from her sorrows. Not long ago he'd have felt cruelly aggrieved, and would've comforted her.

Now, he did not care.

Amongst the wives in Court were various men and women; declared ministers who performed the marriage ceremonies, friends, and witnesses, including Viola's sister, Paulina. When Horatio turned around to see who the other folk were, he noted James Finch with pencil and paper in hand, ready to write down all the proceedings for next day's newsprint.

Horatio was much pleased with the new business. After sending the apprentices to the City and suburbs with newssheets to coffeehouses each morning, they would return with very nice bags of coins for his coffers. For tomorrow's press, he'd have the print in bigger, bolder letters, and afore leaving for court, he'd directed Mister Hammer to create larger typefaces to be set in the form.

The chamber went all quiet like, forcing Horatio round to see what was afoot. He followed the crowd's expectations to a doorway, and frowned.

It was Roger, and without representation. Horatio made certain of that, too.

When Roger was brought in, shackled and guarded by men with swords and pistols, Horatio gazed at Elizabeth who broke into blustery sobs. Then he clapped his eyes on the one playing Betty, and was astounded to see her face pucker up with tears washing down her face.

He had the straw man instill upon her to be filled with emotion, but this was not what he expected. She looked to be truly anguished by Roger's predicament, and realized she, too, must've fallen under his spell. She'd experienced his slick words and the pleasure of his tousling, and collapsed as every other woman did.

Truly disgusted, he turned to regard Viola. Horatio was greatly relieved to see her face cold as stone, and her mouth in an angry line. Remembering how he was growing too fond of her, he cast his brains to her and Roger caterwauling loudly on a bed, and sighed. When he settled on a wife, which he'd have quick need of due to the babe, he'd not have one ever touched by his damned, derelict brother.

A servant of the Court banged a staff on the floor. "Hear ye, hear ye, the Court is to order. All rise to greet His Right Worshipful Sweete."

~ * ~

Betty was brought to the witness box.

"Raise your hand to this here Bible. Will you swear…?"

Betty looked all afeard, and shaking her head declared, "I haven't touched the Good Book since him, your majesty. It'll strike me dead for the ill things I've done whilst I was all alone and tried to survive in this here sodded world."

The barrister, Sir Edgar Wills, gave her a cold regard. "What have you done, girl?"

Shaking and weeping, she stared at her hands on the rail. "I can't say, your royalty. 'Tain't right amongst all these good Christian folk. I'll be cast to the fires of hell and damnation. You'll look upon me as one gone straight to the devil."

And Horatio would be damned if she didn't believe what she was weeping over. It completely confounded him a man such as Roger could have almighty power over a woman in such a short time, and he wondered mightily if she'd confess her sins as being an agent of the straw man.

That could not happen!

He skirted round the standing folk to the straw man, and muttered, "She ain't to admit fraud, you hear me? 'Twill ruin everything, then by God I shall forsake you."

He'd not give the man one farthing for his work.

Horatio stared dead hard at the eyes of the straw man. "You ken?"

He kenned, and of a sudden, raised his hand. "Milords. Me sister's gone to rack over this here terrible business. I'll stand with her to give her comfort."

The girl shook at the rail as the straw man stepped to the box, pulling her close. She whelped, then shivered against him.

The straw man said, "Ask what you will."

The barrister paced in front of the Bench. "When did you marry this here dirty fellow?"

A small man in a black doublet and skirt breeches interrupted, "Pardon, milord, the lady has not yet sworn on the Bible."

Sir Edgar rattled and humphed. "Aye, to it then."

As Betty swore on the Bible, the solicitor passed a piece of paper to the barrister who read it with a scratch to his head. He cleared his throat. "Mistress Sharpe, when did you marry this man?"

The straw man squeezed her arm, and she whimpered. "Five years hence, your royalty."

"Didst thou have a child from this union?"

"Aye, your majesty. A lad. He's sickly, and...," she cried out as if being pinched even though the straw man was patting her arm. "Near death."

Sir Edgar Wills gave her a cold look. "Didst thou know Mister Sharpe, your husband, had run off and married another?"

"Nay." She collapsed against the rail, sobbing.

Horatio felt himself falling into a distemper of heat. The woman was turning into a useless piece of baggage, even with the straw man hulking over her in a menacing manner.

The barrister swung toward Roger, crying out, "Look at the poor woman. She's fraught with anguish. How can you be such a damned rogue?"

Roger rattled his chains. "But I do not know this woman."

Standing still, Sir Edgar looked flustered. He opened his mouth to say something when the solicitor, John Gant, whispered in his ear. After a nod, he said, "Didn't the arrest of your person take place at your own, damned house? Hadn't you been in a state of carnal union, your ass naked and a' waving up in the air?"

Elizabeth cried out in a frightful manner, stopping the proceedings as the publican and his wife rushed to her aid.

The barrister waved the paper their way. "What's this about, then? What's going on in that corner to disturb these proceedings?"

The solicitor, stepped up to him, and whispered in his ear, wherein the barrister humphed and puffed. "Terrible, just terrible."

His Right Worshipful Sweete waved a pomander in front of his face, sending out the scent of nutmeg. "'Tis just a woman, Wills, get on with it. 'Tis getting near me dinner."

Turning back to Betty, Sir Edgar Wills cleared his throat. "I've nothing more to say at this time, Lud, but I'd like to call another witness."

Waving the pomander, Sweete nodded.

The small man in a black doublet and skirt breeches cried, "Mister Wheeler to the witness box."

A scruffy fellow made his way through the throng to the Bench. The man in black gave him the Bible. "Do you swear…"

Despite his dark feelings for Elizabeth, Horatio was torn between hatred and concern. She looked all done in, hunched over and a' sobbing most horrid. The Clarksons seemed concerned, as well. He did not want anything to happen to the babe.

A servant of the Court banged his staff on the floor. "Order in the Court. Order in the Court."

Mister Wheeler was a ragged, dirty fellow with a balding pate, and what was left of his hair fell in greasy strings to his shoulders. Sir Edgar covered his nose with a kerchief as Sweete vigorously waved his pomander.

Wills moved the kerchief away from his face and asked, "Please tell the Court your name."

"'Tis Doctor Wheeler, I am, once minister of Caxton Parish."

"Are you no longer minister of said parish?"

"Nay, Sir. Me home is Fleet Prison these past six years."

Sir Edgar smirked. "And why would you be cast to this prison, Doctor? What heinous crime hath thou committed?"

Wheeler leaned forward over the rail. "The old government cast me out of me vocation for practicing the proper religion. Said 'twas too popish, and stripped me of me ministering papers."

The solicitor whispered in Sir Edgar's ear.

The barrister said, "But that would have been only a three year term. Why have you been in prison for so long?"

"Debt, Sir. When I was stripped of me proper title and profession, I lost income, and am still in debt." He vigorously rubbed his nose with the back of his hand. "Whilst in Fleet I continued with me Godly office during the ungodly times of Cromwell, and even now." He shook his head. "'Tis a sad, cruel world we live in, filled with damnation and lost souls."

Sir Edgar looked confused. "But the rightful church is come back. Why hast thou remained in Fleet?"

"'Tis a welcoming place, sirrah, and more lucrative than after the cold outside. Many a couple come to me for their wedding vows. 'Tis as honest and real as if we was in a parish church, and in Fleet chapel, I do it right and proper with the Book of Common Prayer."

"'Tis a legal marriage then?"

"Aye."

"Do you know the persons of this Court whom you've married right and proper then?"

Wheeler nodded and pointed "Aye, 'tis the lass who was up here afore me and the gentleman in chains. I remember a' cause they seemed so starry-eyed."

Sir Edgar paused, clearing his throat then Gant whispered in his ear. "Is there a record of the marriage? Is there a license registered with the church?"

"Nay, not with the church a' cause the proper church was frowned upon weren't it? That's why I'm in prison, ain't it?" He searched through his pockets. "But I've the license. Filled it out meself." Pulling it out of a pocket, he waved it like a flag. "Here 'tis if you're a' wanting to see it."

The clerk of the Court took it from the minister, and handed it to the barrister, who glanced at it before giving it to the solicitor.

Gant's spectacles slid down his nose as he gave it a look. He whispered in Sir Edgar's ear, who turned to the Court. "Aye, 'tis legal alright."

Roger clattered his chains. "That ain't never true. I never was married to this here woman. All I did was towse her good and proper, and I gave her a shilling for the pleasure of it." He searched the crowded Court for Betty. "Tell the Court it ain't true. You're just a whore for the taking."

But with the straw man standing close, Betty screamed out, terrifying all in the Court. She cried, "Aye, you and I are married. We've a lad whose dying a' cause you deserted us and never come back."

In her distress, Betty wrung her skirts until her ankles showed to the press of men, their eyes goggling most bold. She shrieked, "I love thee, I love thee. Thou must come back to me and the lad. Please come back." And she fell into a swoon on the floor, knocking her head most grievous.

The men standing closest to Betty started toward her when the scream of another woman rang out loud, and a man hollered, "Oh no. Great ill has come upon me kinswoman."

Horatio pushed through the people to see Elizabeth grunting and moaning like an animal near death. Bending over, she near fell off the chair, but the publican caught her in his arms as she dipped toward the floor.

Viola and Paulina stepped suddenly to his side. They said, "Her time is come."

Gazing at the woman whose agony was clear for the whole world to see, he nodded.

A pounding of a staff on the floor reverberated through the chamber. "Order in the Court. Order in the Court."

His Right Worshipful Sweete announced, "'Tis time for me dinner. This Court is adjourned until next fortnight at ten o'clock of the morning, and there will be no more of this here unseemly caterwauling."

Thirty-nine

Two weeks later, Viola followed Horatio into the same chamber as before. Since Court had adjourned, the case had gained notoriety especially since Horatio's bookseller shop spent many hours printing and selling propaganda to coffeehouses.

She grunted. He was a right avaricious person, he was, with no pride whatsoever, not caring one bit if he hurt his own sister-in-law. People stopped Viola in the lane outside the shops and in the market, asking why she'd been so base stupid to marry a damned rogue as Roger.

It made her stark mad to be thought such a fool for the whole world to see, and like a stinging wasp, attacked Horatio for the knave he was. "How can you treat me so horrid, blathering about our personal business to the whole City and suburbs? Your broadsheets are making me into a laughingstock. Stop it at once."

He only laughed. "Nay, 'tis good for me purse, and will only turn more ill for Roger. I intend for him to be locked up in slavery for the rest of his life."

She frowned. "Where will you have him sent? And how do you know he'll be there forever? He could escape."

"Nay, I shall have him sent to the West Indies where he'll work sugar cane or tobacco. It'll be hot and horrid. Hopefully, he'll die of the bloody flux."

"Ooo gore, you're wicked hard," she said with a shiver. The man was nevermore forgiving, and she took serious note never to cross him.

Now, as they entered the chamber, it was already crowded. She looked around for Elizabeth, but did not see her, and she took one of the three empty chairs next to Betty. She looked all done in with a black eye, and a cloth wrapped round her head.

She leaned close and asked, "What ails thee? Art thou well?"

Betty shrugged. "Aye, I'll be fain well enough, I reckon." She pointed to the rag around her head. "'Tis from the fall last time we were here. I clapped me head good and hard when I hit the floor." She blinked away tears. "Me eye was a token from Ned."

Viola did not know who Ned was. She asked, "Who?"

Betty sighed. "The straw man. He's me keeper, and does not like my sudden liking to Roger. I must keep me mouth shut for this here meeting, or suffer for it."

Looking across the chamber, Viola regarded the straw man who looked more the ruffian than ever. He leaned against a wall, smoking a pipe. The smoke drifted from his nose as he watched Betty.

Viola murmured, "What's your name? I know it ain't Betty."

"Can't say. If'n I do, I'll be hit hard across the other eye."

Shaking her head, Viola dismally thought how hard terrible it was for a woman in these here times. A man could do as he pleased with a woman, taking her children from her or locking her up until she crossed the veil if he so pleased, but the minute a woman raised a hand to defend herself...

Well, it was a calamity of the times, indeed it was.

A servant of the Court banged a staff to the floor. "Hear ye, hear ye, the Court is to order. All greet His Right Worshipful Sweete."

And all went quiet as the Dean of Arches entered the chamber.

~ * ~

Viola was next to testify against Roger, and stood when called to the witness box. As before, the solicitor, John Gant, whispered in the barrister's ear afore he said anything at the bar. Viola was clapped by the heels with suspicion John Gant was the one who should be speaking at the Bench, not the other way around.

The small man in a black doublet and skirt breeches stepped up to her, carrying a Bible. "Do you swear afore God the Almighty on His throne in Heaven what you are about to say is the truth and nothing but the truth?"

Placing her hand on the Bible, she said, "I do."

On the box Viola stood quiet, waiting for the barrister to ask his questions, but he was in no apparent hurry. Bent low, he listened to the solicitor for the longest time. After a curt nod from the barrister, John Gant stepped away.

Viola watched as Sir Edgar Wills paced back and forth, reading from a sheath of papers. She could see large handwriting in the form of lists. With him reading and not talking, she was growing a mite tetchy.

His Worshipful waved the pomander. "Get on with it, Wills, get on with it. The day's a' wasting."

"Aye, Lud." He slapped the papers against his hand, and harrumphed, startling Viola. "Mistress Sharpe."

Her heart falling to the pit of her gut, she answered, "Aye?"

"Art thou married to this here fellow?"

"Aye."

"How do you know?"

She turned all vexed. "A' cause I stood with the filthy creature afore a minister, and said I take thee for me husband, and he doing the same. That's how I know."

"Did you say, 'I shall take thee,' or 'I take thee'?"

"I said 'I take thee'."

Roger cried out, "Nay, we said, 'I shall take thee one day in the future'."

Viola gaped at him. Leaning over the rail, she cried, "That was not the way of it, and you know it."

Sweete waved his pomander. The barrister harrumphed and grumped, while the solicitor ran up to whisper in his ear.

Sir Edgar asked, "You understand one way is legal and bound, the other not, don't you, girl?"

His tone ground against her. "Aye, sirrah, I ain't so base stupid as you may think."

The barrister and solicitor both gasped, while Sweete scolded, "You ain't to be an impertinent harpy. Nay, you may not. We can always get the dunking chair for thee, if you ain't careful."

The solicitor smirked then muttered in Sir Edgar's ear. The barrister demanded, "Tell the Court the difference, then."

She set her brains back to Horatio and her discussion over the matter, and the rehearsing they'd done. "To say 'I shall or I will' means a promise for the future. To say 'I do take thee' means I vow afore all and sundry this very moment."

The barrister shot, "Who were your witnesses, then?"

From between two men Paulina cried, "I was there to witness and hear it done, along with our papa who had a pistol pointed at Roger's head."

The Court became very merry.

"That ain't the least bit funny," Roger declared all festered as he rattled his chains. "I could've been kilt. The man's a doddering old fool."

The barrister waved a hand, asking Viola, "Where was the ceremony?"

"In our house."

"Where's your house?"

"On the Bridge."

"Who performed the marriage?"

"A parson."

"Ha!" Roger bellowed. "There's the truth of it. We ain't married, never have been."

Paulina cried, "You cannot say that. Our papa demanded a proper minister, he did."

The solicitor passed a paper to the barrister. "Was the minister from your parish?"

"Nay," cried Roger. "Don't you remember, you damned, buffflehead woman? We got one from Fleet Prison. There weren't no Book of Common Prayer, neither, if that's what you'll say next."

"That ain't true." Pall stepped to the Bench, and falsely stated, "The minister was from St. Magnus, our own Doctor James." Then she stated truthfully, "And the book was aright. We used our mam's." Pall nodded most extraordinary significant. "Me sister and Roger are married alright."

Sweete snapped his pomander, sending out a dusting of powdered cloves and nutmeg. He glared at Pall. "Who the blazes are you?"

The court servant banged his staff on the floor. "Order in the Court. Order in the Court."

Viola scowled at Roger. "I ain't your wife," she declared, not caring at all she was in front of complete strangers of high order. "You've blasphemed and committed bigamy for the whole world to see. You should be clapped in irons for the rest of your days, and hauled off to the gibbet."

Roger stamped his fettered feet. "I weren't never married to that Betty lass, I tell you.

"Aye, you are. She's your one and only with the papers to prove it."

"That ain't true," Roger blustered. "You're me only true wife. I can prove it."

Did she hear aright? "What?"

Paulina cried, "What did you just say?"

Sir Edgar Wills' throat rattled and rolled. "I say, you're a strange one. You just denounced the marriage altogether. Make up your mind what you are, married or no."

Viola ran off the witness box to Roger. "Thou art a villainous piece of dung. May your bowels die whilst you still live, and your death vicious cruel."

Roger beat his chains together. "I love thee. I always have. You art me one and only wife."

From afar, Viola heard pounding on the floor and, "Order I say! Order in the Court."

Someone hollered, "Get the bailiffs. Arrest these hooligans."

Sweete stood. "Who's speaking? This is unnatural behavior. We've already got an arrested man, here."

"Nay! Elizabeth cried, and everyone turned round to see a poor, sad woman.

His Worshipful gazed at Roger horrid hard. "What's this? *Another wife?*"

Viola could not believe the change in her. Elizabeth was all wretched looking and hunched over as if in pain. Her hair was like a wild woman's, and her face was streaked dirty as if she'd been weeping for days.

The Clarksons ran in behind her, blathering, "Nay, nay."

All the Court went quiet.

His Right Worshipful blustered, "Damnit, Wills, tend us to order. Get on with the proceedings."

The servant of the court banged the staff against the floor.

The solicitor whispered furiously in the barrister's ear, Sir Edgar's throat rattling as he slapped papers against his leg.

Everyone watched Elizabeth as she walked up to Roger. "You married me. Why did you deceive me so?"

He laughed. "A' cause I wanted revenge on me brother, the bloody sod." He sneered. "I never loved you. Our marriage was full of base falseness. Did you not see the truth of it?"

He leaned over her. "We never threw the stocking. We never exchanged tokens. The minister did not even have a book to read from. How could you believe I ever loved you?" He cried, "Egad! As soon as the deed was done, I hied off to London."

She went dead calm. "Have you read the Bible?"

"What does that have to do with anything?"

She recited, "Leviticus says: 'And the man that committeth adultery with another man's wife,' as we did, 'the adulterer and the adulteress shall be put to death, and the adulteress shall be childless.'"

Someone cried, "Is that the truth of it?"

The Dean of Arches waved his pomander in dismissal.

Elizabeth smiled ever so sweetly. "The lad we had is a spawn of hell, did you know that?"

Horatio bellowed, "Nay, the babe is from my loins. He's me own son, not Roger's."

Sweete cried, "We've lost control of this here Court. I say, Wills, get us back to order."

Elizabeth never blinked an eye. "Our fornication and adultery shall cast us into the pits of hell."

Roger raised his hands as if to fend off a gust of evil. "You've gone mad, you have." With pleading eyes, he cried, "Look at her. She'll murder me. Save me from murder, I beg you."

Mistress Clarkson burst into tears.

The publican said, "Me kinswoman ain't been the same since the Court a fortnight ago, and the birthing done tipped her clean over. We cannot coddle her nevermore any longer, for she won't see to reason. 'Tis to Bedlam for her, we think."

Gazing toward the heavens, and keening, Elizabeth raised a hand in worship. "And if a man shall lie with a woman having her sickness, and shall uncover her nakedness; he hath discovered her fountain of blood, both of them shall be cut off from amongst their people in death."

A woman screamed. A newborn started squalling.

Horatio snapped, "Where's our baby? Elizabeth, where's the babe?"

She did not hear. Lowering her hand, she said, "I loved thee, Roger, yet you were grave false. We must now die."

She raised a pistol from within the folds of her skirts and pointed it at Roger's heart.

Crying mightily out, he grabbed the pistol from her hand and swinging her around, wrapped the chains of his manacles around her neck. "Nay, it will be I who shall kill thee, thou whore of the night."

A great roar rose from the people as Roger twisted the chain around Elizabeth's neck. Horatio pulled out his pistols and pointed them at his brother.

Viola stared in terror. He'd ruin all. "Nay, what of the babe? Think of the babe."

Clarkson and his wife ran towards Roger and Elizabeth. The publican cried, "Leave her be, or I'll kill you meself with me own pistol."

Roger pointed the gun at the Clarksons.

Pistols went off, smoke and thunder clouding all. Viola dropped to the floor as men and women dashed away, screaming and crying against the explosions of gunfire.

When the smoke cleared, the bailiffs and several men who had fired their pistols stood staring at Roger and Elizabeth as they lay in a heap at their feet.

They were dead.

No one moved as blood pooled and spread across the floor of the chamber. Still as a stone, Horatio stared at his brother and Elizabeth, the muzzles of his pistols wisping smoke. Viola's heart bled for him.

A baby's wails echoed loud through the chamber, bringing all once again awake.

The publican and his wife fell to their knees afore Elizabeth, their sorrow plain for the whole world to see. They hugged their kinswoman, rocking her in her arms, crying out pitifully. Viola couldn't bear it, and turned her back to it. Tears ran down her cheeks.

When her eyes cleared, she saw the chairs where the wives sat, where Betty still sat, holding a tiny bundle. As she walked to Betty with her arms outstretched, the girl watched her. Viola said a silent prayer the girl would let loose of it.

For a moment, Betty hesitated then with a sigh, relinquished her charge.

A staff hit the floor. "This Court is now adjourned."

Forty

Viola stood in the temporary chamber of the King's Bench, waiting for the determination of Elizabeth and Roger's deaths. It had been two days since the killings, and Viola hoped this would come to a brisk conclusion.

After the smoke had cleared, His Right Worshipful Sweete was astonished when almost every man in the chamber had shot their pistols, every man mightily killing the unfortunate persons. Even the solicitor and barrister pulled triggers.

Viola counted twenty men crowding round the witness box before the criminal judge sitting in the great chair.

Standing nearer the men below and shaking his head, Sweete said, "I know not, Lud, whose bullets killed the poor unfortunates. Either everyone must to trial, or none of them."

The judge regarded the men at the box. "I must say, thou art a bloodthirsty lot. I should have all shipped to the new colonies, shackled, and into slavery. But I see some important personages, here, and those dead were not so important." He waved his hand. "Thou art dismissed."

With grins spreading across their faces, the men disbursed out of King's Bench. Horatio headed toward her. "Well, that's done, ain't it? And good and proper, too."

Smiling up at him, Viola agreed. "Aye, and that beastly creature is gone from us forever." She shook her head. "Poor Elizabeth, too."

His face hardened at her words. "She was base stupid to have fallen for the rascal. No good ever came from associating with the blighter. He betrayed all who joined in his company."

Horatio guided her through Westminster Hall that was undergoing a great remodel for the King's coronation. They walked round scaffolds and workmen, and out to the street. It was a bright day, crisp with autumn in the air, people rushing to and fro.

Near beating his chest, he cried, "Great day, me girl. We've got what we wanted, don't we?"

"Aye, but we must to the shops, right and proper. Business is good. Can't leave it to the Finches for long. They've been at it without us too often of late." She looked up at him. "Lucy's gone into labor, and will soon have Simon's babe."

Taking her arms so they faced each other, he said, "Ah, wonderful. It'll be a rollicking house afore long, what with me son and theirs, plus the prentices who ain't all that old to begin with."

He kissed her hard on the mouth.

It was lovely, and she leaned into him, savoring the feel, the smell, until someone hollered, "This ain't no brothel. Get on out of here afore doing what you're about to be doing."

Horatio grinned. "You'll be a right fine mam to Charles, and to all our others."

Viola could not get her brains around what he said. "What?"

"Aye, we'll marry, and be a family."

This was all too strange. The man just finished killing his brother whom he hated beyond redemption, and bore a deep grudge to all who associated with the filthy creature. How could Horatio want her when she had been married to the knave, slept with him, lived with him, gotten with child by him?

She shook her head and pulled away. "Nay, it won't be. You hate all who've been with Roger. How can you say you want a family, and me be a part of it? I'm even sore afeard you'll end up hating your own son a' cause of Elizabeth gallivanting off as she did."

"Nay, I've forgiven her."

"Nay, you have not, nor will you ever. You're a cold hard man, not giving an inch who do you harm."

"We are much alike in mind, Mistress, and both betrayed by Roger. We'll do well together."

Despite what her brains were telling her, to reject this as fast as she could, she was wavering in the heart. "I'm filled with deep suspicions to do so would turn most horrid."

As they walked toward the City, she jogged alongside, and finally cried, "Slow down. Your legs are long and go too fast."

He turned around, almost making her run headlong into him. He said, "It'll be business. You shall be Charles' mam, and if anything happens to me, you'll be independent, running the shops. You'll be Lady Sharpe, and our son will carry on the title."

Now, that was more appealing to her. "Will we lie together?"

"Aye," he said with a grin. "We'll be husband and wife in all ways. A man must empty his cods regular, you understand."

"But you wanted to do it aright with banns and license and such. Whatever happened to your plans of doing it aright as a knight of the realm?"

"It cannot be done aright with you being me wife, now can it? 'Tis against the law to marry the husband or wife of a sibling, dead or alive."

She said, "To do so will be incest."

He started to walk again. "Aye, that it will."

Jogging alongside, she protested, "No proper minister will marry us."

He laughed. "Aye."

"Then, how will we do it?"

"Clandestine, of course, through Fleet Prison."

Meet

Katherine Pym

Katherine Pym divides her time between Seattle and Houston with her husband and puppy-dog. She is an avid reader of 17th century England, particularly of London.

*VISIT OUR WEBSITE
FOR THE FULL INVENTORY
OF QUALITY BOOKS*:

http://www.wings-press.com

*Quality trade paperbacks and downloads
in multiple formats,
in genres ranging from light romantic
comedy to general fiction and horror.
Wings has something
for every reader's taste.
Visit the website, then bookmark it.
We add new titles each month!*